ACCLAIM FOR THE KIKI LOWENSTEIN
SCRAP-N-CRAFT MYSTERY SERIES

Paper, Scissors, Death
* An Agatha Award Finalist *

"A well-turned cozy with loads of scrapbooking tips."

—*Kirkus Reviews*

"Scrapbookers will love the whole idea of forensic scrapbooking and will relish the tips on the craft sprinkled throughout the story."

—*Booklist*

"With plotting as tight as the seal of a decompression chamber and a flow to the narrative that is as smooth as silk, this is a wonderful read."

—*Crimespree Magazine*

"A proper pacy mystery with plenty of tension (and red herrings) that kept me guessing to the end."

—*ScrapBook Inspirations Magazine* (U.K.)

"An engaging mystery."—Donna Andrews, Agatha and Anthony Award-winning author of the Meg Langslow and Turing Hopper series

"Charming, funny, and very enjoyable!"

—J. A. Konrath, author of *Whiskey Sour*

"A page turner who-done-it, filled with colorful characters and scrapbooking tips. The story is filled with insightful glimpses into the heart of a true scrapbooker and a touch of romance."

—Rebecca Ludens, Scrapbooking Guide for About.com

"If you like mysteries, quirky characters, and scrapbooking, you will love this book."

—Angie Pedersen, The Scrappy Marketer, ScrapbookMarketing.com

"Pick this one up if you love scrapbooking or cozies."

—Fresh Fiction

"Fun to read, with laugh-out-loud humor along with tensions and true friendships."   —Mysterious Women

Cut, Crop & Die

"A nicely crafted cozy full of amusing moments, real-life insecurities, and scrapbooking tips." —*Kirkus Reviews*

"Slan fulfills all the promise of her first novel . . . and the book is filled with characters we care about." —*Booklist*

"Another enthralling, interesting, fast-paced mystery."

—ReviewingTheEvidence.com

Photo, Snap, Shot

"A cut above the usual craft-themed cozy." —*Publishers Weekly*

"Slan writes with a wonderful knack for characters and the plot is laid out in a great classic style . . . Treat yourself to a wonderful traditional feeling mystery with characters you will love." —*Crimespree Magazine*

"Intricate and fascinating. Readers will find realistic characters and plenty of tension to keep pages turning right until the end. Award-nominated author Joanna Campbell Slan's series continues to be strong."

—Bookreporter.com

Make, Take, Murder

"The characters are so well developed that each installment leaves the reader yearning for the next." —*Kirkus Reviews*

"Topically relevant and chock-full of side stories." —*Library Journal*

"There are chuckle-out-loud moments as well as wonderful scrapbooking tips and recipes scattered throughout the book."

—RTBookReviews.com

PICTURE
PERFECT
CORPSE

JOANNA CAMPBELL SLAN

PICTURE

PERFECT

CORPSE

A Kiki Lowenstein
Scrap-N-Craft
Mystery

MIDNIGHT INK
WOODBURY, MINNESOTA

FIRST EDITION
First Printing, 2013

Book design and format by Donna Burch
Cover art : Bats: iStockphoto.com/jojo100
        Frame: iStockphoto.com/lolon
        Knife: iStockphoto.com/gokcen yener
        Leaves: iStockphoto.com/Kathy Konkle
Cover design by Kevin R. Brown
Editing by Connie Hill

Midnight Ink, an imprint of Llewellyn Worldwide Ltd.

This is a work of fiction. Names, characters, places, and incidents are either the product of the author's imagination or are used fictitiously, and any resemblance to actual persons, living or dead, business establishments, events, or locales is entirely coincidental.

Library of Congress Cataloging-in-Publication Data

Campbell-Slan, Joanna.
  Picture perfect corpse / Joanna Campbell Slan. — First edition.
      pages   cm. — (A Kiki Lowenstein scrap-n-craft mystery ; 6)
   ISBN 978-0-7387-3538-2
1. Lowenstein, Kiki (Fictitious character)—Fiction. 2. Family violence—Fiction.
3. Scrapbooks—Fiction. 4. Scrapbooking—Fiction. 5. Domestic fiction. I. Title.
  PS3603.A4845P53   2013
   813'.6—dc23   2012050872

Midnight Ink
Llewellyn Publications
2143 Wooddale Drive
Woodbury, MN 55125-2989
www.midnightinkbooks.com

Printed in the United States of America

DEDICATION

To Katigan Campbell Hutts, with love.

ONE

Late afternoon of the shooting

"I'm pregnant?" asked Detective Chad Detweiler, as his face filled with wonder. To his credit he didn't flinch at the news. No, he continued to hold me in those strong arms of his as the paramedic proceeded to shine his flashlight into my eyes.

"I'm going to have a baby," Detweiler repeated what I'd just told the paramedic.

"No," I corrected the big cop firmly. "*I* am the one who is pregnant. You're the daddy."

In the strobing red light of the ambulance, his face registered a series of emotions. Concern. Shock. Surprise. And finally happiness. "Hey, everybody! I'm pregnant!" Detweiler whooped to no one in particular. "I'm going to be a daddy!"

"Ouch!" I winced as the paramedic stuck me with a needle to start an IV. The smell of rubbing alcohol floated above the copper-like smell of the blood running down my face.

"Sorry. Any other health issues I should know about? Allergies? Pacemaker?" said the medic. The blinking red lights of police cruisers imparted a surreal quality to the man's round face. "Any issues besides the baby?" he prompted me, trying to be heard over the crackle of police radios and the screams of sirens.

"Yes!" yelled Detweiler, doing a fist pump. "We're pregnant!"

Two Illinois state policemen paused while processing the crime scene to stare at us. Their Dudley Do-Right mountie hats looked cartoonish, but their expressions were grave.

"I meant to tell you about the baby, but I didn't get the chance! You cut me off when we were talking…" I gasped to Detweiler.

With a firm hand, the medic cleaned the blood from the bullet wound to my head and a pain washed over me. I love color, honest I do, but I could feel myself turning a sickly shade of green.

"Shhh," said Detweiler, taking my hand. "It's okay. We'll celebrate later. Things have been sort of crazy."

No kidding.

"You've had your Hallmark moment. Now move it, bud. This is a crime scene. Don't you have a murder to process?" The medic pushed Detweiler aside and took his place.

"I'm the one who shot him!" I sobbed. "Bill Ballard. I killed him!" Losing all sense of control, I wailed in misery.

"It's going to be all right." Detweiler came around the other side of the emergency worker to stroke my hair. "We heard. The cops who found you are giving their testimony now. It's all over, sweetheart. Shhh. You did good. You did what you had to do. I'm proud of you."

An EMT appeared. In a choreographed effort, he and the medic lifted me onto a stretcher. Detweiler helped, but after they strapped me down, the medic shoved him aside. "We need to get this lady into the bus and to the hospital."

"I killed a man!" I cried to Detweiler.

It was true. I could scarcely believe it, but I'd shot and killed Bill Ballard, the man who masterminded my husband's murder.

After running from the law, Bill had returned to the St. Louis area only to hire a crackerjack attorney who had managed to keep him out of jail. This turn of events left Bill free to hire someone to do me in!

Fortunately, the would-be "assassin" was my friend Johnny Chambers. Knowing I was in danger, Johnny and Police Chief Robbie Holmes had concocted a plot to entrap Bill, a scheme to make sure that Bill would wind up behind bars where he belonged. But unbeknownst to all of us, Brenda Detweiler, Chad Detweiler's wife, had partnered with Bill. Using my mother-in-law, Sheila, as bait, Brenda had forced me into driving over the Mississippi River to a secluded boat dock in Illinois. When we arrived, it looked to me like Johnny might have been drawn into their plot. But he wasn't. He was only biding his time—and he proved his loyalty to me by purposely "overlooking" the gun I was carrying when he patted me down and loosely taped my hands together.

What happened next rivaled the sort of mayhem you might watch in a Quentin Tarantino movie, a scene replete with stomach-churning violence.

Crazy high on drugs, Brenda shot Johnny in the gut. Because Johnny had barely bound me, I managed to work my hands free and remove my blouse to press it against his wound. Meanwhile, Brenda hopped into her car and drove away. I looked up from Johnny in time to see Bill push Sheila face first into a boat. After she hit the bottom with a sickening crack of bones, he jumped in and grabbed her by the throat. With Johnny dying on the gravel and Sheila being choked to death, I had no choice. There was no one left to save us.

It was up to me to kill Bill. Time slowed. As I raised my gun, I became totally focused and in the moment. Even when I heard the crunch of tires, and realized that Brenda had come back, I didn't break my focus. I knew what I had to do.

I had been taught to aim for center mass. But a bullet traveling through Bill's chest would have hit Sheila. Instead, I pointed the muzzle at his head, took my time, slowed my breathing, squeezed the trigger and blew him away. His head exploded in a red mist.

Simultaneously, a bullet from Brenda's gun grazed my temple, and my world went black.

Our wild drama had been witnessed by two off-duty cops who'd planned a quiet afternoon of fishing. That's how I came to be strapped on a stretcher, shivering, shirtless, and disoriented, surrounded by sirens, flashing red lights, and disembodied voices coming over radios. The only comfort was that somehow Detweiler had magically appeared at my side. His coat was wrapped around me, and my fingertips clenched the fabric as though it were my favorite blankie.

"My baby will be okay, won't it?" I asked the EMT closest to me as they carried me to the ambulance. Detweiler was right at the man's shoulder.

"I hope so," said the tech. He turned to snarl at Detweiler. "For the last time. Back off, buddy! Why don't you go arrest somebody?"

"How're Sheila and Johnny?" I called to him.

"Johnny's on his way to the hospital," said Detweiler. "He's touch and go, but I'm pretty certain Sheila will make it."

Almost on cue, her voice cut through the chatter. "You idiot! Get those scissors away from me! You are not going to cut my blouse open! This is silk! Do you know how much it cost? My dry cleaner will have a fit!"

Despite the pain, I chuckled. "Wait 'til she hears I'm having a baby."

"My baby," echoed Detweiler. "I'm going to be a dad!"

TWO

Tuesday, Day 1—morning after the shooting

"You, Mrs. Lowenstein, have a very hard head," said the male nurse, one Ned O'Malley, as he cleaned my wound. The sting of the alcohol wipe was subsiding but the smell lingered.

"That bullet could have done a lot more damage. Instead, it skidded along the side of your skull. Scraped a nice-sized groove in your temple. You'll sport one nasty scar as a memento of your adventure."

His wild, carrot-red-haired head bent over me as he gently pressed a fresh bandage on the wound that ran the horizontal length of my right temple. Finishing his work, he stepped back, looked me over, and nodded to himself.

"Please call me Kiki," I croaked. My throat was dry and my voice was so hoarse that Kermit the Frog and I could have done a duet.

"Kiki," he repeated. "I'm known as Ned the Red, because of the orange hair." He removed his swinging stethoscope and tucked it into a pocket of his bright red scrubs with the dancing Elmo on them. The juxtaposition delighted me. I'm a scrapbooker and a very visual person, so I love putting orange and red together.

"You're a lucky, lucky girl." Easing his way into the seat beside my hospital bed, the nurse leaned forward on his elbows and smiled at me, a bemused sort of half-grin. His face betrayed the fact he'd lived a hard life, what with the creases, sunburned skin color, and pock marks. Probably in his forties, if the crow's feet and the white hairs in his beard were any indication. Mixed with the spicy fragrance of his cologne was a hint of antibiotic soap, the kind they put in the dispensers at McDonald's. Strong stuff that not only killed germs but also peeled the skin right off my fingers.

"Yeah. I feel really lucky," I said.

"I've heard you're a good shot. One of the cops who brought you in nicknamed you 'Dead-Eye Dora.' Believe me, he said it with total admiration." Ned punctuated this statement with a short laugh.

"Thanks. I think." I grabbed the box of tissues on the stand next to my hospital bed and dabbed my eyes.

"One of the side effects of any head injury is strong emotions. Of course, that's also a part of being pregnant."

"How is my baby?" Afraid to hear the answer, I stared down at the mountain range my toes made under the pale green cotton blanket that covered the crisp white sheets tucked over my legs.

"Fine. A mother's body is an incredible vessel. The best space capsule ever. NASA's got nothing on Mother Nature. I doubt your little passenger even knew his mama had been hurt. But I have a hunch these tears aren't about the baby, are they?"

"No," I said hastily, wiping at my eyes. "Okay, maybe. Some. I shot a man. Killed him."

7

"That's what's bothering you?" Ned raised an eyebrow.

"Wouldn't it bother you?"

"How about if I contact someone for you to talk to? Do you have a priest? A minister?"

"Rabbi Sarah Caplin. Montefiore Temple. Over in St. Louis. We're still in Illinois, right?"

"Yes, ma'am. We were the closest hospital to the slough."

"How are my friends?" My heart raced and a cold sweat broke out on my upper lip.

"Mrs. Lowenstein is fine except for a broken collarbone, a fracture of her forearm, a concussion, and bad bruising. Mr. Chambers is in critical condition. His spleen had to be removed to stop the bleeding, and he's in a coma."

"Oh." A tear trickled down my cheek.

"Mr. Chambers did respond to stimuli though, and that's a good sign."

Thank goodness.

Johnny's sister Mert Chambers was my best friend. She would never forgive me if he didn't pull through. Mert was a typical Scorpio. You didn't want to get on her bad side. Once you crossed her, you were toast. And we're talking burnt toast here. She was under the impression that I'd cooked up this whole scheme and put Johnny at risk. Nothing could be further from the truth, but I knew she wouldn't give me a fair hearing. Not now. When someone she loved was involved, Mert led with her emotions. It made her the best of friends and the worst of enemies.

That reminded me: "What about Brenda Detweiler?"

"Brenda Detweiler? Who's that? She didn't come in with you," Ned said.

"Brenda Detweiler is the woman who shot Johnny and me. I'd like to know if she's in custody."

"You probably need to talk with an officer for details on your assailant."

My assailant. Yeah, that described Brenda Detweiler to a T. Although she'd thrown her husband, Detective Chad Detweiler, out on Christmas Day, she'd grown furious when he decided to give in to our mutual attraction. I'd met Detweiler when he investigated my husband's murder. We'd fallen in love despite our best efforts to stay "just friends." But propriety and good sense had kept us at arm's length until Brenda tossed him to the curb. Then, despite our best intentions to go slowly, our relationship moved forward at breakneck speed. In fact, he was all set to divorce Brenda when her father, Milton Kloss, asked him to wait because she'd agreed to go into drug rehab—for the third time. Without Detweiler's insurance, the treatment would have been financially prohibitive. After we discussed it, Detweiler postponed the divorce proceedings. But finding a place for Brenda in a rehab facility didn't happen overnight. Meanwhile she had grown bolder and bolder in her attacks on me.

At the same time that Brenda was making my life miserable, I was also receiving nasty letters and taunts from Bill Ballard.

Ned brought me back to the here and now. "You sure are lucky. Those two off-duty policemen crept through the cattails and discovered a crime in progress. They called for backup and ambulances, but if you hadn't shot Mr. Ballard, both of your friends might have died."

"I killed a man." The words came hesitantly. The tears came easily.

"Listen. I served in Iraq." He rubbed his mouth with a clenched fist. "There's blood on my hands, too. Few people in our society ever are forced to make the sort of choices that you and I have made. But what else could you have done? Would you have stood by and watched your friends die?"

"I . . . I don't know." I blew my nose.

"Sure you do. The news reports call you a hero!"

I covered my face with my hands. "I don't want to be a hero. I just want to be left alone."

THREE

Hospitals are not very good places to recover from an injury. You'd get more rest if you sat on the floor in the middle of Union Station. At times, I wondered whether I was really in a hospital bed, or if I'd somehow been transported to a parade reviewing stand. The stream of people coming in and out of my room astonished me. Last night, right after I was admitted, Police Chief Robbie Holmes brought my daughter, Anya, by to see me and her grandmother.

"We're not going to stay long," said the man who planned to marry my mother-in-law. "But I thought Anya needed to see for herself that you both were all right. Jennifer Moore told me to tell you that Anya's welcome to bunk up at their place as long as necessary."

"Love you, Mom." My daughter had kissed me.

"Love you, too, Anna-Banana," I had said, and they bid me goodnight. I slept soundly until my breakfast arrived, called Anya before she went to school, assured myself she was fine, thanked Jennifer for taking care of my daughter, and drifted back to sleep.

New footsteps awakened me, and I rubbed my eyes with both fists, sure that I was dreaming at the sight of my new visitor. "Amanda?"

There stood my younger sister, almost my spitting image, but three years and twenty pounds shy of me.

"Hey. That male nurse you have told me you're on the mend. What's his name? Ned? Yeah, that's it. I stopped by to tell you that your daughter is fine."

"All the way from Arizona?" I marveled.

"Well, I had been planning to fly here to see about Mom, but before I could book my ticket, she called. Said you'd run off and left her at a stranger's home. Phoned every fifteen minutes to say she was having a heart attack. I got here, took a cab to your mother-in-law's house, and discovered our mother living like a queen. Tracked down your daughter at her friend's house. Anya gave me the low-down. And according to the news this morning, you're quite the hero." My sister propped her feet up on the rails of my bed. Her brown leather flats went nicely with her khaki cargo pants and black knit top.

There was that word again: hero.

I ignored it.

Amanda kept talking. "Have you seen today's newspaper? You're big news, big sister. Here, I'll read it to you." From a fabric bag, she pulled a folded copy of the *St. Louis Post Dispatch*.

"No!" I said sharply. "I don't want to hear it."

"Well, I'll leave it here." She rummaged around inside the bag and lifted out two magazines. "I brought you clean clothes and magazines. I know how much you love magazines."

"Thanks. How's Mom?"

"She went on and on about how upsetting all this was to her. Leave it to Mom to make this her personal tragedy. It's always been all about her, hasn't it?" Amanda chuckled.

"Is she all right?"

"Right as rain, thanks to you. It was really smart of you to take Mom to a doctor. I had no idea she was sick. Physically, I mean. We all know she's not right in the head. But she was even loonier than usual."

"I took her to a geriatric psychiatrist, and he figured it out even before the lab tests came back."

"Who would guess that a bladder infection could cause a personality change?" Amanda shook her head.

"He said it was common in the elderly. He also tagged her as a sterling example of a narcissist." It felt reassuring to be chatting about Mom with Amanda, comforting in a way. My younger sister had avoided me for years thinking I was living the good life while she took care of Mom, but recent events gave us both a better appreciation for each other and our trials.

"I looked it up once, and she fit all the criteria."

Amanda gave me the smirk she'd perfected when we were young. We looked a lot alike, although her hair was less curly than mine, her face more oval, and her eyes a truer blue. "Didn't it ever occur to you that both our parents were nuts? Surely you've figured that out by now. I've been in therapy for years. My counselor tells me I'm a survivor, and I know you had it worse than me. Speaking of surviving, you'll need to take it slow at first."

"Right."

"Lucky you, I'll be around to help."

"You will? How long are you planning to stay?"

She studied the ceiling. "Indefinitely. See, I plan to move here. Actually, it was either that or be unemployed. My boss retired, and the partners in his law firm closed their Arizona office. Fortunately, I had a contact here in the St. Louis area, and they've offered me a job. I'm moving to the area. Weird, isn't it? That we'd both wind up in the same city?" She looked me in the eye. "If that's all right by you, I mean."

"Of course it is. I'd be happy to have you nearby."

"We don't have to live in each other's pockets."

"Amanda, I welcome the chance for us to be close again."

She reached out and squeezed my fingers.

"How does Mom feel about all this? Moving? She's not much for change."

"She doesn't know anything about the move, not yet. If she doesn't want to move with me, and live with me again, she can find her own place."

"I'm betting she'll tag along with you." I paused. "I don't have room for her at my house."

"Don't I know it. Lucky, lucky you."

FOUR

"Good news. We found Brenda Detweiler's Camry. Unfortunately, Brenda wasn't in it." After delivering a courtesy knock on my door, Police Chief Robbie Holmes strode into my hospital room, carrying his police cap in his big hands, his presence foreshadowed by his Aramis cologne. He pulled up the visitor's chair, a beige molded plastic seat with metal legs.

"I'm confused. The *Post Dispatch* says Brenda is in custody," I said. I had given in and read the article after Amanda left.

"The reporter got it wrong." Robbie's large frame dwarfed the chair.

"Does it matter?" Now that he didn't have my daughter in tow, I could give full vent to my anger. He'd ignored my warning that Brenda Detweiler's behavior was getting more and more erratic by the day. If he'd have listened to me, this could have been prevented. Instead, he'd passed over my worries with a patronizing platitude that the problem was between the two of us "girls," treating the violent incidents involving Brenda like small discourtesies.

"I suppose I deserved that. You tried to tell me she was dangerous. I didn't listen. I made a mistake. Will you accept my apology?"

His quick admission of guilt surprised me, and so impressed me that I rolled toward him and quickly answered, "Yes. Of course."

"Good. A farmer found Brenda's car in a field a few miles from here. Seems she'd run out of gas. Probably walked home after leaving it behind." Robbie's voice, always booming, dropped to a near whisper.

"So you think you've found her?"

"No, but she couldn't have gone far. And she isn't at her parents' house. Her mother, Carla, claims she hasn't seen her. The woman is hysterical and had to be sedated. We'll get her in for questioning. Maybe give her a lie detector test. I'm not sure I believe they weren't in contact. But I would guess that Brenda's hiding out at a friend's house. Seeing as how she's from southern Illinois, she has all sorts of resources. But law enforcement officials on both sides of the river are actively looking for her, and she doesn't have any money. Chad notified the bank to cut off her funds. Even if she hitchhikes, she won't get far. Besides, as you know, she's high most of the time. Either she'll need to visit a dealer to get more drugs or she'll run out of dope and do something stupid and obvious. Then we'll catch her."

"Did you check with the Detweiler family? Detweiler's sister Patty Kressig and Brenda are BFF."

"BFF? What does that mean?"

"Best Friends Forever." I looked past him to study the spindly maple tree planted outside my window. Four stakes held the sapling upright. I might need similar help returning to a vertical position. Especially since I wasn't getting any rest.

"Right. I think it's safe to say that Patricia Detweiler Kressig isn't interested in continuing their relationship. Not after the stunt Brenda pulled, drugging her brother and kidnapping you. We've been in contact with Brenda's father, Milton Kloss. He's been up in Chicago this whole time for meetings with the Republican Party. You know, he's running for State Representative, and he's been attending a mandatory get together to discuss campaign strategy for would-be candidates. The Illinois authorities are checking cell phone records on both parents as we speak."

"What do you plan to do when you find Brenda? Treat her with kid gloves like the princess she is?" The lack of sleep and the pain made me snippy. "Or are you planning to bring Brenda here so she and I can 'talk it out'? Isn't that what you suggested we do when I warned you she'd lost her mind?"

After the words were out, I marveled at my own audacity. It was not like me to give Robbie Holmes grief. I liked the man. Liked him a lot. I had watched his love change Sheila Lowenstein from a cold, bitter woman into a loving one. As he'd become a fixture in her household, I'd learned how seriously Robbie took his responsibilities. I gained insight into the difficult political arena in which he carried out his duties. Watching him with Anya, I'd heard about how kind he was, how warm and caring, to a pre-teen who was his "new granddaughter"—at least that was how Robbie introduced people to my daughter.

I'm rarely nasty to anyone, but then again, I've never had to shoot a man in cold blood. I was certainly turning over a new leaf! At this rate, I was becoming a whole new species of plant life.

"No. I'm not planning to bring her here." His sigh was audible. "In fact, we've posted fliers with her photo at every local hospital and convenience store. Your caregivers know not to let her any-where near you."

"Thanks."

"Since this is a continuation of your husband's murder case, I'll be taking your statement." Reaching into his back pocket, he removed a Steno pad. Where he found one I'll never know because they're a scarce commodity these days, but the greenish cover was familiar to me from my two years in college as a journalist major. His pen poised over the lined pages.

"Now start at the beginning."

FIVE

Going through all that had happened was harder than I would have guessed. Especially when I got to the part about killing Bill Ballard. Robbie finally left, but I was too upset to rest.

Nurse Ned came back a few minutes later and took my pulse. "You okay?"

"Yeah." I brushed the tears off my face.

"You've had enough visitors, darlin'. Time for you to take a nap."

Somehow I knew I was safe under his protective eyes, so I wiggled down under the sheets. Ned tucked me in. "Sweet dreams," he said as he turned out the light.

Even when I'm stressed—or particularly when I'm stressed—I eat, so later when the orderly brought the battered plastic tray with my lunch selection, I chowed down. I ate the overcooked Salisbury steak, the watery green beans, the limp lettuce salad with streamers of carrots. When I finished, I faced the wall and fell asleep again.

I woke up to a soft light that bathed the vinyl blinds in a golden glow. Dust motes rose and fell, dancing a slow waltz. The slats were canted enough for me to watch a watercolor portrait of the sunset, indistinct yet softly vibrant. A peacefulness settled over me, like a benediction. The ache in my throat had eased.

I was not alone. I could feel that someone was sitting beside my bed, behind me.

What now? Who else has come to bug me?

That piece of steak sat heavily in my stomach. A powerful thirst nagged at me. The scent of roses filled the air.

Maybe if I ignore my visitor, he or she will go away.

The thirst won out. I fought it as long as I could, then rolled over to find Rabbi Sarah, dozing in the visitor's chair, her chin nearly resting on her chest. Her thick, black curls tumbled over her shoulders. Her hands folded in her lap, the slender fingers knotted at the joints. She suffered from an extreme sort of arthritis, a crippling disease. However, she never let it stand in the way of her duties. The joke around temple was that Rabbi Sarah wouldn't die. Instead, a chariot drawn by heavenly horses and driven by Michael the Archangel would come down and invite her to her reward. Although her face always looked drawn and tired, her spirit energized the entire congregation. To me, she was the epitome of what a spiritual leader should be: compassionate, knowledgeable, humble, loving, inspirational, and a role model. She lifted all of us congregants up, encouraging us to a higher standard of behavior.

Her lashes fluttered and those huge brown eyes focused on me. "I must have dozed off. Did you see these red roses? They came for you while you were sleeping." She handed me the card, and I read, "Love you with all my heart—D."

"How are you?" Rabbi Sarah asked.

"Better now that you're here. Thank you for coming. I know how busy you are."

She smiled, a gentle incomplete grin that belied her worries. "Ned, your nurse, called me. Of course I would come. Care to tell me what's going on? Let's get a pot of tea, shall we?"

To my surprise, she rang the call button and asked for a pot of chamomile and two cups. I didn't know you could order anything! I'd assumed the uninviting photocopied sheet with the menu was all the hospital had to offer. The expression on my face must have given away my astonishment.

Rabbi Sarah laughed, a sound as cheerful as hand bells ringing. "Being a rabbi has its privileges. Not many, but enough to share. How are you feeling? They tell me you can go home tomorrow. How's your head?"

I reported I was fine. My headaches bothered me intermittently, but they were nothing I couldn't deal with.

A woman in a white uniform knocked twice, entered when Rabbi Sarah opened the door, and set a handsome walnut tray on the metal serving arm that hovered over my bed.

"Thank you, Eugenia," Rabbi Sarah nodded to the woman with the coffee-colored skin. "This looks grand."

The server reached over to hug the rabbi. "For you, ma'am, anything."

Astonishing.

I watched Eugenia reluctantly take leave of us.

"She needed help with housing a few years ago. I went to an agency and interceded on her behalf. You can't believe the hoops they ask people to jump through. While I understand the need to monitor usage, and to vet applicants, when a person is hurting any

21

effort is a gargantuan task, and energy is difficult to come by. I paved the way, and she's been grateful."

That was so like Rabbi Sarah. Her spiritual jurisdiction knew no bounds. Although Montefiore Temple was on the other side of the river, Rabbi Sarah's mandate was simple: to serve. Stories about her humanity were legion, like the one about the time she caught two boys vandalizing her car. Instead of turning them in to the police, she worked to fund and staff an afterschool program to keep kids off the streets.

Rabbi Sarah poured us both a cup of tea. "Tell me everything. Don't leave anything out, all right?"

It was quite a data dump—and this time it came easily. I started by explaining how Bill Ballard had sent me threatening postcards, phone calls, and so on. How there were unexplained happenings, such as the time I came home to find a "bloody" pelt on my porch that led me to believe my beloved dog, Gracie, had been skinned. Then I moved on to tell her how he'd avoided prosecution by lying about the time he'd held me at gunpoint. I shared the fact he'd moved most of the money from the business he co-owned with my husband—Dimont Development—into accounts in the Cayman Islands. How I couldn't get at the funds that were rightfully mine. Finally, I outlined the events of the past few weeks. Bill's reappearance in the St. Louis metro area. His vow to make me pay. The plot that Johnny Chambers and Police Chief Robbie Holmes hatched to entrap Bill. It involved me having a mock fight with Johnny, a public disagreement, so that Bill would hire Johnny to hurt me.

I backtracked a little, explaining my relationship with Detective Chad Detweiler, his crazy wife Brenda, and my pregnancy.

Rabbi Sarah said nothing except to nod or ask me to clarify a point.

"Robbie and Detweiler told me over and over that I'd never be at risk. I mean, I agreed he should wait on the divorce so that Brenda can go through rehab, and what happens? She decides to kill me!"

Rabbi Sarah's gentle smile crinkled the corners of her eyes. "No good deed goes unpunished, right? Except there are also great rewards, aren't there? I've been to see Sheila."

"How is she?"

"Fine, but exhausted and in pain. We could only talk for a minute. She told me about how you shot Bill Ballard. She's thankful you did what you did. She owes you her life."

"I'm scared to death about what people will think of me. I'm not a bad person!" I protested. "I'm not a natural born killer! Heck, I don't even eat red meat very often. Well, I did at lunch because that was one of the menu offerings. But normally, I don't! I mean, I know I did the wrong thing to shoot him, but what other choice did I have? How can I live with myself?"

To her credit, she didn't answer right away. Instead, she poured us both a second cup of tea.

"I know you never converted, but I consider you one of my flock, so to speak. You are like Ruth; you chose to follow your husband's family. Let me tell you what rabbinical law says, because I believe that will comfort you. You see, we believe that if you do not take a stand against an aggressor, you are partially responsible for the evil he does. We also teach that to stand by and let someone harm you or others would make *you* culpable. Furthermore, in Exodus, we learn that if a pregnant woman is killed, the assailant must be put to death because he has also murdered her child. So, according to our ways and our laws, you had no other choice but to act as you did."

The tea calmed me, as did her words, but I still felt guilty, dirty, and foul. I told her so. "In the movies, people are rescued. The cops always arrive in the nick of time. Maybe if I had waited, maybe they could have stopped Bill."

"That might have happened. Or one of them or both of the cops could have been killed."

"Yes, but..."

Rabbi Sarah set down her teacup and took both my hands in hers. Her eyes searching mine, not allowing me to hide. "Let's look at this another way. I want you to imagine that Anya was there. That she stood at the scene and saw Johnny bleeding to death. Her grandmother being strangled. Her mother threatened. Let's say that she had a gun. That she shot Bill Ballard. That she feels this overwhelming sense of responsibility and guilt for what she did. What if she came to you and said that she could never get over what she'd done? What if she believed she could no longer live among decent people because she had blood on her hands? What would you say to her?"

This shook me to my core. "Anya? My daughter? Are you kidding? I'd fall on my knees and thank her. I'd tell her how proud I was of her being brave! I'd tell her we ought to celebrate her survival!"

Rabbi Sarah nodded. "Then the real question here, the one we're grappling with, isn't whether what you did was right or wrong. The problem is... why don't you think you have a right to live? What's wrong with you, Kiki Lowenstein, that you can only take blame, not accept gratitude for saving your own life? And the lives of others?"

SIX

RABBI SARAH'S LAST WORDS to me were, "Remember: When you beat yourself up unnecessarily, you are being self-indulgent. You are wallowing in self-pity, not in remorse. If you start to question your part in all this, run the scene again. Put the gun in Anya's hands. That will get you thinking straight."

After she left, I stared up at the ceiling for a long, long time, noticing thin cobwebs fluttering around the fluorescent light fixture. When I started to feel guilty, I did as Rabbi Sarah said. I put Anya in my place.

And when I did, I knew I wouldn't blame Anya for Bill Ballard's death. I would celebrate Anya's courage.

The stainless steel railing around my bed distorted my features. The flesh-toned bandage stuck out like a mismatched bumper on a car. But the eyes that stared back into my own were calm, steady.

If I gave in to despair, Bill Ballard won.

I wasn't about to let that turkey win. Not now. Not ever.

Maybe the time for beating myself up was over. Maybe it was time for me to move on. To grow up and realize that, as Amanda had said, our parents were nuts. What they had told me about myself was untrue. I wasn't a mistake any more than Anya was or this baby would be. Sure, the timing of my arrival might have been inconvenient, but I was definitely supposed to be here.

I sneered. "Take that, Mom and Dad. I'm here. I'm staking my claim, and I'm not a waste of time and space. Boo-ya!"

With that small act of rebellion under my belt (more accurately under the elastic on my panties), I felt a lot better. Tougher. Shifting gears from victim to victor, I moved into "bring it on" mode.

The admitting doctor stopped by to examine me. "I'd like to keep you one more day."

"Please let me go home."

"Head injuries are unpredictable. I really want us to keep an eye on you."

"I don't have insurance."

"I'll fill out the discharge papers. You can go first thing tomorrow morning. One more night won't make that much difference money-wise. We can watch you for another twelve hours to be sure you don't have a more serious injury than we think you have."

Finally, my lack of insurance worked in my favor!

Ned dropped by fifteen minutes later.

"Gosh, you work long hours," I said.

"Three twelve-hour shifts in a row. Actually, I prefer it this way. I usually see patients come in, work with them, and get to see them released. Also, the drive here doesn't take up so much of my workday when I'm here on long shifts."

"Where do you live?"

"Webster Groves."

"Me, too!" That got us talking about our wonderful and eclectic neighborhood. Both of us had a special love for Winston, the stone statue of a dragon who guarded the local library. By the end of the conversation, Ned had promised to drop into Time in a Bottle, the scrapbook store where I worked, so we could go out for coffee.

"Thank you for calling Rabbi Sarah."

"Was she a help?"

"Absolutely."

"Good. Now, time for beddy-bye, little girl. Let me help you to the bathroom, and then I'll tuck you in."

On one hand, it seemed absurd, me being a grown woman and this hulk of a man treating me like a child. On the other, I've never had a loving dad, and Ned's gentle care touched a sore spot deep inside me.

"Don't let the bedbugs bite," he said.

I smiled to myself. How many nights had I told my daughter the same silly thing?

"Are there bedbugs here?" I wondered out loud.

"Nope. Only in finer hotels in New York City. They don't wander out here to the boonies. Now get some sleep." With that, he turned off the light, and I nodded off immediately.

SEVEN

Wednesday, Day 2—after the shooting

THE NEXT MORNING AFTER breakfast, Detweiler arrived. It was the first time I'd seen him since the shooting. "Hey, babe. How are you?" The lanky detective had the good sense to look uncomfortable.

Now that I was safe, I could give full rein to my anger. After all, the stupid idea for me to entrap Bill Ballard had been fully approved by Detweiler, who, along with Robbie, had assured me I'd never be in any danger at all.

"How am I? I am not happy with you, pal. Not at all."

Every muscle in my body was rigid with the force of my dismay. It even surprised me that I was still so angry. Okay, more hurt than angry. Disappointed, too. I'd thought at last I'd found someone to protect me in this life, and it seemed to me that he'd failed.

As quickly as I thought that, I also recognized how irrational and unfair I was being. My father had never been protective. Rather, he had been predatory, and my mother had stood idly by, grateful that he targeted us, not her.

Was I really expecting Detweiler to change my past? That was impossible, and no one knew that better than I.

He sighed. "This whole mess is my fault. I should never have let Robbie and Johnny involve you. I take responsibility for our collective stupidity. All I can say in my defense is that I wanted us to have a fresh start. I wanted all the remnants of your former life, and mine, to disappear. Except for Anya, of course," and he took a shuddering breath before continuing. "She's wonderful and I adore her."

"That's what I wanted, too." Hearing him restate his goals, and recognizing how in sync we were, further dissolved my anger. A long time ago, I learned that a person's intention is what matters, not the outcome. We can't control outcome. You can do your best, but there will always be circumstances you can't plan for. That doesn't mean you did the wrong thing. It's just how life works.

"I withheld information from you, and that wasn't fair."

My head jerked up and I met his eyes. The gorgeous green-gold irises had dimmed a watt. "See, at the station we learned about other, um, situations that Ballard had been involved in, and that scared me. For you. For Anya. So, when Johnny and Robbie came to me with a plan, I went along with it. Probably too quickly."

"What had he done?"

"You don't want to know. Trust me. He was escalating. You were in danger."

"So, you were worried about me? About us?"

He nodded slowly. "Absolutely. I screwed up, and I hope you can forgive me."

He stared at his feet and I stared at mine. Our toes had nothing to say, but we listened intently as though they could talk.

Detweiler sighed and went on. "As for letting Brenda dupe me, I was too eager to be rid of her. She'd promised to sign the papers and trust me to hold on to them, undated, until she got out of rehab. Even when she attacked you in the restaurant, I wanted to believe that once she was in rehab this time, she'd see how crazy her actions were. I didn't want to feel guilty about her. I wanted to move on, and as long as she was running around acting like a whack job, there'd be the chance we'd bump into her. I hated that. I hated the fact that her father held the deed to my parents' farm."

"What?" My jaw dropped. "Pardon?"

"I thought you knew. See, my sister Patty and her husband Paul were underwater on their mortgage when he lost his job at the auto plant. The pressure was destroying their marriage. They got involved in an investment scheme that took all their savings. So Dad and Mom decided to take out a second mortgage on the farm and loan Patty and Paul some money. The bank wouldn't authorize a loan to my parents, but Brenda's dad, Milton Kloss, is on the board and hears about all the foreclosures and so on. He came to Dad and Mom and offered them his personal guarantee on the loan. As collateral, he took the deed to the farm."

This stunned me. The Detweiler farm was a Century Farm, a designation given only to those farms that have been in the same family for one hundred years. I couldn't imagine the Detweilers losing their property.

So the Detweilers were beholden to Brenda's father! This admission knocked the wind out of me. I literally could not catch my breath. Stars danced before my eyes, and the room spun.

"Nurse!" Detweiler yelled. "Kiki? Honey? Breathe. Come on, stay with me."

EIGHT

NED CONFIRMED THAT I'D had a fainting spell, nothing more. In halting words, I explained that my fiancé had told me shocking news. Ned checked my vitals, stood there a few minutes, and pronounced me okay.

"Buddy, you've upset her. I'm thinking I should kick your butt out of here," Ned snarled at Detweiler, getting right up in the detective's face.

"He's my ride." I sighed. "And he told me something I needed to know. It's not his fault. Not entirely."

"Yeah, well, now I'm having second thoughts about discharging you. Especially if this turkey is going to be your caregiver." Ned stuck a finger into Detweiler's chest. "You're doing a pathetic job of helping out so far, mister. Better clean up your act, fast. Now go pull your car up to the front entrance before I take a swing at you."

I said to Detweiler. "I still want that shower before we go."

"How about if I run down the street and bring you a decaffeinated iced coffee from Starbucks while you shower?"

"Make that two," said Ned with a grin.

Detweiler nodded at the nurse. He knew when he was licked.

As Ned helped me back into the bed, I noticed a skull and crossbones tattoo right above the black Swatch on his wrist. What a bizarre set of visual contradictions. Today puppies and kittens turned cartwheels in the bachelor-button-blue background of Ned's scrubs, and a few inches lower a ghastly skull grinned at me.

"Tell me about your tattoo. I know they usually have a special meaning." I pointed to his forearm as he dried it off after turning on the shower for me.

He laughed. "Remnants of another life. I belonged to a motorcycle pack."

"What possessed you to become a nurse? I mean, that sure seems like a u-turn along life's highway."

His expression changed from jovial to bleak. "As I mentioned, I served in Iraq. I couldn't hack it when I got out of the service. So I joined a motorcycle pack. That's where I met Eleanor, and fell in love. We were going to get married, but then she was diagnosed with leukemia. I took care of her, but I couldn't save her. After that, I wanted a way to make a difference, you know? Even though I couldn't keep her from dying, I made her more comfortable. The hospice supervisor told me I had skills in this area. Besides after she died, I never wanted to see another Harley as long as I lived. Survivor guilt does funny things to you. It's harder to remove than a tat."

Ned slipped the pants and top that Amanda had sent with Detweiler onto hangers. "The steam will release the wrinkles. I'll put these behind the door for you."

When the water temp was right, he walked me to the bathroom. "There are railings here by the john and in the shower. After that fainting spell you had, I put a shower seat in there for you. I'll stay right outside the door. Don't hesitate to holler if you feel lightheaded. I promise I won't look."

Along with the hospital gown, I shed a lot of my negative emotions. The water moving down the drain took my anger with it. My late husband, George, and I had kept a lot from each other. Too much. When you think the other person isn't strong enough for the truth, you underestimate your partner. You set a booby trap for your relationship, and no one wants to walk through an emotional minefield. Detweiler and I would be fine. He'd been married twice before. Brenda was his second wife. His first, Gina, had run off, leaving him a note that she didn't want to live her life in a Podunk town in Illinois, married to a cop. As far as I knew, no one had heard from her after the divorce was issued.

I'd been married once.

Between us, we had three marriages. I vowed we would use our histories to be better spouses to each other.

As the water tap-tap-tapped on my back, I thought about how much I loved Chad Detweiler's commitment to family. Brenda Detweiler and Bill Ballard had definitely put our new family at risk. Now Bill was gone, and Brenda would be thrown in jail as soon as she surfaced.

My skin startled to pucker like a prune. I turned off the shower, reluctantly, grabbed the handrail, and stepped out carefully.

"Okay in there?" Ned asked.

"Yep."

Grabbing the sink, I steadied myself. The woman in the mirror sported a black and blue bruise on her temple, circles under her eyes, and a sad expression. Although Rabbi Sarah's visit had gone a long way toward lifting my burden, I still had plenty to worry about. Telling my daughter I was pregnant would not be fun.

I could hardly wait.

Ugh.

NINE

I WANTED TO SEE Sheila and Johnny before I left the hospital. That proved impossible. Sheila was asleep and Johnny was being examined.

"Here." Ned handed me a phone number on a piece of paper. "That's my personal cell phone. I'll check on them both before I leave tonight. Call me tomorrow, and I'll give you the real skinny."

"Will Johnny survive?" I knew Sheila would, but Johnny's condition had been up and down more times than the score at a basketball game. If he got well, Mert might forgive me. If he died, she probably wouldn't ever speak to me again.

Ned shrugged. "The docs aren't sure, but my gut tells me he'll be fine."

"Your gut?"

"When you've been in health care as long as I have, you develop a sixth sense. I can walk into a room where a guy's vital signs are all good and tell you he'll be dead by morning. That's why it's so important to have an RN with experience watching over you. A lot of hospitals try to cut costs by cutting back on their senior nursing staff and replacing us with fresh recruits right out of nursing school. There are talents you can't begin to develop until you've worked in a hospital for years."

"How often are you right?"

"Ninety-six-point-two percent of the time." He grinned and his chin whiskers stuck out like a directional signal. "I keep a chart. When I get off duty here, I go home, fill out my chart, feed my cat Bruiser, and crack open a brewski. Pretty boring, huh?"

"Sounds perfect to me." And I meant it. I wanted a return to normalcy. Boring is wonderful.

Ned escorted me to a wheelchair and made a low bow. "Your carriage awaits you, Cinderella. So does the handsome prince, right outside your door."

Detweiler stood in the hallway. In his hands were two coffees from Starbucks. Ned took his, thanked Detweiler, and nodded to me. "Should I tell this big guy to take a hike? Up to you, Kiki. He better behave, or I'll kick his butt out of here."

Detweiler looked horrified. He wasn't accustomed to being ordered around, but he knew that here in the hospital, Ned held all the power.

I giggled and reached for my drink. "Nah. I think he'd better stick around. My baby needs a daddy."

"Every baby needs a daddy," said Ned, in a conciliatory tone. "And a couple of uncles, too. I've taken a real shine to Ms. Lowenstein here. She's got spunk, and I appreciate that in a woman."

"So do I," said Detweiler.

As Ned pushed me in the wheelchair, the two men engaged in a steady stream of chatter, about the weather, traffic, and the

Cardinals' chances with their new manager, Mike Matheny. Ned interspersed his running commentary with greetings to other hospital staff as we passed by.

When the hospital doors were in sight, Detweiler ran outside to pull up his car.

"He's a good man, Kiki." Ned smiled.

"You've got a Spidey sense about that, too?"

"Yes, ma'am, I do. I had that sense long before I worked in a hospital. You don't ride with a motorcycle pack without learning to read people. Heck, folks see you pull up on a Harley and they have their notions. Some good, some bad. You gotta read them if you want to stay alive."

I sighed. "He is a good man. Does some boneheaded things, but he's a good man."

"That's why we guys need ladies like you. To keep us from being total boneheads. It's the nature of the beast, I'm afraid."

Detweiler pulled the car up, slammed it into park, and raced around to open my door.

Ned helped me to my feet. Spontaneously, I gave the big male nurse a hug. "I am eternally grateful that you chose this as a career. You, more than anything or anyone else here, healed me."

He gave me a kiss on the cheek. "My pleasure, darlin'. My pleasure. You call me if you need anything, hear?"

TEN

EARLY MAY IS A charming time to be in St. Louis. Young tree leaves shiver in their shocking green. House-proud residents line sidewalks and ring their homes in freshly planted tomato-red begonias, sunshine-yellow marigolds, eggplant-purple petunias, and storm-cloud-blue salvia. This spring was coolish, but that would change. On the ride home, Detweiler and I discussed telling Anya about the baby. We decided we should talk to her together, a choice that lightened the load on my shoulders. "After all, I'm equally responsible," said Detweiler, "and happily so. I want her to know that I'm not going to run out on either of you. If Anya's upset, she should be upset with me as well as you. Why don't you call the Moores and let them know we're on the way?"

Instead, I text-messaged Jennifer Moore. She responded quickly with: *Great! See you soon!*

Detweiler looked over at me, his face serious. "How do you think Anya will react?"

"I honestly don't know. I'm bracing myself for the worst. It might be hard for her to give up being an only child."

He parked in front of the Moore's McMansion, and we walked hand-in-hand to the front door. Moving around reminded me that I sported a number of bruises after my altercation with Brenda. My collapse onto the gravel after she shot me left me sore and stiff, but the pressure of Detweiler's hand on mine was warm and reassuring.

"Try not to worry," he said as he pressed the doorbell.

The polished walnut door flew open. Anya launched herself at Detweiler and me, nearly knocking us off the brick stoop.

"I'm going to be a big sister. I'm going to be a big sister," she sang. "Hurrah! We're pregnant! Whoopee! Can I name him, huh? Puh-lease?"

My mouth dropped open so wide you could have driven a dump truck down my throat.

After doing a genuine, certified "happy dance" there on the threshold, Anya hugged me tightly and gave me a huge kiss. "I am so, so happy!" she crowed. "Now I won't be the only Lowenstein! Right?"

A shadow passed over Detweiler's face, but he said nothing. A look went between us, signifying that we would discuss that particular issue later.

But Anya didn't notice. "Can I be there when he's born? Huh? That would be so, so cool!"

Behind her Nicci and Stevie Moore bounced up and down on their toes. They were cheering, "Hurrah! Wow! A baby!"

Jennifer Moore pushed past the teenagers and beckoned to Detweiler and me. "Don't just stand there! I've got sparkling cider to celebrate. Come on in."

When I first met Jennifer, I thought she was the typical Ladue lady of leisure, ultra-thin, über-snooty, and overindulged. As the years passed, I'd come to respect—no, admire!—her greatly. Now tears prickled and threatened to spill as I realized she'd set this happy welcome up for us. She'd heard I was expecting. Probably learned it from Margit, my co-worker at Time in a Bottle, an older woman who had guessed my secret before I was willing to admit the cause of my intermittent nausea. Recognizing how erratic teenage hormones are, Jennifer had prepped Anya. I wasn't exactly sure how she'd done it, and a part of me felt she might have overstepped her bounds, but that passed quickly. Intention. That was the key. Jennifer had hoped to smooth the way for me, and she had.

Anya grabbed Detweiler by the hand as she skipped across the marble foyer toward the large kitchen with its massive vaulted ceiling. As per usual, Steven Moore, Senior, was nowhere to be seen. Probably holed up in his man-cave, watching sports or otherwise fiddling around. Stevie and Nicci danced along beside Detweiler and Anya. That left me bringing up the rear, arm in arm with Jennifer.

"I can't thank you enough. I was so worried." I started, but words failed me.

Jennifer gave me a big hug. "I figured you would be. Kids can be totally unpredictable."

"How did you know?"

She sighed and poured glasses of cider. "I hate to tell you this, but it's all over the school community. I'm not sure how, but everyone is talking about you. Kids? Come on. I'm raising a glass to toast!"

The teenagers joined us, each grabbing a champagne flute.

"Here's to the new addition and to my smart, darling son, who's been invited to take early admission to Dartmouth College."

"Way to go, Stevie," I said. Out of the corner of my eye, I noticed a change in Nicci. Nothing overt. Just subtle.

"That's great," Detweiler offered Stevie his hand to shake. "Your grades must be stellar."

Stevie had his mother's sweet face and his father's classic bone structure. "Actually, I think it was my work starting support groups for the gays and lesbians at local private schools."

Detweiler's admiring smile didn't waiver. "That's important work. Good for you. We get calls all the time when gays are being targeted. Maybe if people are educated earlier in life, there won't be so many adult bullies."

"I hope so," said Stevie, lifting his chin a little higher.

The kids chugged their sparkling cider, grabbed a second bottle, and headed for the great room.

"The other parents are talking about me?" I stuttered. My mouth trembled and the glass clanked against my teeth. "Oh, lord. They don't think I'm some horrible murderer, do they?"

Jennifer laughed, her perfect white teeth flashing with glee. "Are you kidding? Kiki, you're a hero!"

ELEVEN

THE MINUTE SHE HEARD the car door slam, Gracie, my big black and white Great Dane, ran out the backdoor of my house and past me to greet Detweiler by planting her two front paws on his chest. I have no illusions: She loves him best. That's fine by me. I can handle coming in second. Besides, he adores her and I enjoy seeing the pure delight on his face when she slobbers all over him.

"Thank you so much for pet sitting," I said to Rebekkah Gold-fader as she joined my dog in greeting us.

"No problem," she said. "You know I love Gracie. Everybody does."

Like her mother, my boss Dodie, Rebekkah was Amazonian in stature. Unlike her mom, who had lost much of her hair to chemotherapy and radiation treatments for cancer of the larynx, Rebekkah peered out from under an untamed bush of dark brown locks.

"Here I thought I'd won Gracie's heart," she pointed to my dog, who was "hugging" the tall detective with her front paws. "Not so much, huh? I've been thrown over for a dude."

"I'm sure you own a piece of it, but ever since she met Detweiler, she's been all his," I said, smiling at the man and beast as they staggered around my yard. Watching Detweiler love up Gracie always made my heart skip a beat. As tough as he could be in his work, the dog always brought out his soft side.

Finally, Detweiler set the Great Dane's front paws down on the ground and turned to my daughter. "Anya? You need help getting that overnight bag out of the car?"

"Nope. Just give me a minute." With one foot in the police department's Impala and one on the grass, she concentrated on her cell phone. Her thumbs moving quickly over the keys, sending someone a message.

A part of me wanted to shout, "Hurry up!" I was so relieved to be home. All I wanted was to walk inside and plop down on my own sofa. Although we lived in a small place, a garage that my landlord Leighton Haversham converted into a studio he never used, I'd managed to create a warm and homey environment. Not much cash but a lot of dash had gone into the tiny two-bedroom cottage. Every inch of the place shouted, "Kiki Lowenstein lives here!" from the eclectic artwork on the walls to the fun and funky pillows I'd pieced together from wool sweaters I'd turned into felt. Now thoughts of my cozy home drew me closer and closer to my backdoor as though I was dragged along by an invisible magnet.

Detweiler jogged past me to hold the backdoor open.

I walked slowly up the flagstones, noticing the soreness that accompanied every step. When I got to the stoop, Detweiler took me by the elbow and helped me over the threshold.

"Surprise!"

A dozen voices shouted the greeting.

"Huh?" I struggled to take it all in.

A crowd of happy faces smiled at me.

A banner hung from the ceiling. Big letters spelled out, "WEL-COME HOME!"

The shock caused my legs to go wobbly. Detweiler put an arm around me and guided me to the sofa.

My co-workers Margit Eichen and Laurel Wilkins rushed forward to hug me. Behind them came my friend and co-worker Clancy Whitehead. Next Dodie Goldfader, and her husband, Horace, plus store regulars Bonnie Gossage, Elora Johnson, and Rita Romano approached me. Towering over all of them was Leighton, who was holding my mother's hand, which explained why she hadn't already made some sort of a scene to get attention. Flanking Mom was Amanda. Immediately to Amanda's right were Detweiler's parents. Last but not least, Robbie Holmes was squished in the remaining space by my front door.

My place is really too small for that many folks, so I approved when Detweiler suggested that we spill out onto the lawn. Responding to the noisy crowd, Monroe (pronounced MON-roe), Leighton's pet donkey, streaked out of his shed and cavorted around in his pen, kicking up his heels.

"I think someone's very happy to see you," yelled Leighton over the chatter of my guests. The donkey stood with ears quivering and nostrils wide to sniff the air.

How could I resist a love call like that?

Clancy grabbed my arm, and walked me toward the enclosure. Her grip was strong, her gait sure. At one point, she slipped an arm around my waist—an unusually affectionate gesture for someone who generally acts with restraint. I must have been pretty wobbly.

"When you get the chance, Horace needs to talk to you," she said quietly.

"About what?" I leaned close and enjoyed the lingering notes of her signature fragrance, Chanel No. 5. My friend always dresses in timeless style. Today she wore a pair of high-waist slacks in a shade of bone with a cream silk blouse. A simple brown crocodile belt pulled the pieces together. Holy shades of Jackie Kennedy, Batman.

"Horace and Dodie want you to come back to the store. Her health seems to have taken a turn for the worse."

"You're kidding? I only quit three days ago."

"I know. I think she was barely holding it together before all this happened. I've found her asleep at her desk twice in the past two days. Once she was wandering around in the stockroom as if she were lost."

"Has she said anything? I mean, about how she's feeling?"

Clancy shrugged. "You know Dodie. Where's Mr. Detweiler going, I wonder?"

We watched Louis Detweiler walk down my drive like a man on a mission. His wife, Thelma, was busy putting food on a rickety card table surrounded by four folding chairs. "Probably to get something out of his truck. I assume everyone parked around the corner so I wouldn't see the cars?"

"You assume right, but back to the topic at hand. She's not in good shape, Kiki."

Although I'd been plenty fed up with Dodie by the time I quit, my heart ached at this news. Clancy and I both knew it could mean that Dodie's cancer had returned. Clancy didn't say that. Neither did I. Instead, my friend and I scratched Monroe's ears in companionable silence.

Louis Detweiler pulled his silver Ford F150 pickup into my driveway before hopping out and signaling his son. From the flat bed, the two Detweiler men unloaded a wooden picnic table. Clancy and I walked over to inspect the piece.

"Wow! I've wanted one of these for the longest time. Is it a loaner?" I ran my fingers over the surface of the treated wood.

"Nope. It's a gift from all of us," said Detweiler the Elder. "We heard your good news. Thelma and I are delighted about the baby."

I threw my arms around him and gave him a peck on the cheek. "Thank you so much!"

"I'm expecting to eat a lot of good grub on this table. You expect you can make that happen?"

I laughed.

I'm not much of a cook, but Margit is. On an occasion like this, she's in her glory. After I took the seat of honor at the picnic table, she brought me a plate full of sauerbraten with green beans on the side. "Save room for dessert. Rita Romano brought her Sopapilla Cheesecake."

"Oh my gosh," I said, thinking of that heavenly sweet treat. "I certainly will have room for dessert. You can count on it!"

Thelma brought me a glass of iced tea and sat down. "How can I help you? You'll need to rest and take it easy. I'd be happy to drop by and do laundry or whatever."

Her consideration touched me. I shook my head. "I appreciate your offer more than I can say, but right now, with my sister Amanda here, I think I'll be fine."

In a whisper she added, "Does Anya know she's going to be a big sister?"

"Yes," I cupped my hand over my mouth to keep my voice from carrying. "She's happier than I would have ever imagined. Frankly, Detweiler—er, Chad—and I expected her to be upset. Uncomfortable at least, but she's not."

"The old 'I can't believe people your age still do it' routine, right?" Thelma chuckled. "Kids are unpredictable. Especially when they're teens. You never know which way the wind is blowing until your kite is in the air."

She was right about that!

Thelma got up to help Margit serve food, directing folks into my kitchen. Clancy took drink orders. Rebekkah brought out paper plates and cups. Louis set up more card tables and chairs that appeared like magic from the bed of his truck. My friends had thought of everything. While each person visited with me for a minute or two to say, "Hi," I didn't have to move a muscle. If this kept up, I'd have to buy a tiara and practice my royal wave.

Horace shuffled over to sit next to me on the wooden bench. "*Oy vey*, but we were worried about you," he said as his smooth bald head wrinkled. "I have heard that you will be all right. Only you must act with restraint. Is that true? Would you be willing to come back to the store? I ask, in part, because we ... I ..."

His hand flew to his mouth, as if he was holding back a sob.

"It's Dodie, isn't it? What's wrong?" I put down my fork. My stomach knotted with fear. She had been acting very strangely before my run-in with Bill Ballard and Company. Horace's trembling jaw told me all I needed to know. I waited for the words that would confirm all our worst fears.

People walked around us, laughing and enjoying their food, but Horace and I were frozen and alone. Before he spoke, I knew what he was going to say. I'd been dreading it.

"My darling girl, my Dodie. So brave. They tell me to enjoy every minute with her. They say we don't have long."

"It's come back?" My voice cracked.

"Worse. It's gone to her brain."

SOPAPILLA CHEESECAKE

(Special thanks to Julie Failla-Earhart)

2 cans (8 oz. each) refrigerated crescent dinner rolls
2 packages (8 oz. each) cream cheese, softened
1½ cups sugar (divided into 1 cup and ½ cup)
1 teaspoon vanilla
½ cup butter, melted
1 tablespoon ground cinnamon

Set oven to 350 degrees F. and grease a 13x9 inch baking pan.

Unroll one can of dough. Place in bottom of pan. Stretch dough to cover bottom of pan, firmly pressing perforations to seal.

In medium bowl, beat cream cheese and 1 cup sugar together until smooth. Beat in vanilla. Spread mixture over dough.

Unroll second can of dough. Carefully place on top of cream cheese layer. Pinch seams together.

Pour melted butter evenly over top. Mix remaining ½ cup of sugar and cinnamon. Sprinkle evenly over butter.

Bake 30 minutes or until center is set. Cool about 20 minutes. Refrigerate for easy cutting.

Serve warm with a dollop of vanilla ice cream.

TWELVE

To keep from bursting into tears, I grabbed my iced tea and took a long swallow. Out of the corner of my eyes, I watched Dodie take a seat next to my mother. Although my boss wobbled a bit on her feet, her face was animated and happy.

"Are they sure?"

He nodded.

"D-d-does she know?"

Horace picked up a paper napkin and blew his nose. "No."

"Are you going to tell her?"

"I haven't decided. There are signs that her cognitive ability has been compromised. Perhaps it is God's blessing that she does not know what is ahead."

"And Rebekkah?" I watched as their daughter walked over to grab another cold Coca-Cola from the cooler someone had set outside my backdoor. Could I detect sadness just from the girl's walk? Probably not. Like many women who are tall, both mother and daughter hunched over as if that would reduce their height, in a posture that hid their faces.

"She knows her mother isn't doing well. I have not..." He stopped. "I have not had the courage to tell our daughter everything I know."

"Of course I'll come back. I'll help you in any way I can!" I grabbed his hand.

"You are a true friend," Horace said. "That reminds me, I asked an accountant friend of mine to handle the books for a while. He'll be calling you. That way I am free to spend all my time with..." His voice trailed off.

"Does Dodie want me back?"

"Yes. But I admit to a small deception. I told her I thought that you would need the job."

"Ha! That's not a deception. When do you need me?"

"Tomorrow?" he asked sheepishly.

"I'll be there when the store opens."

Other regulars from Time in a Bottle took turns greeting me. Then a navy-blue Mercedes C-class pulled up and out hopped Jennifer, Nicci, and Stevie Moore. The teenagers glanced around awkwardly at first, making it clear that any gathering of adults was not their thing. But when Thelma Detweiler intercepted them with a big bowl of chips and salsa, they immediately dropped the attitude and went to find Anya and the colas.

"Long time no see, stranger," Jennifer giggled and nibbled a bit of lettuce from a nearby platter. "This food is delicious. You should get shot more often."

"Hmm. Maybe I'll put that on my permanent 'to do' list, right next to losing weight. Get shot on a regular basis so that Jennifer, who barely eats enough to keep a hummingbird alive, can come to my house and chow down on lettuce." It felt good to be teasing Jennifer. Anything, anything at all to get my mind off of Dodie's condition.

"Actually hummingbirds eat a lot. Up to twelve times their body weight a day."

"Whoa. That's a shocker." I rested my chin on my fist and stared at the teenagers as they wandered over to feed carrots to Monroe. Anya and Stevie were dressed for the spring weather in shorts and T-shirts, but Nicci wore a long-sleeved top and jeans. They were gorgeous kids, all of them. Sweet, too.

"How's Stevie?" I asked Jennifer.

"I think he has a boyfriend. A guy he met at a regional PFLAG meeting."

"Good for them." Stevie had come out only recently. Jennifer had suspected for years that her son was gay, in part because her brother had been, and she saw the similarities in their behavior and interests. Jennifer was Stevie's greatest cheerleader.

"And Nicci?"

Jennifer quit picking at the lettuce and said nothing.

Without comment, I reached down and lifted her hand to examine it. She submitted with a sigh. When she's upset, Jennifer nibbles at her fingernails and chews the skin around them until they're bloody. Reflexively, she curled her fingers into a fist.

"Come on, Kiki," she protested, but I didn't turn loose. Instead I gently pried her hand open. There was the proof: five bloody digits.

"Can I help?" I scanned the people around us. Mom was preening in front of Leighton. Amanda was engrossed in conversation with Clancy, Dodie, and Laurel. Robbie was talking with the Detweilers, until he suddenly reached into his pocket and examined his cell phone. Covering the receiver, he quickly made his excuses and turned away from the couple.

For the most part, Robbie seemed to handle the stress of his job with ease. However, right now, as he walked toward my house, his face contorted with worry. I hoped it wasn't bad news about Sheila. But if Sheila had taken a turn for the worse, he'd let me know immediately. I was sure of that. And he'd do so because we'd have to decide how to tell Anya, since any problem with her grandmother would be devastating for my daughter.

Jennifer interrupted my thoughts, saying, "I know you would help me if you could. If I knew what to ask for, I would. You're probably the only CALA parent I'd feel comfortable sharing a problem with. In the meantime, keep your eyes and ears open, would you? I don't mean to spy on my daughter, but..."

"Right," I said. "I understand."

CALA is the local nickname for the "Charles and Anne Lindbergh Academy," the elite prep school that our children attend. From the outside, it looks like an educational paradise, complete with high SAT scores, a high percentage of students attending college, and a physical plant that any Ivy League college would envy. But the parental community and student body both stagger under the strains of our own high expectations. It ain't easy to be top-notch, or to stay at the tippy-top of the food chain with everyone nipping at your heels. Problems are often swept under the proverbial rug. Situations that should be addressed early on are gleefully ignored in favor of maintaining the CALA brand.

"It's not spying. Our parents had access to everything we did and knew, but this generation is different," I said, watching Robbie return and tap Detweiler on the shoulder to lead him away from the crowd. The younger cop's back was to me, but I could tell that their conversation was intense by the sweeping gestures Robbie made as they talked. At one point, Detweiler turned away from the police chief and raised a shaky hand to his forehead, as if it hurt.

What was *that* all about?

"I know," said Jennifer. "I just hope … well, I hope I'm being an overprotective mother. That's all."

———

"Kiki? We need to talk," Robbie Holmes put a heavy hand on my shoulder.

"What? Could we do this later? I'm getting tired. I'd like to lie down." Between the news about Dodie and the recognition that Jennifer suspected Nicci had a problem, I felt tired. Perhaps I should have stayed in the hospital, no matter what the cost. Then all these troubles and tribulations would have taken another twenty-four hours to reach me.

"I know, but this is important." Robbie offered me assistance in getting up. "Will you excuse us, Mrs. Moore?"

With the change in my elevation, my head started pounding and my limbs felt weighed down.

"This can't wait?" I leaned against him to keep my voice from carrying.

"I wish it could. I got a call from the Illinois State Police. They've found Brenda."

THIRTEEN

DETWEILER STOOD AT THE side of my house, white-faced and solemn. Robbie motioned us away from the crowd. "Let's sit on Leighton's front stoop."

"Isn't this rather extreme? I mean, we could go into my bedroom and shut the door."

So what if Brenda came after me again. I would stick to home and the store. Gracie would be by my side, and she wouldn't let anyone hurt me. Although my big dog didn't bark often, she could get aggressive when confronted by an intruder. She'd proven her mettle in the past.

The two men didn't respond, so I sighed and fell into step between them. Oddly enough, Detweiler didn't put an arm around me or reach for my hand. Most of the trek, he stared down at his feet with his hands shoved deep into the pockets of his jeans.

We sat on the stoop, a brick pad facing one of the shady tree-lined streets that makes Webster Groves such a desirable town. Positioned like "Hear No Evil, See No Evil, Speak No Evil," we dutifully lined up, shoulder to shoulder. Although the surface of our seat was unforgiving, the view was lovely. Leighton loved flowers. Each spring he added colorful impatiens to his collection of day-lilies. The riot of blood-red, tangerine-orange, and lemony-yellow always lifted my spirits.

"What gives? Am I going to have to testify against Brenda? Or appear before a grand jury?" I sounded petulant because I felt that way. I was so tired of Brenda Detweiler.

"Hard to say," said Detweiler, rubbing his jaw so hard that his fingers left a red streak on his skin. When he finished, he scrubbed his palms along the legs of his jeans. As usual, he looked terrific with those long lean legs of his.

Robbie sighed. "You needn't worry about talking with her. That's not on the agenda. Not now. Not ever. A real estate agent was showing a foreclosed farmhouse to a couple. Heard a noise. A buzzing. Flies. Lots of them. The agent walked into a back bedroom and found Brenda rolled up in a blanket."

"Probably sleeping off a high," I muttered.

"No." Robbie sighed. "She was dead."

"Overdose?" I asked, as a queer sort of chill startled in my solar plexus. The sensation spread, numbing my fingers and toes. Reflexively, I clenched my hands in my lap.

"No." Detweiler's voice was strange. Distant. Pre-occupied.

"What? How?" The words stuck in my throat.

"Gunshot wounds. Three to the head. Execution style. An Illinois State Trooper is at her folks' house right now." Robbie spread his big hands wide over his knees and gripped them.

"Oh, lord. I am so, so sorry," I said and I truly meant that. "Her poor parents. And you."

I reached for Detweiler's hand and cradled it in mine. "Do your parents know?"

"We can't tell them yet," said Robbie. "Not until hers are notified. Her mom answered the door, but her father is still up in Chicago. The State troopers were sending someone to hunt him down at the conference."

I squeezed Detweiler's hand. "Believe me, I know you didn't want this. Even with all you've been through, you wouldn't have wanted her dead."

"That's not entirely true. After I heard she was the one who shot at you, I would have cheerfully throttled her with my bare hands." He shook his head. "As they loaded you onto the bus, I called her and left her a message. I told her I could just kill her."

"But you didn't mean it!"

He shrugged. "Doesn't matter. I said it. Right before I left for my parents' house. I spent the night there to cool off."

"Chad, you and I have talked about this before." Robbie tapped his fingers against his knees as he stared at the hedge across the street. "You mess with drug dealers, you ask for trouble. Those people are ruthless. They have to be to keep their underlings in line."

"That's what you're thinking?" I was happy for the change of focus. "A drug dealer or someone in the supply chain got to her?"

"More than likely," said Robbie.

Detweiler shook his head. "I don't know that she had a supplier. I'm pretty sure she was stealing from the hospital where she worked."

"How? They tracked every last Tylenol I took." I shuddered as I imagined how much I paid for each of those pills.

A car drove by us, its muffler rattling, and for a short while, none of us spoke.

"Nurses with a problem give patients only a portion of the medication and pocket the rest," Detweiler said. "Especially when there's an injection of morphine or multiple pills. Shortchanging the sick sounds ruthless, but that's the nature of addiction. An addict will do anything and hurt anyone to get her hands on more. Sometimes they steal from patients and trade the prescription drugs for other drugs."

"Then it's possible that she quit supplying someone and that person ...?"

"Came after her," Detweiler finished my sentence.

Robbie turned mournful eyes on me. "Or one of Brenda's contacts became frightened. Saw her face on the news and decided things had gotten too dangerous. Maybe Brenda went to one of her pals or customers for money or shelter, or even a fix. Because her face was all over those posters, that person might have decided she was a liability. Or maybe she owed money and, because she was on the run, her suppliers became convinced she would never repay them. There are any number of scenarios."

"Any number of scenarios," Detweiler repeated, wearily, "and all of them end badly."

FOURTEEN

DETWEILER VOLUNTEERED TO IDENTIFY her body rather than further upset her parents.

"I'm still her husband legally, but I'll ask them how they want to handle her funeral arrangements. I still want to be respectful, but it's really their call. This situation is bad enough without making it worse."

"You're right. That's the right thing to do. I'm sure they would appreciate it, if they were thinking straight," I said. "If I don't see you for a couple of days, I'll understand. You'll have your hands full."

"You can say that again," Robbie added. "I'm sure the Illinois State Police will want any names of friends you can give them, Chad. Maybe even a list of her work colleagues or high school pals. I wonder why she went to that specific house? How she knew it was vacant—and why there weren't any signs of forcible entry? I plan to interview a number of confidential informants in the drug trade. They'll do the same over there. Meanwhile, I suggest you keep a low profile. You might want to avoid visiting Kiki until we've got a better handle on this."

"Why?" I asked. His suggestion didn't make sense.

Detweiler scrubbed his face vigorously with both hands, leaving bright red streaks. "Because I don't want to lead Brenda's killer to your door. Who knows? This might be a creep wanting to get back at me. This might have nothing to do with her drug habits. I sure don't want to put you at risk…again."

"I'll have a patrolman keep an eye on the house," Robbie nodded toward my home. "Kiki? Don't hesitate to call nine-one-one if you see anything out of the ordinary. This isn't the time to try to tough it out. Now if you'll excuse me, I promised to go visit Sheila. Here's hoping she'll be able to come home in a day or two."

Detweiler text-messaged his parents that he had an emergency come up, and Robbie walked me back to my party, or what was left of it. While we'd been gone, someone must have decided I'd had enough company for one day. People milled around collecting garbage, putting away food, and straightening my kitchen. Then my scrapbookiing friends said goodbye. Dodie came over, her awkward gait even more so than usual.

"Hey, Sunshine. Glad to see you. You were hurt, right?"

"I'm fine." I hugged her.

"Are you planning to come back to the store? We could use your help," she said.

Behind her, Horace raised his eyebrows, silently urging me to say yes. Rebekkah stood a few feet away from her parents, her body bent under the weight of her worries.

"I could use a job, so that sounds like a good deal for both of us," I said. "Thank you, Dodie."

"Come back to the store," she repeated, like a stuck record. "To the store." A vacancy in her eyes warned me she had no idea what she was saying.

"Yes, I will come back to the store. I can start work again tomorrow."

"Tomorrow."

Horace turned away, staring past me at a future that didn't include his wife.

"I have morning sickness," I said for no particular reason at all.

"Really?" Dodie cocked her head. "I had it, too, although I can't remember why. Was it the flu, Horace?"

"I think you were pregnant when it happened." Stepping forward, he slipped his arm around her. They made an incongruous pair. He came up to her shoulder. Her hands and feet were large, and his as dainty as a girl's. She was once as hairy as the wooly mammoth found south of St. Louis, and he was as hairless as a cucumber. But for as long as I'd known them—and I'd been her customer for years before becoming her employee—they had been lovebirds.

"*Oy vey*! I remember now! With Nathan." Just as quickly, she puckered up as if to cry. "His memory is a blessing."

"I think it's time for us to go," Rebekkah said, rubbing her arms vigorously to ward off a chill. "I bet Kiki needs to rest. Let's go and tell Mr. and Mrs. Detweiler goodbye, okay?"

That was a feint, a move designed to steer Dodie toward the family car. Thinking about the unwelcome news the Detweilers would soon receive, I walked with the Goldfaders, waved farewell to Margit, gave the Detweilers each a goodbye hug and started toward my house.

Clancy intercepted me, as did Laurel. "Woo-hoo! Back in the saddle again!" said the younger woman, giving me a high five.

"Right. But I might not be much use."

"Nonsense," Laurel hugged me and planted a kiss on my cheek before rubbing at my skin gently. "That's some bruise you've got there on the side of your head."

"Kind of matches the colors in your sundress," I giggled.

On anyone else it would have looked girlish, but on her it was alluring. Laurel was a knockout. Her sleek hair, her gorgeous figure, and her stunning features turned heads wherever she went. But even so, Laurel never acted affected by her beauty. In fact, she seemed to ignore it. And if she had an active social life, well, we never heard about it. Eventually Clancy and I had come to the conclusion that Laurel was too busy to date. In addition to working at Time in a Bottle, she had a second job as a waitress in a nightclub on the Illinois side of the river, and she was taking classes at Washington University. Mert had mentioned something about Laurel caring for a sickly mother and cautioned me not to bring that up. "I don't want her to think I was talking behind her back. If'n she wants you to know about her mother, she'll tell you herself."

I smiled at my two friends, thinking what a lovely pair they made. Clancy was just as attractive as Laurel, in an older, classy way.

"Hmm. I'll be the first to admit that the swelling around your forehead has done wonders, dah-ling, for your wrinkles," Clancy said.

"Other people get facelifts with scalpels, I prefer the broad brush approach of a speeding bullet," I said.

"How you feeling?" Laurel asked me.

Gosh but I wanted to spill the news about Brenda! I wanted to absolve myself of the guilt I felt for feeling relieved. After all, she'd been nothing but a major pain in the butt to me. Now she was gone! Detweiler was free! Without her spying on us, without Bill Ballard threatening me, life would be so much easier. As I dithered over how to respond, I caressed my belly and sent my baby a message: "Everything is going to be all right, little one. You'll be part of a loving, happy family."

Laurel smiled at my little bump. "When's the baby due? I get first dibs on holding a baby shower."

"Um, January, I think. I have an appointment with a gynecologist next week."

"Wow. We usually get sleet and ice in January. That trip to the hospital should be exciting. You're going to give birth to a slider!" Clancy grinned.

That didn't sound very appealing to me.

"Does Dodie seem a little lost?" Laurel moved closer to Clancy and me. We waved as the Goldfaders pulled out of my driveway.

I didn't know what Horace had told them or how he wanted to handle the situation, so I restricted my comments to what I'd observed. "Yes, she isn't herself. Usually she's very sharp. Very accurate. She seemed sort of foggy."

Clancy and Laurel exchanged worried glances. "That's what we've been thinking," said Laurel. "She seems to have taken a definite turn for the worse. Yesterday, she put a cup of coffee in the microwave for an hour."

"Day before yesterday, I found her walking around the store and looking at the signs as though she was lost," said Clancy. "I wonder what this means for the business? I asked Margit, and she doesn't know. She's a minority partner just like you."

All I could do was grunt, "Yes, I know." My minority partner status had been a sore spot for quite a while. Not long ago, I had discovered that being a minority partner didn't mean diddly. Oh, you could be proud of the title, but you had no voice in the running of the business. At least, not the way Time in a Bottle, the scrapbook store, was set up.

My mother and sister headed toward me. My friends took notice.

"To be continued," said Clancy as she moved away.

Laurel backed off, too.

Leighton tried to pull my mother aside, urging her to make a detour, but Mom was nothing if not stubborn. He shrugged an apology at me and turned toward his house. As worried as I was about Dodie, as sick as I felt about Brenda, any interaction with my mother was ten times worse than dealing with those crises. No doubt about it, my mom had all the impact of a nuclear blast on an unprepared city.

Or to paraphrase Herman Melville, "Call me Hiroshima."

FIFTEEN

ONCE UPON A TIME, my mother and my sister looked a lot alike. Both had longer noses, and they shared the same shade of auburn hair. Amanda inherited Mom's more voluptuous shape, a very Marilyn Monroe-ish figure. Catherine and I were built more like our father, rather boyish and not so hippy. We all wound up with Mom's curly hair, but mine was the most unruly. Catherine's changed from platinum at birth to a lovely strawberry blond. All of my sisters were three inches taller than I, as was my mother.

Time had whittled Mom down to size.

Now I could stare down onto the top of her scalp and see how thin her hair was. Mom had not aged well. Deep marionette lines bracketed either side of her mouth. Her lips had become so thin that they nearly disappeared. Or maybe her constant state of unhappiness kept them under wraps. Added to this, her nose curved downward, which resulted in a witch-like appearance.

She had been a beautiful woman, but over the years, Mom's sour outlook robbed her of her good looks. As Abe Lincoln said, "Every person is responsible for his own looks after forty."

Of course, my mom wasn't big on responsibility. Her strong suit was blame.

Shaking free of Amanda's arm, my mother stormed me the way the Huns must have attacked the Roman Empire. Her index finger led the charge. "You ran off and left me! I was alone in that big house! How could you? Do you know how frightened I was? Didn't the doctor tell you that I was sick? What did I ever do to raise an ungrateful, unkind daughter like you? I will never, ever forgive you. You're lucky I'm even talking to you."

Lucky. Yeah, I sure was lucky.

My mother hadn't even noticed I wore a bandage and sported a multi-colored bruise.

"Mom, she was kidnapped at gunpoint. Give her a break," Amanda said. "If she hadn't sidetracked that crazy woman you might have wound up dead. Come on, let's go home."

"Home? Ha! You call that woman's house 'home'? I miss my antiques. I want to go back to Arizona. Where's Claudia? What did you do to her, Kiki? You ran her off, didn't you?" Mom's lipstick covered most of her two front teeth, turning her mouth into a big red maw that mesmerized me as it flapped open and shut.

"Mrs. Montgomery, the woman you knew as Claudia Turrow was a con artist. Her real name was Beverly Glenn, and she specialized in stealing from lovely people like you." Robbie Holmes stepped between my mother and me. With his huge mitten of a hand, he gently pushed her angry, pointed finger away from my face.

At his touch, Mom simpered and did a little "pshaw" move of her hand. "Oh, that's just the kind of nonsense I'd expect Kiki to tell you. The truth is that Claudia loved me more than she loved anyone on earth. She told me so. I was the mother she never had. A con artist? You must have heard silly rumors. Of course, my friends were very, very jealous of me—and my relationship with Claudia. They probably made up stories about Claudia to drive us apart." Mom batted her skimpy eyelashes at Robbie Holmes.

"Yes, ma'am, I can certainly believe that people would be jealous of you. Beauty runs in your family. And you have a wonderful daughter who risked her life to make sure you didn't come to any harm."

Mom smiled at him shyly. "Isn't Amanda wonderful?"

SIXTEEN

Thursday, Day 3—after the shooting

THE NEXT MORNING AMANDA swung by in her rental car to see how I was doing. "I'll drop Anya off at school and take you to the store. Chad mentioned that you shouldn't be driving. At least, not yet. Mom's still in bed, so we can grab breakfast at a drive-through if you two want."

Chad? Oh, she meant Detweiler! I'd have to become accustomed to people using his real first name!

"The dog comes with." I nodded at Gracie.

"No problem. I love dogs. I almost married two of them."

The offer of a breakfast burrito from McDonald's thrilled Anya, even if going to school didn't. She suffered from a bad case of "I'm-ready-for-school-to-be-out"-itis. I struggled with a bad bout of morning sickness. I buried my nose in a cup of hot tea and nibbled on an English muffin so my stomach wouldn't misbehave. Amanda ordered a big breakfast sandwich that she ate with one hand while Gracie drooled over her shoulder.

Following our instructions, my sister drove to CALA. As we turned into the circular drive, Amanda struggled not to gawp at the palatial administration building, class buildings, and expansive grounds. "This is some school," she whistled.

"Sure is. Have a good time," I told my daughter as I kissed her goodbye.

"Right," Anya snarled. "Like taking algebra and French are loads of fun, Mom."

"Do her moods always swing from high to low so quickly?" Amanda asked as Anya walked toward the building.

"Nope. Usually they cycle faster. Any leads on finding a place where you and Mom can both live? Does she realize she's moving here?"

"I told her last night. She started to have a cow, but I reminded her that your nice neighbor, Mr. Haversham, showed a real interest in her, and then I pointed out that a long-distance romance might be hard on both of them."

"You weasel, you. Leighton will have to peel Mom off like chipped nail polish."

"He's a big boy. He can handle it. Listen. To deal with Mom, I've become a crackerjack liar and a nearly professional-quality manipulator. Otherwise, I'd be battling her every day, all day. With any luck, I'll find a place that's move-in ready before your mother-in-law is released from the hospital. That or I'll have to rent one of those short-term, executive-stay hotel suites."

"Let me know how I can help you. If I can."

"Huh. I always thought you were overly sensitive about her criticism, but after watching her lay into you yesterday, I've been forced to revise my opinion. You're right. Our mother really, really doesn't like you!"

My sister came into the store and wandered around while I went through the process of opening our door for another day of retail selling. The craft gene—a variation on the XX chromosome that's yet to be mapped—skipped a generation with my sister Amanda. Nothing in the place particularly appealed to her, so she gave me a hug and left for an appointment with a real estate agent.

Horace walked in with Dodie, settled her in the big black office chair behind her desk, and gestured to me for a private powwow. "Rebekkah will bring her lunch. We have another doctor's appointment at one."

"Horace, I am so sorry. I mean, after talking with her yesterday…" I stopped. What could I say? I couldn't find the right words. "Look, whatever I can do for you, I will. The baby isn't due until January, but I can work until I go into labor if that will help."

His face crumpled as he said, "That won't matter."

"What do you mean?"

"I mean she doesn't have that long."

SEVENTEEN

DODIE STAYED IN HER office for most of the morning. I looked in on her and found her arranging paperclips. At one point, she wandered out and looked around as if she were lost. "What are you doing?" she asked me.

I invited her to take a stool across from me as I worked at the craft table. "I thought I'd come up with a new class idea. You love my class ideas. We always get a lot of customers to sign up. That means money for the store."

As she sat across from me, she picked up various things, a pencil, an eraser, and a colored marker, one at a time and dropped each of them on the floor. With every "thunk," I stopped my work to retrieve the lost object. It reminded me of babysitting a toddler who had just realized she could train her minder to play fetch.

I deftly moved the Fiskars scissors and the craft knife beyond her reach, hoping she wouldn't notice they were gone. The last thing I needed was for Dodie to drop a sharp blade into her own flesh. Or mine. If it hit me, I might very well faint at the sight of my own blood. Or puke. Or both.

I don't know who named this malady "morning sickness." Probably some squirrel of a doctor who couldn't tell time. I happen to get sick all day long. Just when I would forget about my pregnancy, I would start to heave.

At some point, I had to do something to quell my nausea, so I ran to the back and got Dodie a Coke and myself a Zevia Ginger Ale, a no-calorie cola sweetened with Stevia.

To fill the silence between us, I made yet another trip to the back, returned with her radio, and tuned it to a classical music station. That's how we spent our time until eleven when the front door flew open and a young woman walked in.

Probably in her mid-twenties with a slender frame, long blonde hair, and perfect features, the customer wore an elegantly simple dress, and sky-high heels. Most of our ladies are more interested in comfort than in style, so she surprised me.

"May I help you?" I brushed a few stray pieces of scrapbook paper off my khaki pants. This morning I'd done the old "extend the waistband" trick by looping one end of a rubber band through the buttonhole and the other end over the button. It works but it pinches. I wiggled two fingers down as I stood and tried not to grimace.

"I'm looking for Mrs. Goldfader. I heard this is her place." The visitor's red-rimmed eyes suggested that she had been crying, and the distracted way she scanned the store told me she wasn't a scrapbooker.

"She's right back there. At the worktable."

"Oh. Okay. Um," she said as she walked in the direction that I'd pointed.

As my boss heard the footsteps, she half-turned on the stool to face the girl.

"A-a-are you Nathan's mother? I mean, um, were you?"

Dodie nodded, slowly. Painfully.

"I killed him."

"Excuse me?" Dodie squinted at the girl. "What did you say?"

The girl shivered. "I said I killed him!"

And she turned around, ran past me, and out the door.

EIGHTEEN

DODIE'S SOBS SHOOK HER so violently that I decided to move her off the stool and into the office where she could sit in her desk chair.

I hurriedly dialed Horace's cell phone. When he answered, I stuttered, "You have to get here right away. Dodie's had a shock. It's not a medical emergency, but she needs you."

"I am coming."

As best I could, I comforted my boss. "Shhh, shhh," I said as I tried to rock her in my arms. "It was a prank. A cruel prank. That's all."

It seemed to take Horace forever to get to the store, but by the clock he must have run several red lights to arrive so quickly. I explained what had happened. By then, Dodie had calmed down, somewhat. Leaving them alone, I ran to the refrigerator to get her yet another cold Coke, the first-aid choice for any problem that happens at the store. Returning with the can, I knocked before entering the office. Horace knelt opposite his wife, holding both her large hands in his small ones, and talking to her in a low voice.

Dodie didn't seem to notice I was there, even though I popped open the drink and put it next to her. She kept saying, "Don't try to hide it from me. I know what is happening. I know!"

Horace whimpered, a noise like a dog might make when you kick it. I slipped out of the room.

"Kiki!" she yelled.

"Yes?" I trotted back in and put a hand on her shoulder.

She turned wet eyes to me. "Promise me. One thing. Promise?"

"Whatever you ask of me, I'll do." I debated adding, "If I can," but under the circumstances quibbling was cowardly.

"I am trusting you. I don't have much time left. I know it. Promise you will find that girl. Promise you will learn what really happened to my boy."

"But you know what happened," Horace said. "He was out with other kids. They partied and he dove into a gravel pit. God works in mysterious ways."

Dodie looked up at me. "That is what they say, but none of it ever made sense."

"Don't," begged Horace, his voice breaking. He stopped to wipe his eyes. "Teenagers. They are young. They are foolish."

I passed them the box of tissues we keep in the office. First I short-stopped the box to grab a handful for myself. We all sobbed loudly, and it occurred to me that if a customer wandered in, we would certainly scare her or him off quickly. In short order, I started hiccupping because I was crying so hard. Dodie's recognition that she was dying cut me to the core. She and I have had our problems over the years, but in retrospect, I owed her everything. After my husband died, it was Dodie who chided me, "You have a child to take care of. You cannot afford to stick your head in the sand and wave your backside around. Grow up!"

She had been so right. Many times I resented how harsh she was, but hindsight is the best vision-corrector around, and I could now see how she had forced me into adulthood, kicking and screaming at her all the way.

Now I faced saying goodbye to my dear friend and mentor. My chest ached so badly I could barely draw a breath.

"Nathan was a good swimmer. A smart boy. Smaller than his classmates, because he skipped a grade. He was always cautious. Why would he do such a thing? Why jump off a cliff in the dark? That is not like him. You know it, Horace!" She pounded her fists on the desktop.

"Oyf eygene kinder is yederer a blinder," Horace mumbled. Turning to me, he said, "When it comes to one's children, one is always blind. Perhaps he was not as careful as we thought he was. Or maybe he grew tired of being the cautious one."

"Why? Tell me! Is that like our boy? No! Even as a little boy he thought first and then acted! Always so solemn. So thoughtful. You said so yourself when they told us what happened. Remember?"

Horace grabbed her hands again, kissed them tenderly, and brought them close to his heart. "Yes, my love. I said it did not make sense. But the older I get, the more I accept that life does not make sense. We plan and God laughs. That is the way of it."

"No! Finally someone has spoken out. There is more to the story. More to Nathan's death. He would never willingly jump like that! I tell you, a mother knows!"

Again, she looked to me, her eyes hard and demanding. "Promise! I know you are good at solving puzzles. I know you won't give up, even if it is very, very hard. Promise me, Kiki, and I will die happy. Promise!"

What could I say? "I give you my word, Dodie. I will find out what happened."

NINETEEN

"A copy of Nathan's high school yearbook might help us. You could go through the photos and see if you recognize our visitor," I said.

Dodie nodded. "Yes. In my diary I have all the names of the others who were with Nathan. I can look at them and then at the photos. That is a very good idea, Kiki. I can also have Rebekkah see if she remembers anything about the girls who were with my son that night."

"How much older was Nathan than his sister?"

"Three years," said Horace.

"That's good. Any longer and she probably wouldn't know much about the other kids, but a three-year age difference isn't that much. She's bound to remember something, and if not, perhaps she can talk to schoolmates who were a year ahead of her, and who might remember personal details."

The smallest hint of a smile started on Horace's face. "You really have gotten good at this, haven't you?"

That broke the tension. "Believe me, it was never my intent to become a good snoop."

In chorus, we all repeated, "Man plans and God laughs." The silliness gave a well-needed sense of relief.

"Look, Horace, why don't you take Dodie out to eat? Bring me back a salad, would you? You know what I like." I was eager to get them up and moving and out of the store. Sitting here and obsessing about our odd visitor wouldn't help anyone.

"Let me wash my face," Dodie said. As she stood, she grabbed at the desktop. With both hands spread wide for balance, she lurched from desk to door frame and out into the stockroom. Her lack of coordination shocked me, and I guess my reaction showed because when I turned to Horace, he said, "That's one of the signs she's doing poorly. Her fine motor skills are eroding. She has no balance. Her mind gets stuck like an old vinyl record with a deep scratch on it."

"I will do everything I can to make her comfortable here, but is the store a good place for her? I mean, today doesn't count. I'm sure she won't have an unsettling visitor every day."

"As long as she wants to come here, I think it's a good idea. Any semblance of normal life will help us all. Does her presence create a problem?"

"No, I just don't know how to care for her. I mean ... if she needs something ... will I know what to do?"

"Here is the phone number of the hospice nurse assigned to our case." He wrote a number on a sticky note. "Her name is Sally. Sally Lippert. She's very nice, and she can answer any questions you have."

"I've never been around someone who is ..."

"Dying?" Horace supplied the word for me. "In the United States, we like to pretend that everyone will live forever, so we shuttle people off to a hospital as soon as we can. That way we don't have to watch them struggle. We can maintain the illusion that they will get better. It is all very neat and sanitary, but it is also cruel. Too often while we ease our suffering we prolong theirs."

I had no idea what he was talking about. Not a blinking clue, so I nodded my head and decided I would either call the hospice nurse or my new friend Ned as soon as possible. My stomach rumbled, and my hand automatically went to my belly. How odd would it be, having my life bookended by birth and death. But then, that was the natural order of things, wasn't it?

After the Goldfaders left, I straightened the store, paying attention to what was selling and what wasn't. As usual, when I discovered merchandise that wasn't moving, I would design a class around those items. "Turn," which is the retail term for moving merchandise in and off of the sales floor, is critical to success in any retail operation. Think of it this way: Would you rather get paid once a year or twelve times? The higher your turn, the more times you collect the profit from your sales. If the item isn't turning, it needs to be replaced with a product that does, promptly. Otherwise, it's like having money sitting in a drawer rather than in a bank account where it can draw interest.

Our colored markers hadn't moved. Neither had the hypotrochoid art set, a novelty drawing tool that I was confident our Zentangle® enthusiasts would love once they saw how the interlocking circles worked. That got me thinking. I wasn't really keen on how we packaged our pen sets. As a person who whipped out her Sakura pens to tangle at any spare moment, I knew that those plastic clamshell packs were a pain to open. Instead, I went online and found clear zippered bags that would be perfect for carrying pens.

I was placing the order when Robbie Holmes walked in.

The dark circles under his eyes aged him twenty years.

"Sheila?" I asked and jumped to my feet quickly. I stood up too quickly. I gripped the worktable to steady myself. That's what immediately came to mind. I figured my mother-in-law had taken a dramatic turn for the worse. Then another thought: "Johnny?"

"No. There's no change in either of their conditions. Could you close the store? We need privacy."

I turned the sign in the front door from OPEN to CLOSED. "I'm all ears."

His legs practically buckled beneath him as he sank down into the tall stool. Robbie couldn't meet my gaze. A sick tremor started in my hands. "What is it? Detweiler? Is he okay? Was he shot?"

This was my worst fear, an accident in the line of duty.

"No."

I breathed again. I knew it wouldn't be about Anya or the school would have called.

"Then what?" I leaned toward him, as though I could pry it out of his mouth.

"The Illinois state troopers' Crime Scene Investigators found bullet casings scattered around Brenda's body. The lab ran tests. They're a lot quicker than we are, but I guess since her dad's a big contributor to the local politicos, this was a fast turnaround even for them."

"So they have an idea what kind of gun was used to shoot her? That's good, isn't it? They might be able to trace the gun, right?" I was excited. Perhaps Anya and I wouldn't need that extra patrol.

"Right." Robbie sounded bleak.

"Why aren't you happy about this?" I wondered if he was just tired. He'd had a rough couple of days, just as I had.

"You're right. They can trace the bullets."

"Good deal! Hot dog!" I stopped abruptly when I saw the misery written large on Robbie's face.

"They came from Chad's service revolver."

TWENTY

"You're kidding, right? There's been a mistake. Or you're joking around. I mean, that's ridiculous, isn't it? Why would Detweiler shoot her? And with his own gun? That would be totally stupid. You know him. He'd never, ever do anything like that. Ever. Come on, Robbie. Get real." I couldn't even focus, the shock was so great. My stomach convulsed and I thought I'd vomit on the craft table, right then and there. Instead, I raced to the john, rinsed out my mouth and splashed my face with cold water. Then I grabbed a Coke for Robbie and a Diet Dr Pepper for me.

On second thought, I decided the artificial sweeteners might not be good for my baby, so I grabbed two regular Cokes. Robbie gratefully took his from me and turned his head as the pop-tab sizzled.

"As much as I find this hard to believe, the evidence speaks for itself. The lab couldn't have made a mistake. They are spent casings from bullets fired out of Chad Detweiler's gun. The marks prove it. And rational people can do irrational things in the heat of the moment. It happens every day of the week."

"What?" I yelped, and I spilled a bit of my Coke. "Robbie, you don't believe that for a minute!"

"You're right; I don't. But what else can I think? There's no question that the striations on the casings are a match. Maybe Chad thought her body wouldn't be found. With that electric blanket around it, the time of death is nearly impossible to pin down. If a real estate agent hadn't wandered in, Brenda's body might have been there for months. Decomposing. Making it harder and harder to tell what happened. Maybe in the heat of the moment he forgot to search for the spent casings. Who knows? Stranger things have happened."

"But not to Detweiler! You know him, Robbie. He'd never do anything like this. Ever!"

"Be that as it may, they are planning to take him into custody about now." Robbie rubbed at a spot on the leg of his navy police uniform. Even after the spot disappeared, he kept rubbing the same place, over and over.

I hopped up and down like a deranged bunny rabbit, all the while waving my arms as if to get his attention. "You can't let this happen. You have to stop them! A cop in jail? You know how dangerous that'll be for him? He'd never do anything like this! You know it! You have to do something! Robbie? Are you listening?"

I grabbed his shoulders and shook him. Correction: Tried to shake him. He's too big and solid for me to have bothered.

Batting away my hands, he said, "Kiki, here's the thing. You can't imagine how upset he was when he heard you'd been hurt. He was furious. I've never seen him like that. Ever. At the scene, two state troopers had to restrain him. He even took a swing at one of them! Chad's usually one of my more level-headed officers, but even I was worried about him when he found out what happened." Robbie paused to pinch the bridge of his nose. "And threatening Brenda when the Crime Scene guys were there? It wasn't smart. Not at all. Chad was definitely on a rampage."

"Maybe you misunderstood him. What exactly did he say?" I perched on the stool so I could steady myself by gripping the craft table. Stars swam across my field of vision. This was too much to handle coming on top of Dodie's meltdown.

Suddenly my environment seemed silly. Trite. Meaningless. The pretty paper. The cute embellishments. What was I doing here? The guy I loved was going to jail. For life. Falsely accused. Whatever the ballistics testing said, I knew that Detweiler couldn't have hurt Brenda. That wasn't like him. No way.

But then again, I'd only seen him angry twice. And I couldn't imagine how upset he must have been over Brenda's participation in tricking me—and in the shootout at the slough. Worse yet, I shivered as I imagined how he might have reacted when he realized that she'd endangered our baby.

"Have the Detweilers hired an attorney for him? I mean, they need to get him out as soon as possible."

"I've talked to them. They're doing everything they can, but their resources are limited. You heard about the second mortgage on the farm? Because Brenda's father co-signed, Chad's folks are between a rock and a hard place. If they irritate Milton Kloss, he could call the loan. They would lose their home and the farm. If they don't help their son, they'll never be able to live with themselves. It's an unholy mess." Robbie ran a hand through his hair, causing it to stick out like porcupine quills.

I tasted bile, and it choked me. "What about a public defender? Or someone who owes Detweiler a favor? Anyone who owes you one?"

"He'll need an attorney who's passed the bar exam in Illinois. My contacts are all here on the Missouri side."

I buried my head in my hands.

Robbie tapped my shoulder. "Sometimes the only thing left is to pray. I know that sounds simple. I know it sounds like I'm giving up, but on more than one occasion in my career and my life, I've had to come to terms with the truth. We do what we can and we leave the rest to God. Try not to worry so much, because it'll stress your baby. Say your prayers. Light a candle, and turn this over to the Lord."

TWENTY-ONE

BY THE TIME CLANCY and Laurel showed up to relieve me, I had gone berserk, returned to sanity, and broken down sobbing several times, going through those phases like a washing machine clicks its way through various cycles.

As they listened, I spit out the news about Brenda's death and how the bullet casings matched those from Detweiler's gun. If I'd been more in control of my emotions, I might have spoken more prudently, but I trusted both women and I couldn't restrain my emotions. So I let it all out, the entire ugly mess, complete with the news that Detweiler had threatened Brenda in front of other cops. In the midst of my meltdown, my phone rang, but I didn't recognize the number so I let it go to voice mail.

"Where's Dodie?" asked Laurel, looking around.

"Horace came to get her. She was distraught and so was he!" That admission started a fresh round of tears as I explained what happened with our strange visitor.

"When it rains, it pours," Clancy said. She isn't a toucher, but she patted my shoulder awkwardly.

Laurel went to the refrigerator and brought me a bottle of cold water. "Text-message your sister and tell her I'm giving you a ride home. You need to lie down, sip a cup of chamomile tea, and chill out. Clancy can watch the store until I get back."

I tried to argue, but I was too tired—emotionally and physically—to put up much resistance. Although my manual dexterity is good, you'd never know it by watching me punch in a text message. There are more misspellings than a D-student's term paper. Eventually, I patched together a couple phrases that would make sense to Amanda.

I also checked the message on my phone. It was an accounting firm. Probably the person Horace had hired to do our books. Well, that person could take a number. Literally and figuratively.

Gracie needed to go for a walk before we put her in the car, so Laurel put the leash on my dog, and the three of us wandered along the broken concrete sidewalks in the transitional neighborhood where Time in a Bottle is located. As we ambled, Gracie dutifully peed and sniffed at every bush. When I wobbled, Laurel gripped my arm if I were a doddering old lady.

"Everything is going to be okay," she said. "You'll see."

"Besides all this, Mert won't even speak to me," I whined.

"Aw, Mert's like that. She gets mad and withdraws. But Johnny is going to get well. I just know it. When he does, she'll relax."

"What if he doesn't?"

Laurel stopped walking, which effectively prevented me from moving ahead. "Kiki, you know he will. You have to have faith that he's going to be all right! Here's the deal: You aren't helping anyone by being a basket case, girlfriend. No one. Not yourself and certainly not anyone who loves you. Detweiler and Dodie both need you. There's a lot to be done, but none of us can move in the right direction if you don't get your act together. So knock it off, okay? As for Johnny? Send him positive energy, not your doubts and worries. And Mert? Leave her alone. She'll come around in her own good time. She's a slow processor, a person who needs to mull over her emotions and thoughts before finding closure."

"But you don't know what I've been through!"

"No, and you don't know what I've been through, either."

"What?" This certainly wasn't the answer I expected. At first I thought I'd heard her wrong. Her hazel eyes flashed with anger, and I stepped away from her in shock. Laurel is typically so kind, so accommodating, that I wondered, "Who is this? Has she been hijacked by an alien?"

But, no, it was a new side of Laurel, that's all. There she stood in her skinny jeans and her azure and maroon blouson top with that long hair of hers spilling over her shoulders like a shawl of palomino gold. Yep, it was Laurel, only she lacked her customary smile.

"Look, you aren't the only one who's had tough luck in this world. Leave it at that. This isn't the time for the story of my life. Point being: All of us go through stuff. Hard stuff. Challenges. Disappointments. Things that should never happen, happen. Stuff that's unfair. Stuff we didn't ask for. Big deal. At the end of the day, it's all about moving on. Do you wear a big, stinking sign around your neck that says, 'Poor me'? Or do you pull up your big girl panties and keep going? It's so very, very easy to play the victim. To want sympathy. You know what? Victims are weenies. Weak people. Something happens to them and then they put out the welcome mat and invite other yucky stuff to happen over and over again. They never move forward. They are defined by the crap that happened. Victims play an endless loop tape that says life is unfair, especially to me. Is that what you want? Or are there other things you'd like? A happy home? A loving man? Friends? Or do you want to hang onto your victimhood and drag it around like a security blanket, using it as an excuse for a miserable existence?"

I had never heard her talk this way. With a bolt of surprise, I realized that I'd never looked past her beauty. If you had asked me about her, I would have said, "She's as pretty as a centerfold," but I wouldn't have commented on her steady personality or her habit of turning lemons into lemonade.

I'd never really been fair to her. They say, "Don't judge a book by the cover," and that witticism is intended to keep us from discounting folks with less than desirable appearances. But the opposite is also true. We judge extremely attractive people and decide they are stupid. Or vacuous. Or superficial.

None of that was true about Laurel, but I'd never spent much time really getting to know her.

"Let's get back." She tightened her grip on my elbow and we resumed our walk.

I didn't like what she said. Didn't like it at all. She was calling me a whiner when I had a perfect right to feel sorry for myself.

Even as I tried to shake off her comments, deep down, I knew she was right. I was making a choice. I could either drag around my garbage bag of hurts or let it go and move on.

After all, Dodie and Detweiler needed me.

TWENTY-TWO

I HAD INTENDED FOR Laurel to drive me home immediately after our walk, but Rebekkah had shown up at the store while we were out. Clancy convinced her to wait for our return. Opening a burgundy faux-leather book in the middle of the worktable, Rebekkah pointed to one specific photo in a line of formal portraits. "That's her. The person who told Mom that Nathan's death was her fault. At least that's the girl Mom identified."

I grabbed a magnifying glass and bent closer. "Yes. I think so. Her hair is different, and she's older, but I think that's her."

I asked Laurel if we could postpone leaving until after I'd talked with Rebekkah. Clancy got busy straightening the rubber stamps in their rack, while Laurel grabbed a handful of promotional postcards and took them to the front counter to address to customers.

Pulling her bushy hair back from her face, Rebekkah leaned over the yearbook, located a dog-eared page, and flipped to another photo, a candid picture of the girl chatting with a group of students. The description read, "Cherise Landon, class president, discusses issues with her constituency."

"Cherise Landon," I said. "That's definitely the girl who dropped by."

Rebekkah nodded. "Mom recognized her immediately. Didn't even have to put on her glasses. Nathan had a huge crush on Cherise, and while she was nice to him, she was out of his league, and he knew it. There's always an 'in crowd,' isn't there? The best-looking kids. The ones with athletic ability or lots of money."

"Is she Shep Landon's daughter?" I'd heard the name on TV.

"Right. He's the senior partner at Landon, Paisley and Humphreys, the law firm that advertises on TV. She was class president, as you can see, also the May Day Queen. The All-American girl that every guy wanted to date. Nathan followed her around like a lovesick puppy."

"She was there the night he died?"

Rebekkah reached into the hip pocket of her cargo pants. "Uh-huh. This is a list of the kids who were there. At least, it's the official list."

"Meaning?" I read the cramped writing.

"Meaning that I suppose they could have lied and omitted a name, but I don't think so. By the time the authorities arrived, the kids were all sober. Their stories all matched. Since no one was to blame there wasn't any reason to lie about who was there. Also, they'd taken one car, so if there was another person, how did he or she get home?"

"What exactly did they say? About what happened?"

Her brownish-green eyes swam in a puddle of tears that she hurriedly blinked back. "Do I have to?"

"Look, I hate to ask, but I need to know if I'm going to try to figure out what gives here."

"It started with a party at Spenser Sutherland's house. There were five kids. Nathan, Spenser, Cherise, Tiffany Perotti, and Jeff Horton. I mean, maybe there were more kids at the start of the evening, but most of them had left before someone suggested going for a ride in Jeff's car. His parents had just bought him a Pontiac GT in bright orange, and he loved showing it off. They piled in and drove around St. Louis for about an hour. Then, they got the idea to drive to the Pacific Palisades Conservation Area, in the Meramec River watershed."

"Why there?"

"Because Jeff had heard the road leading to the gravel pit was haunted. It was all the rage at school. Everyone wanted to get in touch with dead spirits. Personally, I think the boys wanted to put a scare into the girls. To spook them. On the way to the conservation area, they decided to buy a case of beer. They stopped at a convenience store and found a customer who agreed to make a purchase for them. They also bought sandwiches and chips."

"Was Nathan a drinker?"

"He would have a beer or two at parties, but booze didn't agree with him. Gave him headaches. Mainly he'd grab a can at the start of the evening and sip it all night. You know how it is. He wanted to fit in. I mean, he got teased a lot because he was little, like Dad, see? And smart. Really smart."

"They drove to the gravel pit and then what?"

"There was a full moon. After telling ghost stories, the boys challenged each other to jump off the cliff and touch the moon. Supposedly, they went several rounds without incident and then it was Nathan's turn. There was a thunk, a splash, and nothing else. Cherise grabbed a flashlight out of Jeff's car. The girls trained it on the surface of the water. The boys swam out, but couldn't find Nathan."

"When was the last time you saw Cherise?"

Rebekkah closed the yearbook. "Four years ago. Her last day of high school. She got into Princeton. Studied international finance, I think. Must have just graduated last month."

"But why visit your mother today? Especially…" I stopped. I didn't know exactly what Rebekkah knew about Dodie's condition.

"When Mom's dying?" Rebekkah's voice stumbled over that last word, giving it the harsh treatment it deserved. "Dad and I went to our appointment with the hospice worker this morning. She's coming to talk with all of you later this week. See, we don't want any misguided heroics."

"What do you mean?" Clancy interrupted us by sticking her head around the corner. "I'm going to be working with your mother and so is Laurel. What expectations do you have? I think we have a right to know."

On occasion, Clancy was not very diplomatic. However, I valued her straightforward approach. She was right: We needed to know what was ahead.

Laurel's sigh could be heard from two display racks over. Her purple ballet shoes slapped their way across the floor as she came our way. Putting her hands on the hips of her skinny jeans, she said, "Let me translate. Rebekkah is telling us not to call nine-one-one if Dodie passes out or starts to feel unwell."

"Right. Because if you do, the emergency technicians will go to any length to prolong Mom's life, and we don't want that." Rebekkah shoved both fists into the pockets of her cargo pants and looked away.

"I don't want Dodie to die." I could barely spit out the words.

Laurel tilted her head, stared at me, and spoke very slowly. "Whether we want it to happen or not, Dodie *is* going to die. The cancer is taking her from us. But if the EMTs respond to an emergency call and come get her, they'll put her on life support systems. That's their mandate, but it will prolong her suffering. Hospitals and doctors view death as the enemy. So they might give her a blood transfusion or oxygen or whatever, none of which will be gentle or comfortable. In the end, all their invasive treatments will only slow the natural process of her death. Nothing they intend to do will buy her quality time."

"But it could buy her more time, right?" I asked.

"But not quality time. Maybe longer in a coma. More time in and out of consciousness on high doses of morphine. Certainly more time in pain. But not time when she can function or enjoy us or live the sort of life she wants to live."

"So, if I'm working with her and she collapses, I'm supposed to stand here? Do nothing? That's what you want?" My voice went up a notch as panic grasped me around the throat.

"If Dodie collapses, by all means, make her comfortable. Then call Horace and Rebekkah. Call the hospice nurse. But do not call nine-one-one. Hospice and her family will work as a team to give her palliative care."

"I don't know what that means," I said, flicking away tears with the back of my hand.

"Palliative care aims to relieve a patient's pain rather than try to restore her to health. You see, no one can make Dodie well, so it's a matter of going slowly and painfully, or dying quickly with less misery," Laurel explained.

I put my hands on my hips. "How do you know all this?"

"Because I've watched a loved one die of cancer. In my humble opinion, given their limited options, the Goldfaders have made very good decisions. I suggest we respect their wishes."

TWENTY-THREE

I'D HAD ENOUGH OF Laurel. Reached my limit. And the expression on my face must have telegraphed my feelings because when Clancy offered to drive me home. I didn't care that Laurel had been planning to give me a ride. I'd had it with her. What a know-it-all! First she lectured me on my attitude and then she spouted off about how we couldn't help Dodie.

Clancy watched me as I opened the door of her meticulously clean silver Avalon and helped Gracie climb onto the back seat. "Laurel's right, you know."

I bit my tongue so I wouldn't tell Clancy how Laurel had scolded me for whining.

I climbed into the passenger seat. As if to comfort me, the big dog settled her rump on the back seat and rested her muzzle on top of my shoulder. "Does Margit know all this? About Dodie?"

"It's on my 'to do' list to call her this evening. Today she's with her mother. It's her mother's ninety-fifth birthday."

If my mom lived that long, I'd celebrate by poking myself in the eye with a fork. Putting up with her for another twenty years would be the death of me. During the day, I'd checked my cell phone and found three messages from her complaining about how I'd mistreated her at HER party. She also suggested that I was keeping Amanda busy so my sister wasn't around, and gee, didn't I realize how lonely Mom was there in that big house of Sheila's all by herself? How could I?

Very easily.

My cell phone rang. I nearly didn't answer, thinking it was my mother frustrated by my silence. But at the last minute decided that with two people I cared about in the hospital, one on his way to jail, and another with one foot in the grave, maybe I should pick up.

"I have a phone number for you," said Laurel before I could say, "Hi." She rattled off a number and added, "I'm going to send it to you via text, so you don't have to scramble for a pencil."

"And I should call this number why?" I sounded petty because I felt that way.

She laughed. "Okay, okay. I deserve a little attitude. At least you're acting spunky again. That's the phone number for John Henry Schnabel. He's the best criminal defense attorney in Illinois, and he's agreed to take Detweiler's case pro bono."

My phone landed on the floor of Clancy's car. "Oh, gosh, oh, I'm sorry. I dropped my phone. You there? Laurel?"

"Yes," she chuckled. "I'm here."

"How? Why? I mean, thank you, but…"

"Like I said, I've been through stuff. We'll discuss that later. Schnabel has never lost a case when the client is innocent. He's on his way to the Sangamon County jail right now, but he's expecting your call. He needs the phone number for Detweiler's parents because if they've already engaged counsel, he might need to back off."

"Th-thank you."

"You are welcome. Now call him so he can get to work."

"I assume you need something to write on." Clancy had overheard. She pointed to her glove compartment. "Pen, pencil, notepad are all there."

Thelma answered on the first ring.

"It's Kiki—"

"I'm sorry, hon, but I don't have time to talk, we're on our way—"

"Wait! Listen! I have the name and phone number of a criminal attorney who'll handle your son's defense pro bono. It's John Henry Schnabel and he's on his way to meet you at the Sangamon County jail."

There was a long silence.

"Did you say John Henry Schnabel? How on earth did you get him to take this case? We don't have that kind of money, Kiki!"

"It's pro bono."

"How on earth … ? Never mind! What's his number?"

She stuttered her thanks and promised to call me with any news. Then I filled Clancy in on what had transpired.

"While you and Laurel were out walking Gracie, I called Amanda. She will pick up Anya from CALA, feed her, and drop her off later. I'm planning to come in with you and see that you get that cup of chamomile tea." With a flourish, she reached into her purse and waved a plastic baggy filled with teabags.

"Let me guess. Laurel gave you those."

"Wonder Woman strikes again."

"I bet she owns one of those costumes with the red bustier and blue trunks. How does she do it? Laurel's like my life coach, my personal mentor, and my personal assistant all in one. Geez, I always thought she was competent. Never seen her botch anything. Watched her smooth the ruffled feathers of the most disgruntled customers. But I didn't suspect she could work miracles. Yet she has."

"How much do you know about Laurel?" Clancy raised one perfectly shaped eyebrow at me.

"Uh, Mert recommended her."

"Ever noticed how much alike they look?"

I rolled my eyes. "Piffle. You need new glasses."

"Think about it. Has she ever talked about her personal life?"

"No."

"Ever invited us to her home?"

"No."

"Have we ever met anyone she's dating or any member of her family or any friends?"

"No, no, and no. What are you driving at?"

Clancy shrugged. "I'm not sure what I'm driving at. She's an enigma. I always thought that maybe you knew her better than I did. Or that Dodie did. Or that she was a friend of Rebekkah's. But she's not. She's like this elusive shadow. An invisible-visible playmate who works with us and then—poof!—she disappears."

A fly landed on Clancy's windshield. It marched over, around, up and down. She hit the wipers and brushed it away. I knew almost as much about Laurel as I did about that fly.

No, that's not true.

"Here's what I know about Laurel: Whenever we've needed her, she's been there. She's always been a trooper. Always been upbeat and positive and helpful. If she has a past she's running from, frankly, I don't care. Sure, she ticked me off. But maybe she said what I needed to hear."

"I missed something." Clancy turned over her palms to indicate she was lost.

I filled her in on Laurel's lecture about whining.

"She's right, you know. You've been a great friend to me, and I think the world of you, Kiki, but you do have a tendency to whine a lot."

"Nothing like kicking me when I'm down."

"See what I mean?"

TWENTY-FOUR

CHAMOMILE TEA TASTES LIKE grass clippings. Under Clancy's stern gaze, I drank two cups, but it wasn't the high point of my day. Sitting on my sofa, with my dog at my feet and our two cats curled next to me, I could almost pretend that all was right with my world. Almost.

"I can't stop thinking about Detweiler," I told Clancy.

"Then you need a distraction. I heard everything Rebekkah told you about that girl who upset Dodie. What are you planning to do?" Clancy came over to the sofa and picked up Seymour, Anya's gray tabby. She returned to her chair and stroked his head as he pressed his little pink nose into her hand.

"I haven't the foggiest."

"Take a guess. You're pretty good at solving puzzles."

I thought a minute. "I think I'll go over to CALA and ask Ruth Glazer in the alumni office what she knows about those kids."

"They went to CALA?"

"Yes."

"How did Dodie and Horace afford the tuition? I never got the impression they were terribly well-heeled."

"At the start of seventh grade, students all over town take the ISEE, the Independent School Entrance Exam. To keep academic standards high, CALA accepts students who score well. See, they can't control the quality of the legacies, because whether those kids are smart or not, they're guaranteed a spot, so adding high-scoring ISEE students to the mix keeps CALA's overall SAT scores above average."

"Let me guess. They also offer scholarship or tuition help to these imported brainiacs."

"You got it. Nathan and Rebekkah both attended CALA. That's how Dodie and Sheila knew each other. That and they attended the same temple. Sheila changed temples after Harry died. She'd never liked the rabbi at their old house of worship, and how he conducted the funeral service didn't sit well with her."

"What do you expect Mrs. Glazer to tell you?"

"Beats me. It's possible there were rumors after Nathan died. Stories about what really happened."

"That's assuming something really did happen other than the official version. Cherise Landon could have felt guilty because she didn't stop Nathan from jumping off the cliff. Or because she invited him to the party, if she did. Kids are great observers but poor interpreters. What she thinks, how she feels about Nathan's death, might have very little to do with the actual circumstances."

Clancy understood the dynamics at play better than I, because she'd once taught high school. As she scratched under Seymour's throat, his rich purr filled the room. Seymour could sound like a cello soloist when he was happy.

"Here's another idea," Clancy said. "Why not track down the students who were there, one by one, and tell them that Dodie is not doing well? That you'd like to make an album for her. So you need to collect any memories they have of Nathan."

"What if they are scattered all over the country? I doubt they'd respond well to a strange woman calling them."

"What if Rebekkah asks them? If she goes on Facebook and asks them?" suggested Clancy. "The kids love Facebook."

"You think they'd be forthcoming?"

She shrugged. "What did they teach you in journalism class about asking tough questions?"

"I didn't get that far in college. However, I'm a big fan of Piers Morgan. Did you see his interview with Robert Blake? Or with Mike Tyson? Wow."

"How does he do it? The tough questions?"

I thought a minute. "He starts with easy questions. Then he usually couches the tough ones in 'Can you see why some people might ... ?' so he isn't the bad guy. It's usually pretty effective. When the guest turns on him—and I've seen a couple turn on him, like that woman who had a baby by John Edwards, that presidential hopeful—he stays cool. 'Then set the record straight,' he'll say."

"Could you do that?"

"I don't know. I wish Sheila was out of the hospital. She knows all these old CALA families. Wait!" I sat up straight. "Hand me my phone."

TWENTY-FIVE

Jennifer listened to my question and said, "Sorry. I can't help you. I didn't really get involved with CALA until Stevie started school there. But since you called, how are you feeling? Any word on Brenda? Is she still out there? Posing a threat?"

"No. Just dead silence on her part." I groaned inwardly at my pun.

"I've been listening to the radio all day," Jennifer said. "The news media in Illinois are saying that a woman's body has been found and that the identity is being held pending notification of the family. Could it be her?"

"Could be. Who knows?" I hurried to change the subject. "How's Nicci?"

"More and more withdrawn. I hope this is the response to her breaking up with her boyfriend."

"Boyfriend?" News to me.

"More like a crush than a real boyfriend. She and he text-messaged each other. Met at the mall. He would join her and Anya at movie theatres with other kids. Remember when a whole tribe of them went a couple of weeks ago?"

Yes, I did.

"I guess this boy, Reston, and Nicci would sit by themselves away from the others. To her, that was real love. But things changed. Stevie tells me the kid is being a real creep to Nicci online. Teasing her. Making fun of her. Sharing personal info that's inappropriate. That's how kids are, right?"

"Wow. I am so sorry." This was almost a standard refrain from me. In fact, I said these exact words, with exactly the same intonation, so often that I should probably trademark them. Or print them on a sign and flash them at folks.

She sighed. "Makes me long for the good old days when we walked ten miles to school in the midst of blizzards. Well, I didn't. Our housekeeper drove me, but you probably did. Seriously. Back then, a guy would dump you and tell your friends, but pretty soon, people moved on. Now, whatever he says that's cruel, it's there for others to read for years to come on the Internet."

"What do you intend to do?"

She hesitated. "Would I be overreacting if I sicced my IT guy on this little creep? To report this little jerk to Facebook and Twitter and whatever so he's banned. I could ask our IT department to erase all negative comments about my daughter."

Jennifer was the CEO of a large company that manufactured and sold sports memorabilia.

"Are you asking my personal opinion? Because I'm living in scorched earth mode these days. If you have the resources to nail his scrawny backside to the wall, go for it. Better yet, tell him you know a gunslinger and that once she's killed, she's hungry for her next victim. Go ahead! Teach the twerp a lesson."

She laughed and we said our goodbyes.

My fingers itched to call Detweiler's parents again, but I figured they had enough on their plate without talking to me. After all, Thelma had promised me she would call.

Clancy had gotten up during my conversation with Jennifer. I walked into my kitchen and found her scrubbing Gracie's water bowl. Her neat-nik tendencies make her restless when she visits, so we've agreed she's welcome to clean anything she wants whenever she's here. Oddly enough, that seems to make her happy.

Works for me!

She turned and asked, "Could Robbie Holmes get you a copy of the police report? The one with statements taken the night Nathan died?"

"Maybe. Robbie has been on the force for thirty years. He might also remember what was said that didn't make it into the report. Even if he won't share it, he could find it and answer a few questions for me. That is, if he has any time. Running back and forth from here to the hospital in Illinois has to be a big pain in the backside. But Sheila's supposed to be home soon. That should help."

"And she'll give your mother and sister the boot."

I had considered this. "Until Amanda finds a place to rent, it's possible that Sheila might want them to stick around. Linnea, Sheila's maid, won't be able to babysit Sheila around-the-clock. I don't know how debilitating a broken collarbone is—"

"I can tell you. I tripped over a student's backpack when I was teaching and broke mine. The doctor told me it's the most commonly broken bone in the human body. Unless you have a compound fracture where the bone pierces the skin or a comminuted fracture where the bone is broken into several pieces, surgery isn't necessary but complete immobilization is. Sheila shouldn't be walking around, reaching for things, or doing any strenuous activity. Having your mother and sister at the house would be helpful, I'd think."

"If Mom doesn't drive Sheila nuts."

Clancy grinned. "There's always that."

TWENTY-SIX

AMANDA BROUGHT ANYA HOME, and I hoped we could talk, but my sister needed to hurry back to my mother's side. My daughter didn't have much to say about her day either.

"Whenever you're ready to talk, I'm willing to listen. In fact, I want to talk to you about what's been happening."

"Not in the mood." Anya picked up her backpack and headed for her room.

Digging around in my change jar, I found exactly enough money to pay for a Domino's Pizza. I ordered Anya's favorite, thin crust sausage and pepperoni. We ate while watching *The Mentalist*. Although the food seemed to do Anya good, she still seemed preoccupied.

Thelma called at quarter to eight. "Mr. Schnabel is a godsend, Kiki. You worked a miracle."

No, but Laurel did. I'd have to thank her.

"He's out? Everything's okay?" I got up and took the call into the kitchen. I hadn't told Anya about what was happening with Detweiler. Over the course of the evening, my energy had leaked out the way air escapes from a helium balloon. I couldn't handle whatever emotions were bound to come with this worrisome news. Anya had never run into Brenda, but she'd heard plenty about Detweiler's wife's drug use and bad behavior. I was being a big chicken not to tell my daughter all the ugly details, but from the depths of my memory came a line from H. Rider Haggard's *Cleopatra,* "Peace, Slave! Leave matters of the world to rulers of the world." Of course, Anya wasn't a slave and I wasn't a ruler, but the accusations against Detweiler would be hard for her to handle. She didn't need to bother with them. Not yet.

"There will be a bond hearing tomorrow. Milton and his wife, Carla, will be in the court to give their statements. Then we'll see if Chad can be released."

"But his safety! They can't put him in with criminals!"

"They'll put Chad in solitary confinement, away from the general population. We got them to agree to that at least."

"Oh, Thelma. You must be so upset. How's Louis taking all this?"

"Hard. The sun rises and sets on Chad. On all our children. Louis can't imagine how Chad's spent casings could have been found at the scene."

The words flew out of my mouth before I could stop them. "Someone could have planted them there."

"Who picks up spent casings?" Thelma wondered.

"Believe it or not, there was this couple that went to Atlantic City on a killing spree. They murdered another couple. But they were caught because she—the female killer—kept evidence of their crime to scrapbook! The news reports hinted she picked up empty bullet casings."

A long silence. "You have to be kidding me. I'm glad I stick to my knitting."

"People think that all scrapbookers are nice people, and typically we are, but hey, we're a broad cross-section of the population. Most of us are nice, but a few … not so much. I mean, it happens, right? Are they checking the casings for DNA?"

"I guess they're checking them for all sorts of stuff. But the evidence found at the scene had to be sent to a lab outside of Chicago where there's a backlog."

"So Schnabel is being helpful?"

"Oh, my, yes. He knows his stuff, Kiki. Started on the phone making calls with investigators, questioned the lab results regarding the ballistics, questioned the chain of evidence, waded right in. I don't know how on God's green earth you convinced him to come to our aid—and pro bono at that!—but what a relief. That silly public defender they assigned Chad couldn't help a cat sneak out of a pillowcase."

She paused and asked, "How are you doing, hon? You okay? Everything all right?"

What a trooper she was. I assured her that I was fine.

"Keep your fingers crossed. Say prayers for us."

She promised to text-message me as soon as the bail hearing was over. I told her to give Chad my love and hung up.

"Are you as tired as I am?" I asked Anya as she sat on the sofa staring at the TV. Her colt-like legs were tucked under her and both cats, Seymour, and Martin snuggled in her lap.

"Yes." Her eyelids looked as if they were ready to pull down the shades and call it a day.

She got ready for bed, and I went into her room to tell her good-night. Seymour curled his gray-striped body next to her head. Martin, the yellow tom, nestled in the crook of her legs.

After turning off the light, I hesitated. A powerful impulse drew me closer to my little girl. Gently, I sank down onto her bed. "You sure you're all right? You've been awfully quiet, Anya-Banana."

"Just thinking."

"About what? Did you have a rough day at school? Worried about exams?"

"Not really."

I waited. As I did, my eyes adjusted to the darkness of her room. The silhouette of her dresser and her desk became visible. At last she said, "Mom, why would someone hurt themselves?"

So she was thinking about Brenda and her drug use.

"They don't see it as hurting themselves. They are running away from pain."

"By causing themselves pain? How does that work?"

I took a deep breath. "I'm not entirely sure of the mechanism, but people choose activities that distract them from their real problems."

"But it makes new ones!"

"Absolutely. So when a person keeps buying stuff he can't afford, for that moment when he's contemplating the purchase and handing over the money, he's not thinking about his troubles. When the bills come, wham! Then he's in distress again. So he goes out and buys something hoping to feel better. It's a cycle."

She didn't say anything. Her breathing had become slow and regular. I tucked her in and crept out of the room.

TWENTY-SEVEN

Friday morning, Day 4—after the shooting

I woke up with the dawn, after a night of bad dreams where Bill Ballard's head exploded again and again, leaving me covered in sweat. My teeth ached from clenching my jaw. Overnight the bruise on my temple had turned shades of blue, black, and green, a great look for a Mardi Gras party. Otherwise, not so much.

After letting Gracie out and fixing myself a cup of instant coffee with those nifty flavored Folgers crystals, I called the hospital, thinking I'd check on Sheila. To my surprise, the switchboard put me right through to my mother-in-law.

"Hello?" Her voice was raspy.

"Sheila, it's me, Kiki! I'm so glad to talk to you! You must be feeling better." My fingers clutched the warm coffee cup as I buried my toes in the fur on Gracie's back.

A pause. "Don't be silly. I'm fine."

Yes, she was! Crabby as ever! Back to her old self. Relief washed over me.

"When are you coming home?"

"That stupid doctor hasn't told me. Says he needs to see how I'm doing. What nonsense! I'll be much, much better if they let me out of this place. Why on earth they didn't take me to Barnes-Jewish? I mean, really. What were they thinking? Out here in the middle of nowhere. Surrounded by cornfields. None of my friends can drop by and bring me matzo ball soup! Poor Robbie has to drive miles to see me! My granddaughter can't pop in. And the sheets are horrible! Like sandpaper on my skin!"

I pinched myself so I wouldn't start laughing. "I could drive over with Anya."

"Don't be stupid. You shouldn't be behind the wheel. Robbie told me about that bullet you took to the head. Good thing you have a head like a brick. Came in handy, didn't it? That crazy woman. No wonder Chad Detweiler wants to be rid of her. Whatever possessed him to marry her in the first place? Don't you just wonder? Speaking of Detective Detweiler, what's this about you being pregnant?"

Oh, boy. I took a long swallow of the coffee and sat up straighter in my chair. The day of reckoning had arrived, and sooner than I expected. "I meant to tell you. I wanted to get past the three months. You know how that goes."

Another silence. I braced myself. I could imagine her scalding me with her tongue. And she could do it, I knew she could! My mind returned to the first time Sheila and I met. I've been in blizzards that were more enjoyable. I still recall the frosty stare she gave me when her son introduced me and explained I was carrying his child. After one drunken night of passion, George Lowenstein had felt obliged to marry me—and told his parents his plans. But Sheila Lowenstein felt no obligation to accept me. None at all.

It had taken her years, the death of her child, and a lot of water over the dam before she decided I was a worthwhile human being. Now I could feel the tension crackle along the miles between us. Would our relationship go back the way it was? Would she think poorly of me?

"I can't imagine you not using protection. I can only assume this was an accident."

"Detweiler called it equipment failure."

She laughed, a hearty belly laugh. "That's a good one! That's how I'll explain it when all my friends want to know the gory details."

I silently ran through an exhaustive list of curses. Sheila could be a notorious gossip, and I wasn't thrilled about being on the receiving end of her tongue-wagging. Especially since most of it would be shared with CALA alumni. "Sheila, I certainly didn't mean for it to happen. I wasn't being careless. It's embarrassing and—"

"What difference does it make? We'll deal with it. It'll be okay. Does Anya know?"

"Yes, and she's thrilled."

"That's all that matters. Might be good for her to have a sibling. I always regretted that George was an only child."

"I . . . I appreciate your understanding."

"I didn't say that I understood. I said that we'll get through this. You are planning to marry him. Before the baby is born. Right?"

"Uh, no." And I explained what I intended to promise Anya.

"Whew." She blew out a sigh. "You're caught between a rock and a hard place, aren't you? Well, you'll marry him eventually, right?"

"I hope to." Obviously, she hadn't heard he was charged with murder. I decided to let sleeping Dobermans lie. This didn't seem the time or place to spring bad news on my mother-in-law.

"How're you doing?"

"Okay. Better now that I hear your voice. It's good to … to know you're all right. Really all right."

I allowed myself the luxury of one drippy tear and blotted it with a paper napkin.

"Thanks to you." Her voice sounded curt, but I knew her well enough to know that was her way of hiding emotion.

"I wouldn't let anything happen to you, Sheila. I couldn't! You know that."

"I wouldn't have blamed you if you hadn't come to my aid. After all, you had Anya to consider. When I saw you climb out of that car, I couldn't decide whether you were brave or just plain stupid. I still can't decide."

"You don't have to. You don't have to do anything but get better and come home."

TWENTY-EIGHT

AMANDA CALLED AND OFFERED to come by and pick me up, but I was sure I could drive safely. If I had a problem, Anya could help me. She had actually done a bit of practice driving in a parking lot with Robbie Holmes. "Good for her to know the basics," he'd said, and he'd been right.

"If you're sure," Amanda pressed the point.

"I'm sure. How's Mom?" I asked.

"Ornery. Any idea when Sheila is coming home?"

"I hope she'll be released in the next day or so. Even when she's home, she's going to need help around the house. With a broken collarbone, she's supposed to stay immobile. Her maid only works six hours a day. Robbie has an erratic schedule."

"Are you suggesting that Mom and I might be able to stay here awhile?"

"I don't want to get your hopes up. Sheila will need the help, but Mom can be such a pain in the butt that your staying might not work."

I could imagine my sister nodding on the other end of the line. "I understand. I guess I'll take it one day at a time. The agent lined up four houses for me to tour. None of the ones I've seen so far would work. Either too big, or too expensive."

That gave me a thought. "Clancy's mother is in an assisted living facility. Her house is vacant. How about if I give you Clancy's number? She might be willing to rent it rather than let it sit vacant. As I recall, her mother didn't trust her with power of attorney, so she actually can't sell it without her mother's permission."

"Let me guess. Her mother still thinks she'll be moving back in any day."

I sighed. "You've got it. Mrs. Clancy and Mom are mixed message martial arts experts. I love you, I hate you, I want to live in my house, I want you to move in with me, ya-da, ya-da."

"Will she be moving back? I don't want to get settled and get kicked out in short order."

"Mrs. Clancy will move back in when Ponce de Leon finds the Fountain of Youth and sells her a jug of the water. She has severe osteoporosis, heart problems, dementia, and vertigo caused by high blood pressure. Other than that, she's as spry as an eighty year old, and meaner than a junkyard dog with a sore tail."

"Sounds like you think a lot of this woman?"

"If the cops gave me back my gun, I'd shoot her and get a medal for it."

"Speaking of which, have you seen today's paper? That's why I thought you were calling. To tell me to hide it from Mom."

My stomach lurched, and I reached for a kitchen chair. "No. What did it say?"

"That your boyfriend off-ed his wife in cold blood. That he drove her to drugs by cheating on her with you."

"WHAT!"

"That despite desperate pleas from his father-in-law, Detective Chad Detweiler refused to encourage Brenda to get help. Says here, 'Detective Detweiler preyed on his wife's weaknesses and used her as bait to entrap drug pushers, for the sole purpose of furthering his career.'"

"Who said that? T-t-that's ridiculous!"

"Her father. There's a huge photo of him crying on the front page. The headline reads, 'Loss of a Daughter Causes Candidate to Suspend Campaign.' Kiki, I thought you'd heard this on the news. They led off with it at ten last night."

I groaned. "I don't watch the local news at home. Dodie used to keep the TV on in her office. She was always informed and told me what was happening. Last night, I turned the ringer off on my cell phone so Anya and I could get a good night's sleep. She was in a bad mood, and I was tired."

"Oh, boy."

"Is it really that bad?"

"Not entirely. Police Chief Holmes spoke up in your behalf. He says you had agreed to help them apprehend a dangerous killer. That you agreed to get in the car with Brenda Detweiler to save the life of your mother-in-law, and that it was a courageous and selfless act."

"What did he say about Detweiler? Surely he stood up for Chad!"

"He refused to comment. He said that Detective Detweiler is temporarily relieved of his duties pending an investigation by the

Illinois State Police." She paused. "But later in the article, it quotes anonymous sources in Illinois as saying that spent casings from his service revolver were found by her body."

A gasp escaped my lips. "How did that get out?"

"You knew this? I have to say that it sure looks bad for the hunkster."

"I knew it, but I don't believe it. Chad Detweiler would never shoot Brenda, ever!"

A creaking sound caused me to turn in my seat.

Anya stood two feet behind me, listening to my conversation.

TWENTY-NINE

"WHY DIDN'T YOU TELL me? Huh? When was I going to find out? At school? When the other kids teased me? They're already saying I'm the daughter of Annie Oakley. They want to know if I carry a gun, too!"

I gritted my teeth. "That's not fair. To you or to me."

"Tell me about it! Every day the kids in my algebra class tease me! Mr. Phillips doesn't say a word. He thinks it's funny. He smirks while they do it! And now this. Well, I've had enough, Mom! It's not fair for you to keep secrets from me! What if Detweiler really is a killer, huh? What if he got sick of her and shot her?" Anya's hands curled into angry fists as she clutched them at her side. Gracie came over and sat down beside her, whimpering and turning big brown eyes on my daughter.

"I never meant to keep it a secret. I tried to talk to you last night—"

"Baloney! You should have told me it was important. You should have said it couldn't wait."

"I thought it could. I was told that Brenda's parents hadn't been notified, so the press didn't know her identity."

"That's a bunch of garbage, and you know it! What difference does that make? Whether they knew or not, they were bound to find out! That's why you were sneaking around, taking your phone in the other room, and talking to Mimi Detweiler, isn't it? You were trying to keep it from me. You think I'm just a stupid kid! You didn't even tell me the truth about the baby! It's going to be a Detweiler, isn't it? Huh? Nicci and Stevie said it will be. They're betting you and Detweiler will get married so it won't be illegitimate, and that means it's going to be a Detweiler and I'll be the only Lowenstein left on the face of this earth!" With that, she broke into a howl, a yodel of pain, and leaned against the door frame to cry her eyes out.

Nothing I could say would help. She was too overwrought to hear me. The clock showed I needed to be dressing for work, but that didn't matter. Anya did. The trauma of my shooting, the absence of her grandmother, the appearance of my mother, all of it factored into my daughter's emotional upheaval.

"Come on, honey." I led her to the sofa. The keening noises from her throat had to hurt, but I realized it was good for her to let it all out. Slumping next to me, Anya cried and cried, while Gracie stuck her nose under her arm, trying in her own doggy way to comfort her mistress. Seymour crept out of Anya's room and raced across the carpet, hopping nimbly onto the sofa. He patted Anya's head with one paw.

That broke the evil spell.

"W-w-what?" The love pat surprised Anya. She jerked her face out of her hands and twisted to catch the gray tabby with his paw extended. Leaning close, he rubbed his cheek against hers, his white whiskers tickling her skin. From the hallway, Martin crept toward us. Suddenly deciding that he didn't want to be left out, he raced over and bounded up the side of the sofa, but quickly became hung up as his claws caught in the fabric. Anya reached down and gently untangled the yellow cat.

I was never so glad to have feline intervention!

"I can't make this better for you," I said. "But I can tell you—cross my heart and hope to die—that I will NOT marry Detweiler before this baby comes. Despite what your friends say, this baby will be born a Lowenstein. I promise you that."

"Why? Because of me?" Those denim blue eyes of hers looked purple because they were so red.

I shook my head. "That's only one reason. See, I married your father when I was expecting you, and I always wondered if he really wanted to be my husband or just wanted to have a family. This time, the man will have to wait. If Detweiler still wants me after I have a baby, then we'll make plans. I won't have him marry me just to give his child a name. The baby will have a perfectly good name, Lowenstein."

Anya's mouth curved into a tremulous smile. "I say it like a prayer: 'Lowenstein, Lowenstein, Lowenstein.' From the *Prince of Tides*. Pat Conroy. Your favorite author."

"Favorite living author," I corrected her. "And our name is a prayer. Don't you forget it."

Slowly, she relaxed and let all her weight rest against me, snuggling down under my arm, finding her spot as she curved into me. "I won't. I don't think Detweiler did it, Mom. Do you?"

"I know he didn't."

"Then you better help them prove he didn't, because I think he's in trouble."

124

THIRTY

Reversing our usual order of events, I stopped by work, dropped off Gracie, and then took my daughter to CALA. On the way to the school, conscious that Anya would walk in late, we talked strategy. No way was I going to put up with my child being teased because of me or Detweiler. I knew enough about CALA to know that a strong pre-emptive strike was in order. After parking the car, Anya and I walked into the school together, the solidarity of our bumping shoulders making both of us feel more powerful than if either of us had been alone.

"Mr. Phillips? May I speak to you?" I called to the pasty-faced little nerd who taught algebra, Anya's first class of the day. I have no idea where they found this turkey, but I'd already observed that he took his time grading the assignments, making it difficult for his students because if they didn't understand one concept, and he went on to the next, how could they keep up? They couldn't. I also knew he was a nasty little jerk because I'd seen his hand-scrawled note on one of Anya's assignments, "NOT up to par. Maybe you weren't listening in class. Or is it because you're blonde?"

That one I'd let slide. But his day of reckoning had come.

As I waited in the doorway, he straightened all the papers on his desk and lined up his pencils in his drawer. Once finished, he pursed his lips in irritation and sashayed my way. I nudged Anya so she'd take her seat. The other students stared at the teacher and at me. I think they guessed what might be coming because Anya walked past him with an air of confidence.

Once the classroom door was closed behind us, I faced the twit and said, "Mr. Phillips, I don't know if you read the paper or follow the local news, but my fiancé has been wrongly accused of a crime. I am mentioning this to you because I trust that you will not allow the other students to tease Anya."

He shifted his weight from one foot to the other, as he clasped his upper arm with one hand, twisted his whole body in a girlish way. "I can't babysit my students, Mrs. Lowenstein. I suggest that if Anya has a problem, she take it up with the dean."

I took this in. I nodded. I was perfectly willing to be civil, but then… he smirked. That did it. I leaned forward and poked him in the chest. "You better listen and listen good. I killed a man last week. Shot him in the head and blew his brains from here to eternity. Either you do your job and protect my child, or I'll hunt you down and blow you to Kingdom Come. Ka-powie! And I'm a very, very good shot, buddy boy. Got it? Don't give me that 'I can't babysit my students' trash. You're not much of a teacher in my estimation, so you ought to be good for something—and if it isn't protecting my kid, you better be good at hide and seek, because I am coming to get you. And I always get my man. Are we clear?"

He couldn't decide whether to faint or pee his pants.

"Yes," he squeaked.

"Good, because I've got you in my sights, pal."

With that, I walked away two steps, pivoted and headed back toward him. "Oh, and about talking to the dean? Don't bother. I'm on my way there now. Ciao, Charlie."

When I talked to Dean Rucklehouse, she assured me, "It's one of CALA's guiding principles that we will not put up with bullying or teasing. Period. End of discussion."

"That so? You better hold a staff meeting and remind your teachers of that because that Pee-wee Herman look-alike you hired to teach algebra hasn't gotten the memo."

Dean Rucklehouse sneered. "Surely you are mistaken, Mrs. Lowenstein."

"No, I'm not. But you are. And just in case you haven't heard, I shot a man last week. Yes, I did. With these two hands. Guess what? You know how they say that once you've taken a life it's easier the second time around? I totally believe that's true. So I better never hear of ANYONE in this school standing on the sidelines with their thumbs up their butts while my daughter is teased. Are we clear on this? I hope so, because if I have to repeat myself, well …" and I pantomimed pointing a gun, aiming it at her, and shooting it. "I'll have to resort to taking care of the problem all by my lonesome. And believe me, I can do it!"

Needless to say, I left the Dean's office chuckling to myself. There was no way CALA would kick out a Lowenstein. My daughter was a legacy student and brighter than ninety-nine percent of the student population. Not only had I scared the snot out of them, but Sheila would finish the job of wiping any boogers off their faces.

Feeling very, very proud of myself, I marched down to Mrs. Glazer's office. The door to the Alumni Office was locked, so I scribbled a note and slipped it under Ruth Glazer's door: *Dropped by to see you. Need help with a project. When might I come back by? Kiki L.*

Squaring my shoulders and holding my head high, I walked out of CALA. Before I climbed into my ancient BMW convertible, I blew the school a nice big raspberry.

THIRTY-ONE

BACK AT THE STORE, I explained to Gracie about the threats I'd delivered. She put her paws on my shoulders and licked my ears, which I'm sure translates into "Bullies only understand being bullied. You done good." I also told her about Detweiler, and those sad brown eyes led me to believe my Great Dane was worried, too. "But it's not all gloom and doom," I said as I rubbed her velvety ears. "Thanks to Laurel we've got a great attorney for him. I'll hear from Thelma later today. Maybe we'll drive over there tomorrow. You like going for rides, don't you?"

Dodie had taken to keeping dog biscuits for Gracie in a special snap-top plastic jar with black paw prints all over it. I retrieved one and Gracie dutifully sat for her yummy.

Once she was in her doggy playpen, I washed my hands. My reflection in the mirror showed a tired-looking woman sporting a huge black and blue bruise peeping out from under a flesh-toned bandage. Of course I looked whipped. Nightmares disturbed my sleep. My muscles ached from my struggle to survive. And I was pregnant, which sent my entire body into a tizzy.

But Laurel was right. Whining about my problems wouldn't help anyone. I'd done everything I could for everyone else in my life. Detweiler had an attorney. I was checking on Johnny and Sheila, and sending them both prayers. I had a plan for finding out what I could about Nathan. My sister was taking care of my mother. I'd laid down the law at CALA. My daughter and I were communicating.

With that summary of "This is your life, Kiki Lowenstein," I girded my loins, that is I snapped my bra straps, and decided to take on the day.

I started by turning on the television in Dodie's office. A reporter questioned Milton and Carla Kloss about their daughter's death. Milton accused Detweiler of setting his daughter up and possibly shooting her as revenge for harming me.

As the interview ended, Milton reached for his wife's hand in a gesture of solidarity. Carla Kloss had been standing slightly to one side and behind her husband during his rant. Her face had been turned away from him, rather than paying attention to what he said.

I noticed a distinct tension in their body language—and when Milton reached for his wife's hand, she shrank away from him.

Why? What dynamic was at play there?

People grieve in such individualistic ways. The loss of a child usually damages a marriage beyond repair. In a survey by Compassionate Friends, 57 percent of those couples who lost a child were not together one year later. Did that include the loss of an adult child? I didn't know.

While reflecting on that sad reality, I opened the store, going through the procedure laminated on a big card. We'd had the procedure written down for some time, but Margit suggested laminating the card to make it more durable. She also threaded a long red ribbon through a hole punched in the top. Thanks to that dangling stripe of bright color, we never lost the laminated directions. For closing, she fixed a similar card with a bright blue streamer attached.

Although Margit and I hadn't gotten along when she first started at Time in a Bottle, we'd come to appreciate and enjoy each other. She tended to mother me in ways unexpected and very much appreciated. Lately she'd taken to cooking extra portions for me to take home. Twice she'd knitted cute tops for Anya, one sweater and one camisole. My daughter now raced to give Margit a warm hug whenever they saw each other.

Margit brought skills to the store that were quite different from mine. Her strong suit was numbers. She was teaching me Quick-Books, our accounting system, and I was encouraging her to try papercrafting, even though her true love was fiber arts. "One day, I would like us to sell yarn," she told me. "I love knitting. Crochet, too. I would hold classes for beginners and special sessions for those who run into problems when working on a project."

"Then we wouldn't be a scrapbooking store."

"*Nein.* We would be a crafting hub. Like the center of a wheel. We would teach a variety of classes and stock all sorts of supplies." She smiled shyly. "That is, if I had my way. It is unlikely, *ja*?"

This morning she came through the backdoor carrying two big Tupperware containers of her fabulous plum küchen. "One is for the crop tonight, and the other is for you to take home."

I thanked her profusely. "I've been thinking, Margit. Maybe we do need to expand our offerings to include yarn. But how could we do that in a store this size? We barely have enough space as it is."

"There is much wasted area in the stockroom. If I keep a thumb—" and she pushed down with her digit to illustrate "—on our ordering, we would not need to stock so much. Most of our supplies will drop ship. Merchandise arrives in two days or less. Think of it, Kiki! There is too much on those shelves! It sits there. We forget what we have! Bah, such a waste of money."

After her rant, I wandered through the stockroom. Margit was right: Most of the space was wasted. During our last inventory, I found an old box of paper with edges that had curled because of moisture. By my calculations, we wasted $125 of potential profit there. A few of the boxes were stored too high for me to reach. I never accessed what those held. Making a slow circle of the stockroom, I visualized display units. If properly positioned, there would be enough space for a cozy circle of knitters. Drop-ins could use the craft tables near the front of the store. Most of our scrapbookers wanted to crop, or have scrapbook parties, at night after work. But many of the knitters I'd met were retired. They could come during the day.

In fact, the longer I wandered through the metal shelves in our backroom, the more possibilities I saw. We could knock down the back wall of our existing sales floor, leaving the support beams, of course. I'd watched enough episodes of *Holmes on Homes* to know how important those were! Opening up the back would give customers an easy access to the new space.

The cash register could be moved to the middle of the store. Big mirrors could be added to the corners, ones like those at blind intersections. With mirrors in place, one person could keep an eye on the whole store. Dodie had installed security cameras to be monitored from her office, but if you were ringing up a purchase, you might not know a customer in the back needed help.

Electrical plug-in receptacles had been sunk in the center of the sales floor. The last time we moved the fixtures for cleaning I'd seen them. Moving our checkout counter wouldn't be difficult at all.

How smart of Dodie to name our store Time in a Bottle rather than something with scrapbook in it! Because our name offered such latitude, we could easily expand our mission and thus, our sales.

Yes, I saw a world of possibilities, and all of them excited me. Instead of focusing solely on the problems at hand, I had something upbeat to dream about. Suddenly, the day got a lot brighter!

THIRTY-TWO

OUR FRIDAY NIGHT CROPS are legendary for the food, the fun, the fellowship, and the great projects. They are also a whole lot of work. Mainly for me.

Every scrapbooker has paper she no longer likes/needs/wants to use. Tonight I intended to demonstrate ways to use unwanted paper as a backdrop for Zentangle® designs. If the pattern is subtle, the tangles (patterns drawn in pen) work wonderfully well as backgrounds. If it is more bold, tangles can be drawn around the existing patterns.

Besides a technique demonstration, we also host a special project at our Friday crops. Several weeks ago, Dodie purchased a case of simple, unpainted wooden boxes with inset lids. I planned to turn these into cool boxes that would be nifty for jewelry, stashing trinkets, or holding stationery supplies. Actually the list of uses was endless.

I'd been working on the tangle designs for our project right up until the time I quit my job, so it wasn't hard to pick up where I left off. To prep for the crop, I would transfer these designs onto a handout, making it easy for our crafters to finish the project at home if they ran out of time.

With any luck, creating the handout would be so absorbing that I'd lose track of time. Detweiler wouldn't have his bail hearing for another hour, and I'd begun to watch the clock. Cops don't do well in jail. Criminals blame everyone but themselves for their incarceration. Once word gets around that a law enforcement official is behind bars, things get really ugly. I knew that Detweiler could handle himself in a fight. But what if an inmate with a homemade shiv attacked him? It wasn't unheard of.

I couldn't go there. Instead, I rubbed my belly and took several deep breaths to calm down. "Silly!" I chided myself. Why was I doing all this heavy breathing when I could be tangling? Research had proven that tangling helped people cope with anxiety. Wasn't that exactly what I was feeling? Sitting down to do some intense tangling, I quickly slipped into a zen-like state. Pretty soon, I felt much, much better.

At noon, Clancy presented me with a shopping bag from St. Louis Bread Co., which delightfully rhymes with "bread dough."

"Eat," she said, withdrawing a smaller bag and shoving it toward me. Inside were a half a teriyaki chicken sandwich, a container of minestrone soup, and an iced green tea. She reached inside and pulled out an iced green tea and a salad for herself. We perched on stools at the worktable. That way we could keep an eye on the front door while Margit finished calculating our sales figures and worked on new supply orders.

"What do I owe you?" I asked Clancy.

"Not a thing. In fact, I owe you. Commission on renting my mother's house."

"You're kidding me!"

"No, I am not. The agent I hired to rent out Mother's house hadn't even had a nibble, but you managed to find me a responsible tenant. In fact, I won't even have to move most of my mother's furniture into storage. Your sister plans to sell most of their furniture in Arizona, because the cost of transporting it is prohibitive. The family antiques will be shipped here, of course, but that's it. So Mother's things can stay. Between the real estate commission and storage, you've saved me a bundle."

She hesitated. "I suppose you've seen the papers this morning. And the TV?"

I shook my head. "I'm trying to avoid as much of it as possible."

"Good luck with that! Milton Kloss must have hired a public relations firm."

"What do you mean? Doesn't a public relations firm handle good news?"

"Not necessarily. There's a whole branch of the practice called crisis management. Milton was on every channel, and the radio, and in the newspaper. If he didn't have a public relations firm sending out news releases, I can't imagine how he managed to cover so many outlets. I bet they held a press conference."

"I still don't get it. His daughter is dead. If something happened to Anya, I'd be a basket case. I wouldn't care about talking to the media. I couldn't be coherent!"

"He's plenty coherent. According to him, you and Chad Detweiler conspired to drive poor Brenda to drugs."

"What!" Shades of my conversation with Amanda. Call me stupid, but these accusations still held the power to shock me. A sharp punch to the stomach couldn't have hurt more than these lies. "That's ridiculous. She'd been in and out of drug rehab many times before Detweiler and I even met! We kept our relationship platonic until she kicked him out of their home!"

Clancy raised her eyebrows and answered me with a dismissive snort. "Look. He has to blame somebody. His daughter is dead, and his campaign is dead, too. Typical politician, he's using this tragedy as a way to further his career. You knew he was running for State Representative, right? My neighbor, Calvin Tyson, works for the Republican Party as treasurer for the local candidates. He told me that Milton was behind in the polls and out of money before this happened. Now, he's got the sympathy of the entire party. Even if he withdraws, he'll be a darling with the local politicos."

"I wonder where Milton was when his daughter died."

"Up at the Palmer House."

"That's what he says..."

"He flew his own plane into Midway. It hasn't been out of the hanger since he arrived. Calvin told me this morning that Milton's name was on the roster for the session held on social media. He'd signed in to the morning session. In fact, Milton was in a session on campaign finances shortly after lunch when the Illinois State Trooper came to tell him his daughter had been found."

Clancy continued, "Milton sent an e-mail to the leadership of the local Republican Party, explaining he wants to keep them informed. According to him, the authorities best guess about Brenda's time of death is between seven and eight, the morning after the shooting. Milton was in an educational session for new candidates at eight. People saw him."

"How does this Calvin know all that? Usually the authorities withhold information to help with the investigation. But now you're telling me that your neighbor even knows Brenda's time of death. That's weird."

Suddenly my appetite was gone. I knew Chad had spent that night at his parents' farm, because he'd told me as much. Could he have gotten to the empty house in time to shoot Brenda and go back home?

"Milton Kloss went on to say that his son-in-law wanted to get rid of Brenda so he could remarry, and that Brenda had resisted the divorce, hoping they'd get back together. He said that Detweiler wasn't interested in upholding the sanctity of their marriage, but that Brenda was."

"Let me guess. He mentioned that I'm pregnant."

My friend gave me a slight nod of her head, a move full of regret and sadness. "I'm sorry, but yes. Kiki, the whole world knows you're pregnant. Milton told the committee members that Detweiler wanted to marry you to give his baby a name. I guess your honey has made no secret of the fact he's crazy about kids."

I opened my mouth to tell Clancy that I'd promised Anya I wouldn't marry Detweiler until after the baby came, but the store phone rang. And my cell phone rang. And the door minder rang. And in walked two reporters with microphones in hand.

"I'll take care of them," Clancy said, with a nod to our uninvited guests.

KIKI LOWENSTEIN'S MEMORY BOX PROJECT

Wooden keepsake boxes are available at many big box craft stores or online from www.craftandplay.com. Of course, you could also use a cardboard box and adhere the tangle to the upper lid!

1. Paint the boxes with acrylic paint or cover them with Duck Tape. (Tip: Duck Tape also comes in flat sheets that are very easy to adhere.)
2. Create a tangle design large enough to fit in the inset. (Tip: If you aren't using a box with an inset, create a tangle that is 1" smaller than the lid all around. This allows you to "frame" or mat your finished design.)
3. Cut a clear plastic report cover to the corresponding size of your design. (Tip: If using a box, cut the report cover ½" larger than your tangle all the way around.)
4. Adhere the clear report cover to the tangle with a clear-drying glue. (Tip: If using a box, center the tangle and use clear-drying glue to adhere it to the plastic report cover. Then attach the tangle and clear cover to a piece of background cardstock. Glue the tangle unit to the lid or use brads to secure it.)

Note: "Duct" tape is the term for that silver adhesive tape used in construction. "Duck Tape" is a brand name for a tape that comes in a variety of patterns and colors. It's strong like duct tape, but more versatile.

THIRTY-THREE

WHILE CLANCY HANDLED THE reporters, I scuttled into the backroom like a cockroach runs from sunlight. As I checked the number on my cell phone and recognized it as belonging to Thelma Detweiler.

"Oh, Kiki," she groaned. "I wouldn't wish a morning like this on my worst enemy, and he was there: my worst enemy. I don't know when Milton Kloss grew horns, but I saw them with my own eyes. That man was nasty. Blames all Brenda's problems on Chad! Accused Chad of all sorts of mischief! His wife, Carla, couldn't look us in the face, and it's no wonder. I never liked that man, never felt comfortable with him, but I thought it was just me. Now I know I have good reason to hate his guts."

"What did the judge decide?" As much as I wanted to hear all the gory details, I couldn't stand the suspense. Thelma needed to cut to the chase.

"Chad is remanded to our custody. Basically under house arrest. But he has to wear an electronic monitoring device. An ankle bracelet. Of course, he also surrendered his passport, which is silly, and he also can't go to work over in Missouri because he can't cross state lines. What a bunch of hooey. I suppose I should be relieved, and I am, because the only reason Judge Imbert agreed to the ankle bracelet is that a crooked cop up in Cook County was strangled to death last week while in jail, and that wonderful attorney Mr. Schnabel pointed out that there was very little evidence linking Chad to Brenda's murder."

All this came at me way too fast. Detweiler and I were doing more than our share of dodging bullets these days. This one definitely sailed right past us.

"Have you seen the newspapers?" I asked.

"Great day in the morning. Can you believe it? Milton knows none of that is true. That man even held a press conference on the steps of the courthouse before we got there. Crying about how poor Brenda deserves justice. Of course, she does! We want to see her killer caught as much as he does, but honestly, she was playing with fire, doing drugs, meeting with dealers, stealing from the hospital and who knows what else. Chad begged her. We did an intervention. My daughter Patricia, who was once Brenda's best friend, sobbed and begged her to get help. But Brenda had her own agenda. Always did. That girl wanted out of the house and out from under her daddy's heavy hand in the worst way."

She stopped. "What in the world is wrong with me? Kiki, hon, you aren't worried about what Milton said about you, are you? No one believes that. Anyone who knows Chad or knows about the situation knows you aren't to blame for one iota of this. Not one jot."

I closed my eyes and tried to block out the image of the reporters barging into our store. "I appreciate that, Thelma, really I do. However, the news media on this side of the river is right out there on our sales floor, hungry for blood. My blood. Worse yet, my daughter is getting teased at school. So whether people believe Mr. Kloss or not, he's sure doing a good job of making all our lives miserable."

Then I remembered I was talking to a woman whose son was accused of murder and felt ashamed of myself. I added, "Not that it matters. What's important here is making sure that Chad is safe. The Illinois State Police will figure out that he didn't do this. As long as your son isn't in jail, isn't in danger, justice will take its course."

Thelma's laugh was tinged with bitterness so sharp it crackled over the phone. "Ha! Kiki, the man in charge of the investigation here is an old friend of Milton's. They went to that military academy over in Indiana together. When Chad left the police force here, his old boss took it hard. Bad-mouthed him up one side and down the other. Ever noticed that Chad's a particularly careful driver when he crosses the state line? That's because a few of the state police here know their boss hates my son. Trooper Jeffries thought Chad would be his lackey forever and ever. But Chad wanted to work for Robbie Holmes. Heard how professional Police Chief Holmes is. When Chad decided to leave Illinois, holy heck broke out. He didn't tell you that?"

"No," I whispered.

"I guess he didn't want to worry you. Anyway, Mr. Schnabel is on top of the situation. He's contacted an investigator to go to the crime scene. He's talking with experts about how a ballistics test could be wrong. Also creating a time line. See, Chad came to after being drugged and called you. When you didn't answer, he called the St. Louis Police Department. Heard what happened. Drove to the slough. Got there in time to watch them load you into the ambulance. Followed the bus to the hospital. Was turned away. Came here. We were with him. He spent that night here, and most of the morning. Brenda was killed that morning. The coroner puts the time of death at seven or eight a.m. The only time we didn't have our eyes on Chad, he was out taking a run."

"When was that?"

"Around seven-thirty. But he couldn't have run that far. Or that fast. He's good, but we're not talking about Usain Bolt!"

This was worse than I expected. If Detweiler's only alibi was his parents, he was in trouble. Big trouble. After all, he could have pretended to go running, hopped in his car, shot Brenda, and gotten back in time for a hot breakfast. The air left my lungs, and I couldn't breathe.

Was it possible that Chad Detweiler actually did shoot Brenda?

THIRTY-FOUR

"Why don't you come on over and have dinner with us?" Thelma suggested. "I know Chad would love to see you."

"That's kind of you but I can't. Not tonight. I'm in charge of the crop. We have twenty-two scrapbookers coming. I need to get projects ready and double-check the arrangements. My boss, Dodie, has cancer. We thought she had it licked, but it's come back and attacked her brain. There's a lot to do here at the store, and I'm trying to make life easier on her."

Thelma sighed. "Puts everything into perspective, doesn't it? My son is alive. You're alive. The baby is all right. Sure, this is inconvenient, but we'll cope with it."

I smiled to myself. I liked Thelma's calm, matter of fact approach to life. Actually, Louis was the emotional one in the family. From the outside he seemed like a hard-working farmer, a man who made a living by the sweat of his brow. An updated "American Gothic" with the stoicism common in those who wrestle a living from the earth. After getting to know him better, I understood he was the romantic, the dreamer, the one who suffered emotional highs and lows. Thelma stood quietly by his side, with both her feet planted in terra firma. A clear-headed realist, her hand on Louis's shoulder kept him heading on the right path.

"Hang on, hon." She left the phone for a minute. "Chad wanted to talk to you but poor baby, he wandered off into his old room, fell on the bed, and went to sleep. I tried to rouse him, but he couldn't do more than grumble at me."

My heart hurt, thinking of him. The night I'd spent in the county jail had been a nightmare, and no one had paid any particular attention to me. Being a cop behind bars must have scared the living daylights out of him. All it would take was one renegade guard and his cell would change from a safe haven into a trap.

Before Thelma and I said goodbye, I promised I'd come over for an early dinner the next day, Saturday. "When Chad wakes up, tell him . . . tell him that I love him."

"I'll do that, hon. I know that'll cheer him up. I'm sure he knows how you feel. We can all see it in your eyes. And again, thank you so much for getting us John Henry Schnabel."

I still couldn't imagine how Laurel managed to pull that particularly big rabbit out of her hat. The schedule said she would be in at one-thirty to help us prep for the crop. With my gratitude in mind, I decided that for our Monday night crop project we would create a "thank you" card, a note of appreciation. That way I could make two samples and give one to Laurel later today. The project was bound to be a big hit because a lot of our papercrafters love making cards. It's a great way to practice scrapbooking skills on a small scale, to use up extra paper, and to save money because really nice cards can be pretty expensive.

First I needed to check out our supplies. Fortunately, puttering around in the backroom would keep me out of sight if the reporters were lurking. This was the perfect time to poke into those boxes on our uppermost shelves.

Grabbing the stepladder from the back closet where we kept cleaning supplies, I dragged it over to a unit and pulled down a box. This one had "cards" written on one end in a thick marker, but the handwriting wasn't familiar to me. It must have been relegated to that top shelf long before I came to work here.

Inside sat unopened packages of plain white greeting cards with matching envelopes. "Perfect!"

On Monday, we could make card toppers, designs that could be later adhered to the front of a card. Card toppers are a smart way to stockpile different designs. Since most of them are flat, they are easy to store. You don't need to own an endless supply of card "bodies" and envelopes. When an occasion comes up, you simply go through your stash of card toppers and choose one that is appropriate and attach it to the card "body."

Excited about my find, I did a quick inventory. Satisfied we had more than enough, I grabbed a set so I'd have the proper dimensions. After text-messaging Clancy and discovering the coast was clear of reporters, I took the card body over to the worktable on the sales floor. While Clancy helped a customer find embellishments for an upcoming trip to Disney World, I went to work creating a topper that our customers could copy.

As I waxed creative, Clancy handled a steady stream of customers. Nothing overwhelming, but enough to keep her busy while I worked on a design and a handout. Luckily, the media didn't come back. I mentioned that to Clancy and she snickered. "That's because I text-messaged Robbie Holmes and he sent an officer by to remind them this is private property."

"Good old Robbie!" I laughed.

When Laurel came in at one-thirty, I filled her and Clancy in on the bail bond hearing.

"I've been listening to the radio all day," said Laurel. "Brenda's father has been saying horrible things about you and Detweiler. Much of it is outright slander. If you wanted to get an attorney and sue him for defamation of character, I suspect you'd have a good case."

"I think I have my hands full already. All I care about is keeping Detweiler out of jail and finding the real killer so we can move on."

Clancy sighed. "I understand grief and guilt, but honestly, Milton Kloss has gone overboard. He's really trying his best to bury Detweiler, isn't he? Was he always so hateful toward his son-in-law?"

I rubbed the back of my neck because it ached with tension. "Thelma mentioned having reservations about the man, but gosh, he's really turned on Detweiler, hasn't he?"

Laurel's eyes narrowed. On her it looked sexy. She bought all her clothes out of a Boston Proper catalog. Today she wore skin-tight jeans, a low-cut lime surplice top that emphasized her bust, and a gaggle of jangly bracelets. On her feet were tiny lime-green ballet slippers. "Remember that line from Shakespeare? 'I fear he doth protest too much.' I watch a lot of those true crime shows, and usually the in-laws stick by the guy, even long after the evidence has shown him to be a valid suspect. Seems to me that Brenda's father has decided that Detweiler is Public Enemy Number One— and he's come to this conclusion awfully quickly. Too quickly for my taste."

"Look at it from his viewpoint. His daughter is dead. We don't know how much he did to dissuade her from using drugs. Or how quickly he realized she was an addict, and whether he hurried to get her help. Maybe this is major misplaced guilt," Clancy said. "He can't blame himself, so he's blaming Detweiler."

"Mr. Kloss knew that Brenda was willing to go into rehab." I paused to mull this over. "He asked Detweiler to stay married to Brenda so the police department insurance would cover the costs of rehab. Otherwise it was going to come out of Mr. Kloss's pocket. Unfortunately, the county employees' insurance has a limited number of treatment providers. Brenda couldn't go in until a spot opened up."

"Maybe he's blaming Detweiler because Brenda had to wait for a spot to open up, right?" Laurel asked.

"Possibly. If Milton Kloss had been willing to foot the bill, Brenda would have had more options, more places where she could have gone. If so, maybe she would have gotten the help she needed. She might still be alive today. So he's being totally unfair, if that's his beef." I shook my head in disgust.

"Pure speculation on your part. Whatever the reason," said Clancy, "Milton Kloss and his wife are hurting. When people hurt, they strike out and don't care who they hit. I can't imagine losing my child, first to drugs and then to a murderer."

She was right. Put that way, I did feel a lot of sympathy for the Kloss family.

Laurel nodded. "He must be feeling like the world's biggest loser. His political aspirations hit a brick wall, he's burying his daughter, and the whole world knows she was involved in drugs."

"Good point," Clancy said. "Short of his wife leaving him or his stock portfolio going bust, things can't get much worse."

I didn't tell her that the Detweiler family owed Mr. Kloss money. Yet another reason for the man to hate Detweiler. Since Milton Kloss didn't know that Schnabel was working pro bono, the man might well assume he'd never be repaid for the loan he'd given the family, thinking all the Detweiler resources would go to defending their son.

The whole screwed up mess made my head hurt.

Time to change the subject. I handed my friend the card I'd created to thank her. "Laurel, I am forever in your debt. How you managed to get Mr. Schnabel to help us is beyond me."

Instead of explaining how she conjured up Schnabel's help, Laurel said, "This is so cute! I love it. You are welcome."

"Okay, ladies, here's what we need to get done for the crop tonight."

Laurel helped me duplicate handouts, copy coupons, and set up the tables for the evening's crop. For a few blessed hours, my thoughts centered on the store. At two o'clock the front door minder jingled and in walked Ruth Glazer.

KIKI'S CARD TOPPERS

This simple method will yield enough for nine cards. You can use this design with any message: Thank You, Happy Birthday, Congratulations, or even In Sympathy. Changing the papers for the grid will change the mood dramatically.

1. Start by creating a card topper base or background. Cut a solid piece of paper ¼" smaller on all sides than the top of your cards.
2. Cut nine pieces of corresponding paper 1" smaller than the base piece above. These will form the checkerboard of your pattern. For example, you might have three shades of blue, three blue patterns, and three blue stripes.
3. Cut each of those nine pieces of paper into nine smaller, equal-sized squares. (Tip: If you hate measuring, fold a piece of newspaper into nine equal squares and use it as your pattern.)
4. Arrange the squares so you have an interesting checkerboard of colors/patterns. For example, you might have a row of squares that are all stripes, followed by a row of squares that are all solids, and a row of squares that are all patterns. Or you could alternate—stripe, solid, pattern—in each row.
5. When you find an arrangement that's pleasing, glue them down.
6. Add letter stickers to write out: Thanks! (Or whatever!) Or, cut a strip of white paper, add the letter stickers, and glue the strip across the front of the card like a banner.

THIRTY-FIVE

RUTH GLAZER DIDN'T MUCH like me when we first met. Over the years, the staff at CALA has grown accustomed to being mistreated by certain parents. One teacher explained, "Some parents only notice you when they need something. Otherwise, you are invisible. Expendable. You get treated like a tissue that they wipe their noses on and toss in the trash. After a while, you learn to stay aloof to protect your feelings. We do have feelings, you know."

There were those parents who treated the teachers and admin people at CALA as an extension of their personal staff. One woman famously called a fundraising director and instructed him to pick up her dry-cleaning. Seems she was scheduled for a meeting at the school and thought that if he wanted her participation and her money, he wouldn't mind playing errand boy.

Since so many movers and shakers in St. Louis sent their offspring to CALA, the archival files in the Alumni Office held dark secrets, the backstories of problems usually kept carefully hidden away. Awhile back Dodie had "loaned" me to the school, suggesting they put me to work as a writer for their alumni news-letter. She surmised, correctly as it turned out, that I could learn a lot about the place, become indispensible to the school, and drum up business for our store. Access to the files gave me all sorts of material to use when making family albums or memorial albums.

But to gain that access on an unsupervised basis, I had to earn the trust of Ruth Glazer. Ruth had seen a lot of volunteers come and go, primarily because they wanted to poke around in the personnel files of the teachers, administration, and students. She kept a careful eye on me until deciding I could be trusted.

While I wouldn't embarrass the school with anything that I'd learned, I admit to having used the files to solve a couple of crimes that touched the CALA community. I considered that a win-win, but Ruth might not have, if she'd have known.

On the other hand, maybe she *did* trust me to use whatever I learned to benefit the school. After all, wasn't that the point? The whole reason for hanging onto those slips of paper, handwritten notes, and other ephemera was to assist the school in doing its job. (Translation: To help it raise money and keep attracting students. That is, to perpetuate itself.) When a teacher died under mysterious circumstances, when a parent's anger led to a sniper attack, the information in those files helped me solve those crimes—and the rhythm of the school continued with only a tiny blip. Certainly, CALA's fundraising didn't suffer.

So it's entirely possible that I wasn't fooling anybody, especially not Ruth. And maybe, just maybe, that's why she'd finally decided she liked me.

Her visit during the middle of the day came as a surprise. Usually she only stopped by in the evenings. Since I'd shown her how to scrapbook photos of her grandkids, she'd become one of our best customers. But this afternoon was different. A certain clip to her walk told me she was on a mission.

When we first met, Ruth would greet me with a curt nod. After I earned her seal of approval, Ruth started offering me a stiff hug as she did today. She managed the embrace very awkwardly as if to say, "I'm trying to be warm and fuzzy, but this is the best I can do!" Today, her hug was more effusive than usual as she whispered in my ear, "Thank goodness you are all right. Just look at that bruise on your temple! I never did like that William Ballard. Honestly! Such a bully as a kid. I'm not at all surprised he was in the middle of this."

Her gray pantsuit and printed blouse copied an outfit I'd seen on Clancy, but up close you could tell the fabric wasn't very good. The statement necklace around her neck sported big plastic beads rather than natural stones. A pang of pity overtook me. Out of her natural environment, I could see Ruth for who she really was, a proud woman who wanted to be like the wealthy parents who employed her.

To quote that naval hero, Popeye, "I yam what I yam." Didn't she realize she didn't need to compete?

But then who was I to give her advice about fitting in?

Instead, I gave her a little extra squeeze of affection. "You don't think of me as a cold-blooded killer?"

"Gracious, no! I would have done the same! I mean, I certainly hope that I would have had the presence of mind to do the same. Tell me, how is Mrs. Lowenstein? She nearly died, didn't she?"

"I talked with her this morning, and she was grumbling about this and that, so I'd say that's a PRS."

"A what?"

"Positive Recovery Sign. I made that term up."

"Oh, you!" Ruth swatted my arm. "I got your message. What can I do for you? Do you have another project in mind? Another memorial album? I suppose you could make one for Bill Ballard, since he was an alumnus."

"I think I'll pass on that."

"No doubt!"

"Could we go in the back? My question is sort of delicate."

As we walked past Laurel, I asked the young woman to keep an eye on the sales floor. "We'll be in Dodie's office."

Of course, our private talk mandated a stop by the refrigerator so I could grab a Sprite for Ruth and a bottle of water for me. I'm not adverse to drinking water, but I have to admit, I looked longingly at that ice-cold can of Diet Dr Pepper. Six months and counting until I could enjoy my favorite diet beverage again. Sigh.

Margit offered to leave when she saw us coming. Once I'd closed the office door, I told Ruth about Cherise Landon's visit. As I spoke, my guest fiddled with the pop top from her can. I wasn't sure what she was withholding, but clearly, she wasn't eager to share information with me. I decided to tell her the truth, that Dodie was dying.

"What a shame! I've always liked Mrs. Goldfader. She's wonderfully down-to-earth, isn't she? Dear, dear."

"She's asked me to find out what really happened to her son, Nathan. I have an inkling that I won't be able to do that. After all, he's not around to talk, and I doubt that anyone who was there that night wants to confess. But I promised her that I'd find out. Honestly, Ruth, I couldn't tell her no."

Ruth frowned at me. "Are you certain you want to pursue this? Shep Landon is not a man to be trifled with."

"I don't care about him. I care about Dodie."

"You need to stay away from that man. When this happened, he wouldn't let Cherise talk to anyone. He threatened the school with legal action if we linked Cherise's name to the accident in any context. You see, she was a minor at the time. After she graduated, he came and cleaned out her files. All we have is her grade transcript and test scores. Mr. Landon is a very thorough man, and a protective father. He made it perfectly clear to the school that Cherise wasn't involved, and that was that."

"But she told Dodie it was her fault!"

Ruth fingered the rim of her soft drink. "Guilt leaves a creeping stain. I'm doubtful that Cherise caused the accident, although she might still feel remorse that she was on the scene when it occurred."

"You're telling me that she's not at fault no matter what she says? That she's simply feeling the sort of normal guilt we all do when something bad happens, whether it's our fault or not?"

"How do you feel about Brenda Detweiler's death?"

She had me there.

"Okay, okay," I muttered.

"I've come to like and admire you, Kiki. Honestly, I do. Speaking from my heart, with genuine affection for you, I urge you to drop the subject. Right here; right now."

THIRTY-SIX

AT THREE O'CLOCK, ANYA called. "Mom? Could you pick me up from school? Could I come help with the crop?"

"Don't you want to stay at the Moore's house? I thought you and Nicci planned to watch a movie together."

Silence.

"Anya? You there?"

"Mom, please? Can't I come to the store? I'd like to sleep at home tonight. Isn't that okay?" A fissure in her voice betrayed her stress.

"Of course, honey. I'll come get you right away," and I did.

After she climbed into my car, Anya rested her forehead against the window on the passenger side. I tried to coax a conversation out of her, to no avail. Finally, I settled for taking her to Bread Co., hoping that food would oil the hinges of her jaw, since none of my encouragements were working.

No such luck.

The wisest course was waiting her out. Years ago, parenting experts talked about quality time, suggesting that the amount of time you spend with a child is not as important as "quality time," those special moments of import.

Ha. What a crock.

With a kid, you never know when quality time will happen. And if you aren't spending enough quantity time, you might very well miss the opportunity to connect when it comes your way. Anya would talk when the mood struck her, if I was willing to be both patient and flexible. That was the key, listening. Being fully present. Not just giving her lip service or nodding and tuning out.

As I parked my old red BMW in the parking lot of Time in a Bottle, I took my daughter's hand in mine. "I don't know what you're thinking. I realize we've had a lot happen these past few days. You must not be ready to talk, and that's okay. Just know that I love you with all my heart. I'll always be in your corner. When you're ready to talk, I'll listen. Nothing that's happened so far—and nothing that can ever happen—will change my love for you."

In her eyes, doubt lingered. The pale denim blue of her irises darkened to navy with concern as she frowned and said, "Do you remember when Dad told me to keep his meetings with that woman secret?"

My husband, George, had been carrying on an affair with an old sweetheart, Roxanne Baker, for most of our marriage. At some point, he decided to include Anya in his outings with Roxanne, so he swore Anya to secrecy. It was a good thing that George was already dead and buried when I learned about his duplicity, or I would have strangled him with my own two hands.

"Um, I'm not likely to forget about that ever."

"It can be hard when someone asks you to keep a secret. I mean, what if you promise them you won't tell?"

I bit my tongue. I wanted to blurt out, "I'm your mother! You can tell me anything!" But I didn't. Instead, I struggled. Finally, I said, "You are right. That's a hard one. You know from experience that it's not always fair to ask another person to keep a secret. Is it?"

"No." She turned to look out the window, instead of at me.

"Do you know what therapists do? They keep a person's secrets unless that person is going to hurt someone."

Her head whipped around. "What? Tell me that again. I'm not sure I understand."

"There's this rule called 'patient confidentiality.' It means that what you say to a therapist is sacred, just like when you talk to your rabbi or priest or lawyer. But if you tell a professional that you plan to hurt someone, all bets are off. If you tell a priest that you plan to kill someone, the priest has an obligation to go to the proper authorities."

"Always?" asked Anya. "What if you were going to hurt yourself?"

"You mean like commit suicide?" I asked. My heart did a free fall into the deepest regions of my gut. I told myself I needed to stay calm. If I overreacted, I would spook her. She might clam up and not share with me.

"Sort of."

Oh, God! Was she planning to hurt herself? No, she said it was a secret—a plan that someone else had entrusted to Anya.

"Yes, even then. Especially then. Honey, do you know someone planning to commit suicide? If you do, maybe you should tell me. Perhaps we could help him. Or her."

"No." She spoke quickly and firmly. "I don't know anyone who wants to kill herself. I was only asking."

Why don't I believe that? What is she hiding?

More than ever, I was glad she planned to spend the evening with me.

THIRTY-SEVEN

ALTHOUGH I'D SEEN SOME of our regular croppers at my "Welcome Home" party, that seemed like a lifetime ago. For that event, Clancy had only invited a select few. Tonight our customers showed up in droves, which proved to be a bit of a problem because we'd taken reservations for only twenty-two. Rather than turn down the business, Laurel and Anya worked feverishly to put together more kits.

After fielding individual questions about the shooting, I realized we wouldn't get anything done if I kept answering the same queries over and over. It started to become tedious. Finally I tapped a spoon against a glass bottle of green tea and quieted the group down. "If I might say a few words…"

They hushed in eager anticipation. I looked out over three tables of women, many of whom I'd met years ago at crops I'd attended as Dodie Goldfader's best customer. A lump formed in my throat as I considered the changes ahead. What would we do when Dodie died? Would the store close its doors?

I gave myself a hard mental shake. This wasn't the time to think about the road ahead. Instead, I needed to clear the air so we could get down to having serious fun.

"Yes, I was involved in a shooting. No, I never expected something like that to happen. Yes, there was a plan in place to entrap Bill Ballard. No, I didn't make the plan, the police here in St. Louis did because they feared his bad behavior was escalating and more people might get hurt. Yes, I shot Bill. No, I didn't have a choice. Yes, he was going to kill my mother-in-law, Sheila, and Mert Chambers's brother was bleeding to death. Yes, I feel horrible about it. I never willingly would hurt a fly. All of you know that, but I couldn't stand there and watch someone I love—"

And my voice turned so husky I had to grab a swallow of tea. "Be tortured like that. For the rest of my life, I'll have to live with what I did, and I wouldn't wish it on anyone."

I swallowed and pressed my fingertips to my eye sockets so I wouldn't cry. "Yes, I'm pregnant. Yes, it's Detective Chad Detweiler's baby. No, he didn't kill his wife, Brenda. Of that I'm certain. Yes, I intend to marry him, but not until after the baby is born," and here I shot a glance toward Anya. She struggled not to smile and dropped her gaze to examine her shoes very carefully.

"My due date is mid-January. I have an appointment with an ob-gyn next week."

I steepled my fingertips and stared out at the rapt faces. "Does that cover everything? I hope so, because if it does, I'd like to show you this cool project."

"One more question," said Bonnie Gossage. "When can I host a baby shower?"

Laurel stepped up and wagged a finger. "Ah-ah-ah. I already called dibs. But you can be my co-host. How's that?"

Everyone broke into giggles. When they quieted down, I showed them the project.

Anya took a seat next to Bonnie. Light and dark, their heads bent over their paper and supplies. A portion of me rejoiced, seeing how my child fit in. Hillary Clinton was right. It takes a village to raise a child. But in a pinch, a scrapbook store will do.

Anya and Laurel helped me pick up after the event. Clancy would have stuck around, but she was meeting movers the next day to pack up a few of her mother's more valuable, personal items so that my mother and sister could move into Mrs. Clancy's brick home. "If they like it, I plan to convert the half-bath on the first floor to a full bath so your mother can have her own apartment. Your sister isn't much of a cook, and she could share the foyer with your mom so I wouldn't need to add more stairs. I think the house will work well for them."

"You have my eternal gratitude," I said. "The house will be perfect for them. Amanda loves U City already. Mom will be close to a senior center where she can attend 'day care.' They're both close enough to my place that I can visit easily, but far enough that I can have a life."

"Works for me, too. I was able to truthfully tell my mother that I hadn't sold her precious house. That she could move back in, although that was highly, highly unlikely. I told her I hired live-in help to take care of her flowers. She bought it! She's been bragging to all her friends that I'm the best daughter ever. I went from you-know-what on her shoes to an angel overnight. What a promotion." With that, Clancy laughingly bid us goodbye.

Laurel walked Anya and me to our car. More accurately, Gracie walked all three of us to the parking lot. "It was nice to see you, Anya. How exciting! You're going to be a big sister!"

"I know. I can't wait. I hope Mom has a boy."

"Really?" I asked. "Why is that?"

"Because I like being the only girl in our family. And boys get to do cool stuff like catch frogs."

Oh-kay, I thought. Whatever! As long as she was happy, I was, too.

THIRTY-EIGHT

Saturday morning, Day 5—after the shooting

I woke up at six and ran to the john where I spent the first five minutes of my day tossing my cookies. After nibbling on a handful of crackers and sipping a glass of ginger ale, I felt human again. Anya grumbled when I tried to wake her. I couldn't blame her for wanting to sleep in. With her sleepy permission, I left my daughter in the house with Gracie and ran over to Kaldi's to get a latte and breakfast. I thought I owed myself a treat.

After all, I'd had a rough week. As usual, there was a long line at Kaldi's, because the brew is superb. Kaldi's is a local chain that roasts their own beans and bakes great pastries. While waiting my turn in line with other customers, we inched our way toward the newspaper rack.

Detweiler's arrest was front-page news. With trembling hands, I picked up the paper—my rule being if I read what's visible, well, that's to be expected because that's how they hook you, but if I pick it up, I should pay for it—and wrestled the big sheets open so

I could see the "jump" to the inside. My mug shot stared out at me. I'd been wrongly accused two years ago, and I intended to try and get my photo out of the system. But that hadn't been Numero Uno on my "to do" list.

Now everyone in the world could see a picture of me with a booking number under my chin.

I groaned.

The woman behind me said, "Say, aren't you ... ?"

"No! I'm not!" I said sharply. "Mind your own business."

I never, ever speak to people that way. Chalk it up to a queasy tummy, no caffeine, anger, and a sense of general disgust. What had I done to deserve this? Nothing!

After paying for my latte, the newspaper, a huge iced cookie, a blueberry muffin, and a scone, I scuttled to the one empty table in the back and near the restroom. There I read more of Milton Kloss's accusations, including such memorable phrases as, "Mrs. Lowenstein apparently doesn't care whether she's broken up a happy marriage or not. She always gets her man. Even if she has to shoot him!"

Of course, he was equally hard on Detweiler. "He swore an oath to protect and defend. But breaking his word comes easily. After all, he was cheating on my daughter. Breaking his marriage vows. So it wasn't much of a leap for him to toss his conscience aside and shoot my poor baby when she tried to keep their marriage together!"

I stuffed every crumb of food in my mouth, trying to push away my feelings of embarrassment, guilt, and anger. When I finished, I walked to the front counter for more food. On my way, I saw a copy of *The Muddy Waters Review*, the newspaper owned by the family of my old boyfriend Ben Novak. I read through it while ordering an omelet, a side of bacon, and a potato latke. I would have hoped that Ben might ignore my plight and take the high road, but no-ooo. Although Detweiler and I hadn't made the front page, Ben had drop-kicked both of us to the curb in an editorial with the nasty headline, "Killer Cop Deserves Life in Jail."

Instead of waiting for my order, I bolted. I ran to the bathroom as fast as my scuffed up Keds would take me. Then for the second time in less than an hour, I heaved my guts out.

"Poor baby," I said to my bump as I rinsed out my mouth. "You've had a real rollercoaster ride, haven't you?

My eyes water when I vomit, so I stood there blinking and trying to get my digestive system under control. As I did, I looked into the mirror. I saw a woman who had definitely had ENOUGH!

"I'm going to make all of you pay for this. Milton Kloss, watch your back. Ben Novak, you're going to eat crow. A whole flock of them. You two bullies have picked on the wrong woman. My name is Kiki Lowenstein. I repeat it as a prayer. Lowenstein, Lowenstein, Lowenstein. And you both better start praying, because it's payback time."

THIRTY-NINE

Once I was back home, I looked in on Anya. She'd gone back to sleep, surrounded by two cats and one big dog.

I grabbed a huge sheet of blank newsprint, the type most people use for packing. I use it for planning craft projects because I'm too cheap to pay for expensive flip charts. After brewing myself a cup of ginger tea, I drew a mind map, essentially a spider web with a big circle in the center. In that center, I wrote: Who killed Brenda Detweiler?

On the spokes going out from the center hub, I wrote words and phrases as fast as I could. My goal was to capture as many ideas as possible. Once I filled an entire page. I started over on a fresh sheet of paper.

I did this three times. The first time, you dredge up the obvious. The second time, you're getting to the heart of the matter. The third time you complete this exercise, you're hitting pay dirt.

By my reckoning, there were a variety of motives for killing Brenda:

Drug deals gone bad.

Problems at her job. (Since she was a nurse, her drug use made her inattentive at best and wildly unpredictable at worse. I had reason to know this.)

Marital issues.

Money problems. (Maybe she owed money for the drugs and was behind.)

Other.

I could confidently mark off "marital issues." Even if Detweiler was angry with her, why didn't he follow her to her parents' house—where she'd obviously spent the night, despite her mother's claim not to have seen her—and kill her that evening right after the shootout? Why wait until the next morning when he would have had time to cool down? And why kill her anyway? She was definitely headed for jail. She'd be off the streets and out of our hair for sure.

If Detweiler did shoot Brenda, why leave her body in a place where it could be found so easily? Hadn't he told me repeatedly that a missing body was a huge problem for law enforcement? His family owned hogs. So did most of their neighbors. A hog could devour a human body in no time. Why not dump the corpse in the hog pen? Or toss it into the manure tanks where no one ventured because the methane inside was deadly? Failing that, why not weigh her body down and dump her in the Mississippi?

Why would he wait twelve hours, shoot her at a vacant house near his parents' home, wrap her corpse in a blanket, and leave behind bullet casings from his service pistol?

This crime was simply too stupid to be real. Especially if the person committing it was a cop with a lot of homicide experience. Like Detweiler.

Someone had set him up.

Who?

Why?

My phone rang. I looked at the number. The accounting firm would have to wait. My fiancé couldn't.

Who? I circled the word.

It had to be someone whom Brenda knew. Someone who Brenda ran to for help.

Since Detweiler wouldn't offer her sympathy, she probably called on family or friends.

What about Brenda's mother, Carla? She'd been suspiciously quiet since the shooting. Why? Was she content to let her husband make a fuss, or was there another reason? I'd seen how wild Brenda was. Had she run home to Mommy? Was it possible that they quarreled, and Carla Kloss grabbed a gun to defend herself? I could imagine that scenario very easily.

Brenda Detweiler had attacked me twice in public and once in private while I was a patient in a hospital where she worked. So I knew she could be violent. What if she had attacked her mother? Was that why Carla Kloss couldn't join her husband in bad-mouthing Detweiler?

If she didn't go home, where else could Brenda have gone for help? Where had she spent the night?

I kept a map of the St. Louis metro area in the glove compartment of my car. Letting Gracie out for a piddle, I grabbed the folded map and brought it inside. From a closet, I retrieved a cork bulletin board. Opening my laptop computer, I went to my Outlook contacts file. I planned to stick a pin in every Detweiler or Kloss residence within twenty-five miles of Brenda's final resting place. Unfortunately, although that looks pretty cool in the movies, it doesn't work well in real life. I couldn't make out exactly where my pins should go, and when I did figure out the locations, my pins kept falling out.

On to Plan B. I printed out all the Kloss and Detweiler addresses I found in the online White Pages. Next, I went to Mapquest. One by one, I charted the distances from each address to the farmhouse where Brenda's body had been found.

The closest was Patricia Detweiler Kressig's house.

FORTY

ANYA WANDERED INTO THE kitchen and poured herself a bowl of cereal. When I asked about her agenda, she shrugged. "I have homework. I was thinking about just chillin' on the sofa."

Something was definitely wrong. Usually Saturdays were spent with Nicci at one of the local malls or the movie theatres. In fact, I couldn't remember a weekend when the two girls didn't get together.

"Anya? Do you want to talk? Is anything on your mind?"

"Nope."

"You sure?"

"Can't I want to hang out at my own house without being hassled by you?" Her voice was a perfect imitation of Sheila's when my mother-in-law was in a snit. I thought about sending Anya to her room, but decided I didn't want to pick a fight with her immediately before I went to work.

"The Detweilers invited us over for dinner tonight. I was thinking we could stop by and see your grandmother at the hospital. I think she's coming home tomorrow."

My daughter grunted.

"Okay. I'll be home at five. We'll leave as soon as I get here."

Another grunt. I took that as a sign of progress.

"You sure you're okay here alone?"

She glared at me. "Leighton is just across the yard. Gracie weighs more than most men. My mother packs a pistol and shoots people in the head. And my stepfather-to-be is in jail for murder. Who's going to mess with me?"

"Right. Keep your cell phone close by anyway."

The store was quiet when I arrived. Saturday mornings often were. Traffic would pick up as the day went on, so I started my circuit of the premises, straightening and replenishing our merchandise. While arranging a stack of Tim Holtz inks, a brainstorm hit me. The link went like this: Holtz ... Hadcho. As in Detective Stan Hadcho. Why hadn't I contacted Detweiler's old partner and asked him for help? I fished my cell phone out of my pocket and dialed his number.

"I wondered when you'd get around to calling me. How's Chad?"

I filled him in, as best I could. I told him about the Mapquest work I'd done.

"Not good. Not good at all. Patricia is the family wild child. But I can't imagine her shooting Brenda unless Brenda attacked her. If that's what happened, why not come forward and say the shooting was in self-defense?"

"Because it wasn't. It was execution style," I reminded him. That also reminded me why it was unlikely that any family member had killed Brenda. Unless, of course, the killer had consciously chosen to make the murder look like it had been an execution.

"Whatever. Patricia still could have done it. She knew Brenda was making her brother miserable. Chad told me that the two of them had gotten into a knock-down-drag-out fight at Brenda's apartment. I guess Patricia lost all respect for Brenda and told her their friendship was done. Fini. Over. But if that's what happened, why would Patricia frame her own brother?"

Good question.

"Someone had to have planted those bullets," I said.

"Not bullets. Spent casings. The planter didn't necessarily need access to Chad's gun, but he or she did need access to spent casings."

I understood what he was saying. "So it could be someone who was with him when he was at a shooting range."

Hadcho's next words came out as a growl. "Maybe Brenda's killer is another cop."

FORTY-ONE

I HADN'T THOUGHT OF that, and now I wished that Hadcho hadn't brought it up either. But he did, and he kept on talking. "So it could be someone from the force who practiced on the same shooting range as Chad. Even though we only have to requalify every year, Chad prides himself on being a good shot, so he practices more often than the rest of us. Or the person who killed Brenda might have been someone in the department who she met through Chad. Could even be someone in the drug apprehension program. She might have even run into someone from the department who was working undercover. Or a confidential informant, a CI. Maybe this person was worried that Brenda would reveal his identity. She'd clearly gone off her nut."

I started to get sick at my stomach. While he rambled on, I ran to the backroom and grabbed a cold can of Coke, hoping it would keep me from spewing all over the store. What a mess that would be.

Hadcho ignored the *pop!* of my soda can in his ear. "They're sure the gun used on Brenda was his 9 mm Beretta 92F semiautomatic? Like he's using now?"

"What are you asking me? I don't speak Starbucks, I barely speak Wendy's, and I certainly don't speak guns."

"Each of our weapons stays in use about ten years. What if they matched the casings to Chad's gun, but the gun's an old one? I think he recently retired his first gun. Changed it out just last week as a matter of fact."

"Oh my gosh. Wouldn't someone have a record of that?"

"Sure, but what if the record hasn't been updated yet? Or what if the folks in Illinois didn't read it correctly? Each department has different procedures, record keeping, and so on. Let's suppose for a minute that the crime scene people from Illinois handed the casings to their lab. Then they called or emailed the St. Louis Police Department and asked for any records they would have of ballistics tests on officers' guns. The clerk sends them a recent test, but one done before Chad's updated his gun, so they match the crime scene casings to his old gun. Not the one he's currently using."

"I'll share all this with Schnabel tonight."

"Schnabel. Word in the department is that you somehow got him to represent Chad. That so? Wow. If Chad wasn't going to marry you before, he certainly is now. He's going to owe you his life!"

FORTY-TWO

"Laurel deserves all the credit. I guess Schnabel owed her a favor."

"That makes sense."

Did it? What did Hadcho know that I didn't? The door minder rang and I needed to take care of business, so we ended our call with me feeling more unsettled and worried than before.

A stone-faced Rebekkah walked right past me and toward the stockroom. "Over here," I said as I waved to her, but she didn't turn to face me. "How's your mom?" I called to her retreating back.

"Not so hot. She's taken to reading all the spines of books in our house. Moves from one bookshelf to the other. It's like she's lost. Dad smelled this awful stink in their closet. Mom had shoved two half-eaten hamburgers into pairs of shoes." Rebekkah hugged herself. "How do you cope with that? Watch her every second?"

"Let's go up front. I'm the only person in the store. What does hospice say?"

"This is normal. The cancer is interfering with her cognitive abilities." Rebekkah leaned onto the worktable. As usual, she wore a T-shirt with an odd saying and a pair of cargo pants. Both were in dull colors, like camouflage.

She circled her finger on the tabletop. "Tell me I'm not a bad person. I asked them how long it would be. I didn't mean to say I wanted her to … you know … die quickly. I was only wondering, but Dad stared at me as if I were a stranger."

I stretched to put an arm around her shoulders. "You're not a bad person. You are curious. There's that book *What to Expect When You're Expecting,* but no similar guide for how to handle it when a loved one is dying. It's all uncharted territory. But people die as often as people are born. I don't blame you for wanting to know. You were right to ask. You don't want to plan a trip or overlook her last moments because you misunderstood the time frame."

In answer, she buried her head in my shoulder, like a child might. As the sobs came, I rocked her as best I could. Even though the motion was awkward, I knew how instinctively soothing it is. "It's all right, it's all right. Of course you have questions. Of course you are worried and scared. I'm here for you. All of us here at the store love your mother. We'll do anything we can."

She raised a wet, red face. Her hair smelled like strawberries. Her eyes squinted as her lashes were threaded with tears. "Do you have to keep asking about Nathan?"

"Your mom wanted me to. Why?"

"You don't know what it's like. I could never compare to him. Because he was dead, he never did anything wrong, and every time I let them down, I just knew they were wishing … wishing …"

"Wishing what?"

"That he was still alive and that I was gone."

"Rebekkah! You don't really mean that!"

She turned on me, eyes snapping. "Yes, I do! Nathan was a straight A student. Everybody loved him. He was never moody. Always Mr. Sunshine. I had colic, but he was born with a smile on his face. He never gave Mom or Dad a moment's worry. The teachers all loved him. Everybody loved Nathan. Everyone! I would come home with a note from the teacher, and I could just see Mom shaking her head. The only notes he brought home were to praise him! To talk about how brilliant he was! How can I compete with a dead guy, huh? How? And now you're going to dig up his memory. Going to remind everyone that Nathan was the best kid in the world. Never mind that he's been gone all these years. That I stood by Mom and Dad after he died. That every year I help them light the *yahrzeit* candle and pray for him. I can never, ever, ever measure up to him. And suddenly, he's back. Not in the flesh. Nope. He's like your Jesus all resurrected and saintly. Did you know he smoked dope? Well, he did. Mom and Dad never knew that."

The force of her rage astonished me. I did my best to listen to the words and not let the emotion sidetrack me, but I have to admit, her ferocity sent me reeling.

Just as quickly, compassion gave me pause. Rebekkah could never admit these feelings under ordinary conditions. She'd be labeled as selfish, horrible, wicked. In truth, she was a grown-up child who'd never fully coped with the loss of her brother. Now the impending loss of her mother had intensified her grief. Rebekkah was staggering under an emotional load. Nor could she share this with her parents.

"Rebekkah, no one is perfect. Perfect belongs to the Lord. I can't imagine being in your situation. It certainly has to be tough. You are right: He'll never do anything wrong in their minds. They've ushered him into sainthood. You'll have to be a happy second, forever, won't you?"

"That's right. You understand, don't you?" Her face crumpled in relief and a tear ran a silver course over her cheek before sl-loming off her chin. "Why do you have to dig this up?"

I marveled at her question. "Is there something that will tarnish your brother's image? Is that why you want me to drop it?"

She straightened and looked me right in the eye. "My mom won't be around much longer. I don't particularly feel like sharing her with my dead brother."

FORTY-THREE

No way was I going to ask Rebekkah to get on Facebook and help me track down the kids who were with Nathan when he died. Ruth Glazer had warned me off the project. Rebekkah didn't want me to pursue it. I was up the creek without a paddle. All I could do was ask Robbie Holmes to look into the matter. After Rebekkah ambled back to the refrigerator, I dialed his number.

"Hey, when is Sheila coming home?" I sounded oh-so-casual.

"Probably tomorrow if they don't put her out on the curb with her belongings in a plastic bag sooner." His throaty chuckle was warm with his love for her.

"She must be feeling better."

"Yes, and complaining about the quality of sheets on the hospital bed. I finally went over to her house and grabbed a set of Frette sheets for her. Did you know there's some nonsense called thread count? It determines how soft fabric is?"

My turn to giggle. "Not until Sheila educated me. Welcome to the posh life, Mr. Police Chief, sir. I was thinking about stopping by and seeing her this evening. Anya and I have been invited to the Detweilers' farm for dinner. You've heard that he's under house arrest, right?"

"Sure did. You must be feeling better about Detweiler's situation, what with John Henry Schnabel in his corner and all. You ever seen Mr. Schnabel?"

"Nope."

"He's about your height. Wears a polka-dot bow tie. Glasses as thick as cola bottles. Not a lick of hair on the top of his head, only a fringe around the sides and ears. Voice is high and squeaky like a girl's."

That was not encouraging news. In my mind, the attorney was bigger than life. "Is he up to this?"

"Shoot, yes. When the Illinois law enforcement officials heard he was on the case, sales of Maalox shot through the roof. You could let a hungry hyena loose in a preschool and have fewer casualties than Mr. Schnabel can cause in a courtroom. His nickname is 'Blood and Guts' because he eviscerates his opponents. Already the odds have shifted in Chad's favor. Although it sure would help it if we could track down the real killer."

I told him about my conversation with Hadcho.

"Stan is one of my brightest detectives. He's right. When they made their request, I doubt that our clerk checked to see if Chad's file has the latest tests or not. I try to keep updated ballistics info on all my officers. Saves hassle when there's a question of whose bullet did what. Otherwise you need to track down the weapon and it's usually in an officer's possession, so that takes a man out of rotation. As for access to spent casings, of course we have a department range we use, but Chad did a lot of his practice at that range over by his parents' house. The GM, they call it. That's short for great moraine."

I misheard him. "Lorraine? Like a woman's name?"

"No, moraine with an 'm' like 'Mary.' During the ice age, the glaciers picked up rich soil and brought it along with on their slide toward the equator. When the ice melted, that dirt was deposited throughout Illinois. Actually in four places. The transported soil is responsible for the great farming they have."

You learn something every day, but only if you keep your ears open and your mouth shut.

"You're telling me he practiced shooting over in Illinois?"

"Nearly every Sunday. He and his dad would go to the GM and squeeze off a couple of clips."

My heart sank. Now I had another prime suspect, Louis Detweiler. Was it possible that Louis was sick of Brenda's shenanigans? That he wanted Chad to be able to marry me and bring a boy Detweiler into this world? All his grandbabies were girls so far.

More importantly, should I share my worries about Louis and Patricia with Robbie?

I decided not to. I really didn't have enough to go on. Besides, there wasn't much Robbie could do except call over to Illinois and hope to find a sympathetic ear. The man had his hands full, what with Sheila in the hospital and needing to tie up loose ends from the shootout we'd had at the slough. But I was about to lob another ball in the air for him to juggle.

"What do you remember about Nathan Goldfader's death?"

"Not much, why?"

I explained about Dodie's request.

"You sure do get yourself into tough situations."

"What do you mean? Cherise Landon walked into the store and told Dodie that she was responsible for Nathan's death. I didn't ask for this assignment. Believe me, it's the last thing I need right now. But what can I do? Drop it? If I were Dodie, I'd want closure."

"You don't want to be messing in Shep Landon's business. I can't tell you why, I can't tell you all that I know, but trust me, you thought you had problems with Bill Ballard? Shep is ten times worse and Shep has a law degree."

"Meaning what?"

"Meaning I'd rather have my throat slit fast with a razor than have someone tie me down and poke holes in me until I bleed to death. That's how lawyers kill their prey, Kiki. They whittle away at you in court. Shoot, I've watched innocent people wreck their businesses, their marriages, and their health dealing with court cases. I'm an officer of the law, and you'd think that I would believe in our criminal justice system, but I don't. There are too many vagaries that work against a person. Especially if you're a novice who doesn't know the system. Did I ever tell you what I hate most about sending individuals to jail? It's the learning process. They come out better, smarter crooks. They teach each other how to play the system. You and I haven't a clue."

"What am I going to do?"

"Walk away. For once in your life, walk away."

FORTY-FOUR

Anya was in a marginally better mood when I swung by the house to pick her up. Mainly she was happily anticipating a trip to the Detweiler farm. My daughter loves critters of every size, shape, and species. If we could live on a farm, Anya would happily turn her back on her fancy clothes and hoity-toity school. She loves everything about farm living—the sights, sounds, and smells of life in the country. Once I caught her smuggling home a plastic baggy of new mown hay after an overnight with Mimi and Pop Detweiler.

"If I close my eyes and sniff it, I can pretend I'm in the barn," Anya had told me earnestly, fingering the bag with reverence.

Of course, there was another reason she loved going over the river and through the woods to the farm. Chad Detweiler's oldest niece, Emily Volker, and Anya were the same age. From the moment they met, the two girls became fast friends, staying in touch through text-messaging and Skype.

"Why didn't you invite Nicci along? She might like to visit the Detweiler's farm," I asked as I turned over the car engine.

"She's busy," my daughter said far too quickly. There might be legitimate reasons, so I held my tongue. The last time that Nicci came along with us, there had been a touch of awkwardness among the girls. Emily had invited Nicci and Anya to come swim in her above-ground pool, but Nicci quickly declined. Even when Thelma produced a bathing suit that would fit Nicci perfectly, the Moore girl said a very firm, albeit polite, "No."

There is that old truism that three's a crowd. More to the point, Nicci's idea of roughing it is a four-star hotel. Maybe an above-ground pool didn't seem appealing when compared to lounging around the beautiful pool at the St. Louis Country Club. Nicci didn't particularly like getting grubby, playing in the dusty barn, or running through the fields covered with cow patties. Not her cup of tea. Nor was she overly fond of animals. She would go with Anya to pet shops and view critters in cages. She liked our cats and Gracie well enough, but I'd seen both the Moore kids squeal in fear when a large fishing spider crawled onto their back patio. Stevie grabbed a stone to smash it, but Anya tugged at his arm and warned, "Don't you dare! He eats bugs! I'll move him into the bushes."

My daughter showed nascent signs of wanting a career in veterinary sciences or biology. Being around animals gave her tremendous joy. Nicci claimed to want a career in fashion merchandising.

Anya brought me back to the here and now. "I just texted Emily. She says we can saddle up the new pony and go for a ride. Did you know Mimi rescued Apollo? He was bound for the glue factory, whatever that means. And he's not really a pony. He's a short horse. Only fourteen hands high."

Detweiler's parents had given my daughter permission to call them "Mimi" and "Pop" way back at Christmas. They were lovely people, really wonderful, and I was happy that my daughter and I had been welcomed into their lives.

"Hands?"

"You measure the height of a horse or pony in four-inch increments, called 'hands' because it's almost the width of a hand, see?" She held up her palm for inspection, before lecturing me. "While a pony typically has a stockier frame than a horse, the more obvious difference is size. A horse is anything over fourteen-point-three hands high and above. A pony is anything fourteen-point-two and below."

"That's fascinating."

She prattled on about how Apollo had been used as a trail riding mount until the company went bust and decided to shoot him rather than feed him. "Can you believe how cruel that is? Can you imagine? You work your whole life and then—BAM!—right in the brain because you aren't useful anymore. Makes me sick. I want to have a fundraiser at school. Will you help me?"

"Sure," I said. "What's the plan?"

She'd thought it through pretty carefully. Several boys at school had started their own rock and roll bands. Anya thought a "battle of the bands" would be a fun way to get attention for them and money for abandoned horses.

"Does Missouri really have that many horses without homes?"

My daughter rolled her eyes at me. "Didn't you know that in 2007 a court ruling upheld the ban on the slaughter of horses for human consumption? That along with the economic downturn means that more and more irresponsible owners are simply aban-

186

doning their horses in farmers' fields, on the side of the road, and in parks. It's a crisis, Mom. Where have you been?"

"Under a rock?" Is what I said, but I was thinking, "Shot in the head, trying to keep my future husband out of jail, and struggling to hold down a job." But I didn't.

"That creep who's been saying all that mean stuff about you and Detweiler? Mr. Kloss? He's trying to open a slaughter facility on his farm. Wants to turn horses into dog food. Can you believe that? Claims it would be more humane than letting them starve."

"That's true, isn't it?"

"Sure, but there's no guarantee he'll kill the horses in a humane way. He's saying all this because he's greedy. If he can open the first slaughterhouse in the country, think of all the abandoned horses he can turn into cash. I mean, it would be like printing money. Shipping them wouldn't cost much. The cities that are trying to care for the strays would get off cheaper by trucking them to Illinois. It's a central location. His place isn't far from the headquarters of Purina. I bet he could work a deal with them."

My daughter the cynic.

Then I corrected myself. I'd grown up with a Pollyanna view of the world. A messed up assumption that most people were innately good. That when someone talked to you, they were telling the truth. After all, in an alcoholic family if you don't believe the hogwash you're told, someone is going to get hurt. And if you're the littlest person in the family, it'll more than likely be you. So I learned to accept what I was told, to nod my head, and go along.

By contrast, I'd raised my daughter to question authority. Respectfully. The world had taught her to be a skeptic. She had far too much access to information. Or maybe not, because if I could guide her properly, she'd learn to sift through what she heard and come to intelligent conclusions.

"You've been following Mr. Kloss's campaign?"

"Yep. Even before Detweiler's wife got shot. Last time I was at the farm, Mimi told me she hated the man. Couldn't stand him and hoped he wouldn't get elected. She said he's a scoundrel, and I had to look that word up. While he was a county councilman, he voted for development only when it would line his pocket."

"Interesting." I tried to keep my hands steady on the wheel. I wondered what had gotten into Thelma. Here I'd thought her the sweetest person on earth, protective of her grandkids, too, but she'd given my daughter an earful about Milton Kloss.

"Mimi never liked Brenda, either, because of how she treated Detweiler. Emily told me so. See, Emily says that Brenda tricked her Aunt Patricia, too, but I don't know how. Something about talking Aunt Patricia into an investment scheme. How then Aunt Patricia and Uncle Paul lost a bunch of money and almost had to give up their house. And then Mimi and Pop had to get a loan and Mr. Kloss signed it."

"I heard that, too." I gripped the wheel tightly. Illinois highways are notorious for their bad repair. There are only two seasons in Illinois: winter and road repair. The potholes bounced us up and down. I worried that Gracie might hit her head on the rag top.

"Emily told me her Aunt Brenda laughed at her mother when she confronted her about making life miserable for Detweiler. And she was mad at Aunt Brenda about the mean trick she played on Patricia. Really mad, says Emily."

"Ginny? Brenda laughed at Ginny?" Ginny Volker was Chad's other sister, the oldest of the two Detweiler girls, and Emily's mother.

"Yes, Emily heard the whole argument. Her mother told Brenda that she wished someone would shoot her and put her out of her misery."

More Detweilers to put on my suspect list.

FORTY-FIVE

A LATE-MODEL NAVY BLUE Mercedes Roadster sat on the Detweiler's gravel driveway. I pulled in beside it. When he heard my car door slam, Detweiler rushed my old BMW and swept me up in his arms à la Rhett Butler and Scarlett O'Hara in *Gone with the Wind*. I giggled because he was being so darn romantic. He kissed me repeatedly, and at close range I could see how gaunt his face had become. The last few days had certainly been hard on him.

"You okay? How's the baby?" he asked.

"Fine. We're all fine. Just worried about you," and I hugged him tightly.

After setting me on my feet, he threw an arm around Anya, kissed her on the top of the head, and asked, "How's life, Anya-Banana?"

Her eyes brightened at his teasing, but she didn't have much time to react because Gracie had wriggled her way out of the back seat of my car—and launched herself at him. The big girl loves Detweiler more than anyone on earth. Those front paws hitting his chest nearly knocked him to his knees, but Detweiler kept his balance. We couldn't move until Gracie had her ears scratched.

"Gracie, you are such a flirt," I told her. "Get your fat paws off my boyfriend. I'm starving. What did Thelma make us for dinner?"

"A huge pot roast. A piece of meat so big that she had to divide it into two slow cookers. Everyone's on the way. Ginny and Jeff are coming with Emily. Patty and Paul should be here right now."

More red meat. And here I'd claimed I never eat the stuff. Oh, well.

A battered gray Camry pulled in next to my red car. Paul Kressig hopped out to help Patty retrieve two foil-covered bowls and a pan from the back seat.

I never knew exactly how to greet Patty. At our first meeting last Thanksgiving, the air was so frosty, my nose turned numb. But after I helped Patty find her lost necklace, she warmed up. Since then I'd seen her at Christmas and at Easter. She was polite, but in a sort of "I could take you or leave you" way.

Until Anya filled me in on the family dynamics, I had thought that Patty and Brenda were still friendly with each other. I'm sure my relationship with Detweiler had put Patty between the proverbial rock and a hard place.

Since I didn't know where I stood with the youngest Detweiler sister, I hung back. Her husband tipped his green and white Pioneer Seed Corn cap at me in greeting. Patty nodded to me solemnly and said, "Heard you got Schnabel to take Chad's case. Thanks. Thanks a lot. Did Chad tell you there's to be a memorial service on Monday for Brenda? It's at the Penney and Queen Funeral Home. Most of the people who'll be there are either staunch Republicans or owe Milton money."

Paul shook his head and winked at me. "Come on now, Patty. I've voted Republican a number of times. We vote for the candidate not the party, so she and I usually cancel each other's vote out when it's all said and done. What do you say we get this food inside?"

The GPS tracking device, better known as an ankle bracelet, bulged under Detweiler's pants leg. The hem caught on a thick plastic band that held up a box about the size of a large pack of cigarettes. When he noticed me looking, Detweiler smiled sadly at me. In response, I hugged him, and we stood there arm in arm.

"May I help?" my daughter asked Paul, and he handed her a large glass bowl.

"Is this your corn pudding?" my daughter asked Patty. "Emily told me she hoped you'd bring it."

"It sure is, Sweet Pea. Do you like corn pudding?" Patty asked Anya.

"I don't think I've ever had it."

"Then you're in for a treat." With that, we started toward the farmhouse.

The Detweiler family home, a white clapboard two-story, had been built in the mid-1800s by Helmut Detweiler, a German immigrant. After five long years of working the land alone, he brought his intended, Enid, here from Stuttgart. They married under an oak tree that still stood in the middle of the cow pasture. Few changes had been made to the outside of the house, although the floor plan had seen many alterations. The entire setting with the red barn at our back, the wrap-around porch with rockers, and the American flag flapping at the top of the pole in the center of the circular drive smacked of wholesome, patriotic values. Under twin maple trees in the side yard, three picnic benches with red and white checkered oilcloth coverings beckoned us. Blue and red coolers were positioned between the tables, as was a large aluminum trash can with a black liner. To the coolers, Thelma had taped signs written in bold black marker: Sodas, Water, Beer. I planned to come back outside and take a photo later, as I itched to create a scrapbook page memorializing the scene.

The screen door slapped shut behind us as we entered the house. The noise reminded me of my childhood, when only the wealthy had air-conditioning. Thelma hurried over to help us situate the food and to dispense hugs all around. The rich aroma of the pot roast caused my mouth to water.

The crunch of gravel outside announced the Volkers had arrived. Anya raced out the backdoor to grab Emily and make a dash for the barn. Chad and his mother helped Ginny and Jeff find places for the food they'd brought, two loaves of still warm bread, fruit salad, and freshly picked green beans cooked with ham pieces and new potatoes. A part of me felt guilty for arriving empty-handed, but Thelma had text-messaged me earlier, "I know you'll be coming straight from work, so don't fret about bringing anything. There's always too much to eat."

As I helped Thelma empty ice cube trays into glasses, Ginny put the men to work carrying place settings to the picnic tables on the lawn. The kitchen was buzzing with activity when Chad disappeared for a minute. He returned and tilted his head toward the front of the house. "Pop's in the front room with Mr. Schnabel. I want you to meet him before we go eat. He'd like to speak to all of us. Patty? Can you round up the guys?"

I hadn't known John Henry Schnabel would put in an appearance, but I guess I shouldn't have been too surprised. Surely, I should have guessed when I saw the Mercedes in the driveway. I wanted to thank the man. Already he'd accomplished a near miracle by getting bail for Chad. As for working pro bono, could we ever repay his kindness? Following my honey into the Detweilers' cozy living room, I waited my turn as the super-star criminal attorney gave us each a quick handshake and curt "hello."

"I can't thank you enough," I said.

He waved my appreciation away. His brisk style suggested he had an agenda, but what?

The big old sofa wooshed as Detweiler and I sank into it. The springs beneath it had long since given out. We made ourselves comfortable and settled in. Detweiler put his arm around me and pulled me close to his side, so close, in fact, that I could feel his heart beat.

Thelma's decorating style could best be described as tasteful hodge-podge. She favored shades of moss green and pinkish rose. Antique walnut end tables bookended the sofa. Patty brought in the guys, so Detweiler and I scrunched together to make room. The couch we perched on had been covered with a stretchy material in moss green that disguised the piece's original color and pattern, but the lumps told me it was old as the hills. Crocheted pillows in shades of rose and pink punctuated every piece of furniture in the room. Detweiler told me his mother bought armloads of skeins of rose yarn on sale, and his father challenged her to use them up before moving on to another project. That explained why all the bathrooms proudly displayed pink crocheted tissue box covers.

The Detweiler menfolk looked curiously out of place in such an unabashedly feminine room, but most incongruous of all was the tiny balding hero of the hour, a knight not dressed in shining armor but instead wearing a blue seersucker suit, a white shirt, and a blue tie with bright yellow polka dots. One look at our guest and I started thinking about that movie where Philip Seymour Hoffman stars as Truman Capote.

"Sit down, everyone. This will only take a moment. Thelma assures me that dinner can wait, but her pot roast sings a siren song to my taste buds, and I'm liable to drool like a mastiff if we don't eat soon," said Mr. Schnabel, in a high-pitched voice.

"As you know, Mr. Kloss is attempting to try this case in the media. That works well for us, because if we go to trial—and please note the operative word 'if'—we'll be able to get a change of venue with no problem. That said, I am aware that the media has contacted several of you in a bid to get your side of the story. Mrs. Lowenstein, I believe they showed up at your place of work? Right. Do not talk to them. Not under any circumstances. Anything you say might cause trouble for us later. If you have a question, call me. I'm passing my card around now. That's my private cell phone number. Use it. If the media hectors you, contact me.

"One other thing. Do not under any circumstances communicate with anyone in writing or via text messages about this case. Those could be misinterpreted and used against us. I would also suggest you don't talk about the case to anyone except family members and then only in person. Any questions? No? Because if you say the wrong thing to the wrong person, I will hold you personally responsible for Chad being found guilty of murder."

He jumped up and clapped his hands. "Now, let's eat!"

FORTY-SIX

ALTHOUGH I DIDN'T DOUBT the man was right, I hated having a good meal spoiled by a warning. The speech came across like a threat. I took my place near the back of the food line, just in front of Detweiler. Mr. Schnabel had been invited to go first and fill his plate. The little girls were second. We all took our seats in the picnic area under the big maple trees, where a nice breeze cooled us and tried to steal our paper napkins.

"I saved a seat for you two," said Mr. Schnabel, patting the wooden bench beside him. "Mrs. Lowenstein, come sit next to me."

Great. My first moment alone with Detweiler and I had to share it with a lawyer.

The rest of the Detweiler clan appeared to be avoiding this particular table.

With a quick glance my way, John Henry Schnabel read my thoughts. "I apologize, Mrs. Lowenstein. I am certain that you and Detective Detweiler would have liked some time alone. Rest assured my actions are completely necessary. You will have to forgive me for being so intrusive. However, it has come to light that you, Mrs. Lowenstein, have acquired a reputation as an amateur detective with a talent for getting yourself in hot water. In this situation, your machinations could be very harmful. In fact, you might even cost Chad his freedom. I strongly urge you to leave the driving to me, as it were. Especially in your weakened state. I see you are barely recovering from Brenda Detweiler's shot across your brow."

His pun was intended to ease the tension between us.

It didn't.

"Police Chief Holmes called me about an hour ago. You've already poked your finger into one of the weaknesses in the state's case against your fiancé. By the way, please do make it a point to always call Chad by that endearment, won't you? Fiancé sounds so much more official than boyfriend. It adds an air of legitimacy to your relationship. As such it will be a positive step toward rebuffing Mr. Kloss's insulting remarks about your character."

Thanks a lot, pal.

I nodded and put a piece of Thelma's delicious pot roast in my mouth rather than snipe at him. A petty part of me wanted to turn to Detweiler and say, "In the immortal words of Beyoncé, you need to put a ring on it." Yes, I wanted to marry him, but he owed me a formal request. Of course, one could argue that a baby is a much bigger deal than a diamond, and it is. But still. Call me a romantic, but I still had daydreams about a diamond. These were spurred by the beautiful gem from Mary Pillsbury that Robbie had purchased for Sheila. I daydreamed about one like that. Even if my version was smaller, I knew it could be just as pretty.

In the back of my head, Laurel shook a finger at me and cautioned against being such a whiner.

"To keep you both up to speed, although the casings were not from Detective Chad Detweiler's current firearm, their presence at the crime scene is still, shall we say, problematic?"

"Huh?" That didn't make sense. Here I thought that I had eliminated one of the most important pieces of incriminating evidence!

Chad Detweiler looked at me with sad eyes. "It's true my old 9 mm is out of commission, but instead of letting them retire it, I bought it from the department. I keep it in my car. The Sangamon County District Attorney was tipped off by Robbie's inquiry, so he got a search warrant. They found the gun in my glove box. Bullets from it match the casings found near Brenda's body."

I set down my fork. "Then someone must have planted those! You were here with your parents. You have an alibi!"

Mr. Schnabel shook his head. "Not much of one. Most parents would gladly lie to keep their son from life imprisonment. You see, the time of Brenda Detweiler's death works against us. According to the coroner's report, she died between seven and eight the morning after the altercation with you. And the detective went out for a run at that time."

I swallowed. "But his parents would have heard if he came back for his car."

"This is a big house, Mrs. Lowenstein. His police cruiser was parked on the other side of the barn. They might not have heard him start it up."

My mouth went dry and the pot roast lost all appeal. Since Schnabel himself could so easily refute Detweiler's alibi, and since the bullet casings still matched a gun in his possession, how did he plan to defend his client?

A dull roar began in my head. I wanted to blurt out that Brenda had been discovered suspiciously close to Patty's house. I wanted to tell Mr. Smarty Pants Lawyer that both Patty and Paul had cause to want to see her dead. I wanted to scream that Ginny should be factored into the murderous equation. That she, too, had been angry with Brenda.

Instead I stabbed a chunk of carrot and stuffed it into my mouth. By the time I chewed it and washed it down with ice tea, I'd regained my composure.

"What are you going to do? How do you propose to defend Detweiler?" I asked the attorney point-blank. "You're telling me that he has no alibi. At least not one that will save him. That he owns a gun that produces empty bullet casings like those found at the scene of Brenda Detweiler's murder. What's your plan? How do you intend to save him?"

Mr. Schnabel beamed at me before taking my hand in his and stroking it. "I like spunk. I have a lot of it, and I find it an admirable quality. Please call me John Henry. That's what my friends call me, and if I may, I'd be honored to call you Kiki."

"Of course."

Skip to the chase, buddy, I wanted to scream. My palm ached to smack him.

However, slapping the sass out of this nice man who was working pro bono was not in my best interests.

"What I'd like to do is to start by asking you a favor." John Henry's smile turned tentative, shy even.

"Anything! I'll do anything. Anything to help."

"Good. I'd like you to marry Chad Detweiler as soon as possible."

FORTY-SEVEN

"ANYTHING BUT THAT."

"What?" Detweiler's jaw dropped. He set his iced tea down so hard it jarred the table. "Kiki, I love you. You're carrying my baby. I've asked you to marry me! I mean, we've talked about it. What are you saying? Now you don't want to marry me?"

I did not like being put on the spot. This was our private business. To my mind, John Henry Schnabel had overreacted. Trying to collect myself, I stared down into my plate. This would be a whole lot easier to explain if the pressure wasn't on me. All three pairs of family members at the other tables had quit talking to turn and stare at us. One by one, they resumed their conversation. But I said nothing. The emotions roiled inside me. By turns I was angry, hurt, disappointed, bitter, frustrated, and overwhelmed.

"Of course, I want to marry you. I just don't want to do it now. I mean, right now. Before the baby comes."

John Henry's quizzical look turned to one of deep interest. "Perhaps if I explain my reasoning, you'll change your mind. You see, wives can't testify about their husbands. Although Chad hasn't done anything wrong, your union would guarantee me that you couldn't become a wild card, an unknown quantity during a trial, should this get that far. My second reason is to take the wind out of Mr. Kloss's sails. He's portraying both of you as a Bonnie and Clyde couple, a twosome willing to shoot your way out of any impediments. However, a wedding with you in white or cream and a photo of your delightfully wholesome daughter, will go far to dispel his suggestions. Third, I would like a reason to relocate Chad to St. Louis until the trial takes place. I don't trust the Illinois State Police. They have a grudge against Chad and, as you are well aware, this entire state is rife with cronyism. If I can go before a judge and say, 'This man needs to live with his wife, she's expecting their child, and she can't leave her job,' then I stand a good chance of getting his 'house arrest' under your roof. So you see, my reasons are imminently practical."

"Mine is, too. I promised my daughter that this baby will be born a Lowenstein."

"I'll talk to her," volunteered Detweiler. "I know it's a concern for her, but she'll get over it. Sooner or later, we'll all be Detweilers. I've intended to ask Anya if I can be her legal father. There's never been the right time. You know how much I love you both." He leaned in and kissed me.

"Even so, I made Anya a promise, and I'm sticking to it."

"But you're her parent! You have to decide what's best for her. For us!" The astonished look on Detweiler's face finished his sentence for him. He was wondering if my daughter's disappointment was more important than his incarceration.

This felt like an ambush. And my face burned with fury. "That's right. You've got it. I am the parent. You are not. Nor have you made the commitment to be a part of our lives permanently. And until then, you have no say."

"No say?"

I amended my comment. "Well, not much. Look, I love you, but you weren't around when George died. Oh, you worked on the case, but you weren't living with my daughter day by day. You can only guess at what my kid went through. What I went through. She and I are a team. We will stay that way. When we marry, you'll join the team. But until that moment, I'm keeping my word to her."

A variety of emotions played out on Chad Detweiler's face. One of these was anger. Another was hurt. My words wounded him deeply.

I lowered my voice.

"Everything changes when you become a parent. Everything! You can't imagine that now, and I'm really sorry for the trouble you're in, but that has to do with you and Brenda. I didn't bring this on you. You should have gotten rid of her a long time ago, but you didn't! And even though she's dead, she has reared up out of her grave and bitten you on the butt, hasn't she? Now you're asking me to compromise my relationship with my child so you don't have to pay the consequences of your wife's bad behavior—and the answer is, 'NO.' Sorry. I love you, but my daughter comes first. When you're a parent, you'll understand what I mean."

"Of course she comes first, but we were planning to marry anyway. And this will be good for all of us!"

"Maybe. But not if I break my promise."

"Wow, Kiki," said Patty.

But I wasn't about to hear her complaint. I stood up and faced the stunned family. Of course, they'd overheard all this. "You all got yourselves into this, you can all get yourselves out of it. I am sick of having my life revolve around Brenda Detweiler. I've already faced her down in one unfair fight and I've got the scar to prove it. I'm not interested in going a second round. Come to think of it, I've done more than my share already!"

With that, I tossed down my napkin. I stepped away from the bench, knocking over my iced tea, but not bothering to sop it up.

"Anya? We're leaving. Now."

"Kiki, wait!" Detweiler grabbed for me.

I yanked my hand out of his. I had nothing more to say. Whereas once I'd admired the Detweilers for their loving, cozy family, today I was sickened by their lassitude. If they had stood up to Brenda, maybe this wouldn't have happened.

As I grabbed for my purse and Gracie's leash, everyone started talking at once, but the blood pounding in my ears was such that I didn't hear a word. Instead, I thought back to being a kid in my own household. How my father would abuse me with words and slaps. How no one intervened. Maybe this was a flashback because my mouth was so dry my lips stuck to my teeth. On some level, I couldn't think. I operated on pure emotion, all my energy focused on running away.

"Come on, Anya, hustle." I walked over to where she was sitting and took her by the elbow.

As I marched us toward my car, Gracie's leash caught on one of the picnic tables. With a whipping motion I popped it loose and flipped over a bowl of salad in the process. The lettuce flew up and up like green confetti, then sprinkled down.

Detweiler ran to me, caught me by the arm, and caused me to pivot. "Please, stop! We need to talk. You can't go like this. It's not safe for you to drive when you're this upset."

"From now on, when we need to talk, we need to do it in private, understand? If you want us to be a family, then treat me with respect as a partner. Don't invite me to a gathering and put me on the spot."

I stood on my tiptoes so we were eye-to-eye. "I love you. I care about you, but I will NOT be treated in a disrespectful manner. Nor will I sacrifice my daughter because you are in a jam."

He grabbed my hands and drew me close. "I wouldn't ask you to hurt Anya. You know that. And you are completely right. We should have discussed this in private. In my defense, John Henry surprised me. Yes, he'd mentioned this, but I had no idea he'd spring this on you."

John Henry trotted up to stand next to Detweiler. One hand fought to straighten his bowtie. "I fear this is my fault entirely. I had no idea this would cause you such distress, Kiki," said John Henry, as he panted with exertion.

"Mr. Schnabel, here's news you can use. When I make a promise, I keep it. I promised my daughter I wouldn't get married before this baby came, and that's all there is to it. If I marry Detweiler before the baby is born, then Anya is the last Lowenstein standing. That's very upsetting to her. It feels to her like her whole family is gone. Or will be, when her last name doesn't match anyone else's. I love Chad Detweiler, and if he loves me, he'll be willing to wait."

"Of course, I will. You know that, Kiki. I love you. You and Anya and our baby," and he wrapped an arm around me, so I could hear the soft thumping of his heart.

I rested my head there, loving the comfort of him, but I kept one eye on John Henry. To his credit, the attorney gave me a solemn nod. "I understand."

But when I stepped away from him, Detweiler's face told me that he was very, very hurt.

FORTY-EIGHT

Anya and I moved briskly toward my car.

"I will need to interview you about the shooting and the other problems with Brenda Detweiler," John Henry called after me. "You obviously have an airtight alibi, but I must still ask you a few questions. I hope you won't mind."

"Whether I do or not is irrelevant."

I unlocked the passenger side door for Anya and Gracie, who had to be coaxed inside. She cast longing looks at Detweiler, but I didn't. I was pretty ticked at him.

After getting my passengers situated, I walked around to the driver's side and climbed in.

"Mom? You okay to drive?"

"I think so."

I backed out slowly and did a three-point turn. Detweiler walked over to the side of the driveway. He stood with shoulders hunched, and one hand shoved deep into his jeans pocket. If I hadn't been so angry, I would have burst into tears at the sight of him, seeming so defeated.

But I wasn't about to back down. No way. I waved and drove out slowly, not to seem like I was overly excited.

But I was.

I got lost three times on the way to the hospital in Alton.

I parked under a tree in the visitors' lot. Anya and I cracked the windows so Gracie wouldn't get hot. But even then, since the internal temperature in a car can jump up alarmingly, I couldn't leave my dog in the car.

"How about if you go see Sheila first? I'll wait here. When you come back, I'll go. That'll give me time to calm down."

Anya turned those denim blue eyes of hers on me. Her brows met in a knot of concern. "Will he still want to marry you?" Her fingers snaked over to twine with mine.

Her question caught me off-guard. I tried to answer honestly. "I think so."

"Do you still want to marry him?"

I hesitated.

Flipping her blond hair over her shoulder so it didn't tickle her face, she edged closer to me and rested her head on my shoulder. "Mom, you do love him, don't you? You said you do."

"Yes." That came quickly. "Yes, but you can't bake a cake with sugar as your only ingredient."

"Oh, brother. Why do I sense a lecture coming on? I should have gotten out of the car while I had a chance!" Anya reached for the door handle. She had her father's hands, slender with long thin fingers.

I touched her other hand and held it.

"Wait. You need to hear this. See, it takes more than love to make a marriage work. I know the Beatles wrote, 'All you need is love,' but they were wrong. You have to have the same goals. And respect. Communication. Especially that. I mean, it's not enough to love someone. You have to pull in the same direction, or you'll pull apart."

"I thought you and Detweiler had all that."

"I thought we did, too. I hope we still do. This will probably be our toughest time as a couple. I'm not ready to throw in the towel. Not at all. But I am curious as to how we'll get our act together. There's this marriage counselor who predicts whether couples will stay together. One important trait of a happy couple is the ability for them to make up. Think about it, and you'll see why. Sometimes one person would initiate the forgiveness process. Sometimes the other, but there had to be a peacemaker in every argument, and the other person had to respond in kind. Does that make sense?"

Leaning back, Anya pursed her lips and let her eyes roam the interior of the black ragtop. "Kinda. But here's what really confuses me. You used to never get mad. Never talked back to people. Gran could walk all over you. Anybody could, really. But today, you really gave it to Detweiler. And his family. And his attorney, too! You didn't hold anything back. So I'm wondering, what happened to the old mom?" She sat up to stare at me. "Is this because of your head injury? Robbie told me that can make people weird. Or is it because you shot a man and you're all, like, macho now?"

I'd been expecting her to bring up the shooting. In fact, I'd hoped she would so we could discuss it. Clear the air.

"Maybe both. Maybe neither. I grew up watching Disney films and reading fairy tales. Thinking that a white knight or a handsome prince would rescue me, because, well, my home life was so terrible. When your father came along, I thought maybe he was the guy. But he wasn't. Not exactly. When Brenda forced me into the car, I kept telling myself that Detweiler would find me. Or Robbie Holmes. But they didn't come. I thought Johnny had a plan. That he would take care of … things. Then he was shot. I tried to stop the bleeding, but I couldn't, and I realized he was going to die. And that awful man was strangling Sheila."

I took a shuddering breath. Anya squeezed my hand encouragingly. "I kept thinking, 'I can't shoot Bill Ballard! I can't do this! I'm just a mom! A nice person!' and I started to get angry that Detweiler or Robbie or Johnny couldn't rescue me. And suddenly I had an epiphany. You know what that is?"

She shook her head no. That little face of hers was so solemn, so focused, that I nearly laughed out loud.

"An epiphany happens when you suddenly see the light. When you understand something, especially something you've been struggling with. See, I realized that had Detweiler or Robbie or Johnny shot Bill Ballard that would be okay with me, but I didn't want to be the person to pull the trigger. In other words, I was being a hypocrite. After all, if it was okay for them to shoot, why wasn't it okay for me? Of course, it was!"

I swallowed hard and kept going. "I wish I could honestly tell you that all of this is clear in my mind. Or that I've come to grips with it. But I haven't. Not totally. All I know is that I really, really wanted to see you grow up, and to save my baby, and of course, to save Sheila and Johnny. At first, I was resigned and thought, 'So this is how I'm going to die?' And just as fast, I realized I could save myself. And two other people I love."

I squeezed both Anya's hands, those soft, sweet hands that had trustingly held mine so often. "I asked myself, why was I waiting for a man to rescue me? Suddenly, I saw how silly that was."

She frowned. "So I guess you are different. I guess it did change you. That makes sense. It was a pretty big deal, after all."

My voice dropped to a whisper. I was talking to myself more than to my daughter as I said, "The question is, did I change for the better? I'm not sure…"

FORTY-NINE

As Anya started for the hospital entrance, I let Gracie climb into the passenger seat. As if she knew I needed comfort, she pawed at me, finally resting her large head in my lap where I stroked those velvety uncropped ears. All the drama of the day exhausted me. I must have fallen asleep.

She and I awakened to the metal on metal sound of the passenger door opening. Anya snapped on the dog's leash and let Gracie out to piddle while she rested one hand on the roof and smiled down at me. "Gran is back in fighting form. She'll come home on Monday. Isn't that super?"

"It sure is. Should I go on in and see her? Or is she tired?" In truth, I'd had enough of big emotions for one day. I was angling for an excuse to take a raincheck on seeing Sheila. Any excuse would do.

"She asked for you. Said she wants to talk."

Gracie tugged at Anya, making it clear she wanted to sniff around the lot. I gave my daughter the car keys and told her I'd be back.

The paper-thin skin of the volunteer at the front counter crinkled with concentration as she scanned the computer screen for Sheila's room number. My trip along the medicinal-smelling halls with Ned pushing my wheelchair seemed like a distant memory. But I knew that the minute I laid eyes on Sheila, the whole ugly scene at the slough would come back with a vengeance. Dragging my feet wouldn't help. Sooner or later, I'd have to face my mother-in-law.

After a few wrong turns, I stepped through the partially open door to her room.

The big metal bed dwarfed Sheila as she lay there alone in that sterile surrounding. Thank goodness Robbie Holmes had accompanied Anya on her first visit here. What a shock it must have been to see her strong, vital grandmother in such distress!

Hearing my footsteps, my mother-in-law turned toward me. Her lovely blue eyes crackled with alertness. However, the hair she always coiffed so carefully stuck out at odd angles, in oily clumps. Sheila never goes without makeup. She's nearly sixty, but on a good day looks forty-five. Today was not a good day; she looked every minute of her age and then some. The impact of her pale skin, her limp hair, and her washed-out features hit me hard. Nana would have applied the phrase "death warmed over" to the sad ghost of a woman in the bed.

"Don't just stand there and gawk at me, Kiki. Come sit down. Close the door. I live in fear that someone I know will wander by and see me like this. If they do, I'll have to get myself a gun and hunt them down." A corner of her mouth turned up in a half-smile.

"I wouldn't advise that," I said as I backed into the chair. "You'll be the talk of the town. I am."

She cackled. "That's because that stupid boyfriend of yours didn't dump his drug addict wife a long time ago. In case you're wondering, I've heard all about the charges against him."

"What do you think?" I asked.

Sheila usually smells like Prada perfume, but today the oily scent of her unwashed hair and rubbing alcohol filled the air, making me incredibly sad. Usually her fragrance lingered on my clothes after we parted. Over time, the scent of her had become a comfort, because it was as strong and sure as she always was. Where had that gone?

"Pfft! You and I both know he didn't do it. If he had, he would have been smart enough to count his shots and pick up the casings. No, someone set him up. I'm surprised you haven't stuck your nose into the investigation already." She spoke with effort, her words shortened and wheezy.

"I did. Got my hands slapped." I told her about the gun switcheroo. Then, because I couldn't help myself, I spilled what had happened at the Detweiler farm.

To my amazement, Sheila listened instead of jumping to judgment. When I finished, those blue tractor beams locked on me. "My, my. You have grown a spine, haven't you?"

Tears filled my eyes. "I don't know if I did the right thing." I grabbed a tissue and stopped the flood before it ran down my cheeks.

"You love him, don't you?"

"I do."

"Has it occurred to you that he's acting like a deer that's been clipped by a car? He doesn't know where to run. He's used to being king of the forest, and now he's a wounded beast."

"And you know this how?"

"Because it happened once to Harry. He made a mistake. Wasn't paying attention, didn't face a hard fact. Could have gone to jail. Instead, he had to pay a fine to the attorney general and endure a public scolding. We woke up one morning to see it splashed all over the front of the business section."

"But you knew it would turn out okay, didn't you?" I stood and tugged at a bit of her covers that were slipping down from her shoulders. That's when I saw the splint and sling. The sight of her broken wing caused my stomach to coil into a knot. Luckily, she'd closed her eyes again or she would have seen the expression of chagrin on my face.

"Don't be stupid. I'm not a fortune teller. How did I know what would happen?"

Nice to know she could still fuss at me.

She continued. "What a mess! But I never let Harry know how frightened I was. I kept telling him it would be all right. I stayed calm. That's what he needed, and that's what I did. If two people are in a boat and they both panic, sure as shooting, they're both going overboard. Instead, I became the ballast that kept us steady. I laid low. I reviewed his options with him, and I held my head high when the paper came out. I told him those who knew him would see it for what it was. And they did."

"Is that what I should do?"

Those ice blue peepers snapped open. "Me? Give advice? Perish the thought! You do realize that women are stronger than men, don't you? Always have been. Always will be. There's a line from *Jane Eyre* that I've always liked. 'It is weak and silly to say you cannot bear what it is your fate to be required to bear.' Buck up, Kiki. He's the one facing life in prison. You aren't. If he's lost, confused, and misguided, isn't this the time he needs you most?"

A nurse walked in, holding a paper cup. "Time for your pain pill, Mrs. Lowenstein."

"I need to get going. Anya and Gracie are waiting."

To the nurse, Sheila held up the universal "just a minute" sign, one index finger upraised.

I stood up, leaned over, and kissed Sheila on the cheek. Miraculously, she managed to snag my left hand with her right one. Her grip was surprisingly strong, and her gaze was direct as she said, "It *will* be all right. You'll see."

"I love you, Sheila."

"Of course you do."

FIFTY

Although each step felt like walking through wet cement, I forced myself to trudge up the stairs to the critical care department where Johnny was. The hallway fed directly into the visitors' lounge. Mert's head was bent over a magazine. She didn't see me at first, but I saw her and immediately noticed her messy hair, her rumpled clothes, and the eye makeup smeared onto her cheeks.

A big believer in "displaying the merchandise," Mert always wears push-up bras from Victoria's Secret or Frederick's of Hollywood. Today she wore a sloppy sweatshirt turned inside out and a pair of old jeans. Both her legs were tucked under her bottom, in a childlike pose. A pair of wedges rested on the carpet.

As if she knew she was being watched, her gaze slowly turned my way.

"You."

That's all she said. The accusation in her tone stopped me from coming closer. Her eyes glowed hot as coals with anger. I froze, unsure what to do or say. Here was a woman who'd been my biggest supporter, my greatest ally, and my dearest friend.

I could feel the hate directed my way.

My knees went weak.

She'd warned me about her anger. How when people crossed her, she would cut them out of her life and never change her mind. Mert had many wonderful qualities, but she took a pretty cut-and-dried approach to friends: You were either for her or against her.

"Mert, I never meant to—"

"Of course not. You're like Daisy in *The Great Gatsby*, aren't you? Leaving messes for everyone else to clean up."

I pinched my arm to keep from sprouting tears.

"How is Johnny?"

"Does it matter?" This came out like a hiss.

"It matters a lot."

"Right," she spat the word in my direction. "My brother was in love with you. You didn't realize it, did you? Nope. You were too high and mighty for him. Wouldn't even consider a man who'd been behind bars. And he knew it. Sure he did. But he'd have done anything for you. Anything at all! That's how much he cared, from afar. Look where it landed him!"

For the second time that day, I wanted to run away as fast as my feet would carry me. At the Detweiler farm, I'd been full of spit and vinegar.

Here, not so much.

I turned to leave.

"Coward. You can't even face me." She called to my back.

I stood glued to the spot, unable to move toward the stairway or turn back toward her. A variety of conversations played out in my head, but none of them were satisfactory. None of them ended with the revitalization of our friendship. When Mert was done with someone, she was done, period. No room for equivocation.

Mert did not know that I'd begged Robbie Holmes and Detweiler not to go through with this plan. The idea to entrap Bill had been Johnny's idea from the start.

I was blameless.

But Mert wasn't willing to listen to me now.

She was right about one thing: I was a coward. No way was I going to offer myself up as a sacrifice to her anger.

Instead, I found the strength to walk away.

FIFTY-ONE

SLUNK. THAT'S WHAT I did.

I slunk out of the hospital, moved Gracie out of the driver's seat, and climbed into my car.

The drive back to Webster Groves seemed to take all afternoon, what with the traffic and my mood. Usually Anya works her thumbs over her phone text-messaging at inhuman speeds, but today, she merely stared out the window at the passing scenery, which admittedly is pretty bleak. Highway 64-40 (as the locals call it) splits as you head toward the river. To the uninitiated, it looks like there's a fifty-fifty chance you're in the correct lane. To old hands, it's six of one, half a dozen of the other. Either way will bring you into downtown St. Louis, if you survive the heart attack you have when you think you're in the wrong lane.

After crossing the Mississippi, Highway 40 rises skyward, on a narrow band of lumpy asphalt. A concrete rail guards your car from plunging into the spaghetti bowl of exits and ramps below. Most of the street lights on this exit don't work, so you drive in the pitch blackness, bumping along through potholes. Clasping the wheel so hard my knuckles turned white, I focused on getting past this concrete mess. As my BMW neared the gigantic Anheuser Busch sign with its flapping eagle, my grip eased. Of its own accord, my car turned toward Ted Drewes Frozen Custard on Chippewa, even though we'd taken the long way there.

After parking at the side of the green and yellow building, we took a spot in the line that's an ongoing part of the Ted Drewes adventure. Gracie's nose quivered in anticipation. Anya and I discussed what we'd order. I wasn't keeping a close eye on Gracie.

"Eeek!"

Anya and I spun around in time to watch Gracie gently pluck an ice cream cone from the tiny hands of a little girl with pigtails. The child's mouth fell open as she blinked in astonishment at the dog. Her empty fingers had been parallel to my dog's mouth, and Gracie has never been one to resist ice cream. Especially when it's on her level. She must have thought the cone an offering from the gods.

The child's parents stood there dumbfounded.

Pink streamers of frozen custard ran down Gracie's dewlaps while she happily crunched the cone. The little girl looked from her empty hand to Gracie's maw and back again, as though trying to decide whether to cry.

"I am so, so sorry! I should have watched my dog more carefully. May I buy your daughter another?" I pulled my dog close to my side and bent over to scold Gracie. "Bad dog! Bad, bad dog!"

Gracie didn't care. After rolling a doleful eye at me, she sank down onto the sidewalk, resting on her belly and grunted. She smelled like strawberries and cream.

The girl's parents were wild-eyed, trying to decide exactly how much damage was done. The mom reached for her daughter and pulled her close. The dad puffed out his chest and frowned at me. He raised a warning finger to fuss at me but before he could—

Uuuu-rp!

Gracie belched. A sonic boom of a burp that went on and on. When she finished, she sighed and rested her head on her paws.

Anya burst into laughter. The child's parents looked at each other, looked at Anya and started to giggle. Seeing her parents so tickled, the little girl joined in. So did customers standing around us, watching the scene. Soon everyone had a smile at Gracie's expense.

Or rather at *my* expense, since I bought a replacement frozen custard cone.

FIFTY-TWO

Sunday, Day 6—after the shooting

OUR SUNDAY TRADITION: PANCAKE breakfast! Anya and I dug into our stacks, devouring a little bit of flapjack with our syrup. The cats and Gracie enjoyed their Sunday treat, a small spoonful of wet food on top of their kibble.

I stood at the stove turning leftover batter into thin crepes to be refrigerated when my phone rang. I hadn't glanced at it since yesterday, leaving the gizmo to vibrate in the bottom of my purse, but now I answered the ring.

"Your neighbor is taking Mom to a movie. I need to get out for a while. Take me somewhere only the locals go, please?" My sister sounded incredibly cheerful.

We agreed she'd swing by in an hour. That left me with a lot to do, and Anya still needed to shower and get dressed.

A part of me wanted to stay home and spend time on the Internet where Cherise Landon and her friends might have left breadcrumbs. Anything that might shed light on their past. I did, however, wrestle with the ethics of trying to befriend any of them through Facebook. Should I try to befriend them under my own name and see where I got? Or should I lie?

John Henry Schnabel's warning had worked as a deterrent. I certainly didn't want to make Detweiler's situation any worse. Would my actions on Facebook come back to haunt me? After struggling into a pair of elastic waist jeans and pulling over my head a peasant top that a customer had brought me from Mexico, I put on eyeliner, mascara, and blush.

So Leighton was taking my mother to the movies? I hoped he was merely being nice, and that this wasn't a sign of real interest on his part. He was a wonderful guy, a man that any woman would be proud to marry, so perhaps I should warn him away from Mom. If she didn't get the sort of attention she wanted from him, she would turn on him like a rabid dog turns on its owner and take off his arm.

Not your problem. He's a big boy.

With animals in the house, there are always extra chores. Gracie wanted to go outside. Lately she'd taken to excessive—at least in my opinion—sniffing around. Her bathroom visits took forever. The cat litter box needed changing. I put on rubber gloves to protect myself against toxoplasmosis. According to most experts on the Internet, if I changed the litter boxes daily and wore gloves, I ran very little risk of becoming a host to the organism. And I wasn't taking any chances.

I ran a dust rag over the furniture, finishing not a moment too soon as my sister pulled her rental car into the drive.

"What are you planning to do about your own car? It's back in Arizona, isn't it? How will you get it here?" I asked as she strolled up my walk.

"I have a plan." Her lopsided grin reminded me of when we were kids. I was the serious one. Catherine was the moody one. Amanda was the jokester.

Waving her hands in front of her face, she pantomimed clearing cobwebs. "I see a road trip in our future. What'd you say, sis?"

"I am so out of here."

"Bad times at Ridgemont High?"

"You don't know the half of it. I picked the wrong nine months to quit drinking. If I wasn't pregnant, I'd be drowning my sorrows."

As I took a seat on my over-sized ottoman, she plopped down on my sofa, grabbing Seymour and hauling the gray cat onto her lap while Martin ran and hid. "Here's a bit of good news. You're no longer page one news. That attorney—John Henry Snob?—held a press conference this morning. Tomorrow is Brenda Detweiler's memorial service. John Henry asked the judge for permission for Chad Detweiler to attend. And got it."

"No kidding?"

"Smart dude. He used the occasion to put Chad's story out there. See, Brenda's dad keeps positioning your boyfriend as 'Chad the cad.' That's not helpful to his case. So, Snob-whatever is fighting back." She narrowed her eyes at me. "You should be there, too. At the memorial service, I mean."

"Why?"

"Besides showing support for Chad Detweiler, it sends a clear message that you have nothing to hide. That you are human and mourn her passing. Which you do, I would guess. You always were such a softie. Furthermore, once people get a gander at that divot she plowed in the side of your head, they'll remember that Brenda nearly killed two people. Right now, the entire focus is on her as a murder victim. At least, that's what my old boss would have said in response to your question."

Amanda worked as executive secretary for the best criminal attorney in Tucson until he retired last year. After her old boss left, Amanda was assigned to a junior partner in the firm, a guy she didn't think much of. Neither did anyone else. Consequently, the firm had closed that office.

Tugging at my bottom lip, I considered her advice. "What if the press asks me questions? They came to the store. Robbie managed to get rid of them."

"What if they do? You can handle it. You don't have anything to hide. Let's brainstorm here. They'll ask if you and Chad were carrying on behind Brenda's back. How will you answer?"

"We did nothing until after she threw him out. As a matter of fact, as a couple we decided he should halt the divorce proceedings long enough for her to go through rehab for the third time, no less, on his insurance."

My sister crowed with delight. "Good job. How about this: Is it true she was harassing you? Isn't it possible Detweiler shot her to protect you and your baby?"

"Yes, she harassed me. When I was in the hospital where she worked, she threatened me and shook me so hard I had bruises on my arms. But it wouldn't make sense for Chad to try to protect me after she was wanted for shooting both me and Johnny Chambers, would it? After all, law enforcement officials on both sides of the river wanted to lock her up. She wouldn't have been much of a threat behind bars."

"Excellent. Good job, Kiki." She squinted as she conjured up another query. "What about this: Sure, it would have been logical for him to wait and let her be locked up. But maybe it was a crime of passion. Hadn't she pushed him over the edge? And at the end, maybe they fought about the baby—and he lost it."

"She didn't know about me being pregnant."

"Not your baby, silly. Brenda's baby."

FIFTY-THREE

"WHAT?" I ALMOST FELL on the floor. "Brenda's baby? What are you talking about?"

"Snobby spilled the beans at the press conference this morning. Brenda was almost four months pregnant. She had made an appointment at an abortion clinic for later this week." Amanda grabbed my remote off the coffee table and turned on the television.

I didn't move. I couldn't. My sister flipped from one channel to the next, looking for local news. At long last, I said, "And it's Detweiler's for sure? Chad Detweiler's baby?"

Amanda shrugged. "Who knows? Snobby wanted to get a jump on the Illinois D.A. by announcing it. Got his licks in there. Good job of it, too. Now everyone knows that Brenda Detweiler wasn't the loving, innocent woman her father makes her out to be. She was pregnant, using drugs, and planned to get an abortion. Your attorney did a great job of giving her corpse a black eye."

Anya padded in, rubbing her hair dry with a towel. She squatted beside me, concern written large on her face, her T-shirt damp in spots where she hadn't dried off properly. "You okay, Mom?"

"Yes, sweetie." I took her face in both my hands and stared into those steady blue eyes. How I loved her! I had been so careful when I learned I was pregnant with her. Not a sip of wine. Not even an aspirin. No artificial sweeteners.

And Brenda had wanted to abort her child. That made me sad.

My daughter was, is, and will always be the most precious part of my life. As I let go of her face, my right hand dropped protectively to my belly. I pledged the same love to my unborn child.

What had gone wrong with Brenda Detweiler? How could she have done such a thing?

"You sure nothing's wrong, Mom? You were shouting." Anya frowned.

"Um, you tell her what's up, Amanda. I can't. I just can't." I went into my bathroom for a chance to collect myself. I pulled my phone from my pocket. The text-message light blinked over and over in rhythm. But I backed away from it as though it could bite me. I could just imagine why Detweiler was calling. He was trying to break the bad news to me before I heard it somewhere else.

I turned on the shower full blast to muffle the noise. Tears came hot and hard. I pounded my fist against the sink and growled in anger. The sorrow lodged in a primitive part of me, and I gave it full rein.

Why for once couldn't I just be happily pregnant? What was it about my lot in life that the sky had to fall on my head when I should be radiant with joy?

There were no answers, and I didn't expect any.

After a while, I washed my face and dried my eyes. No, I wasn't cried out. Sometime soon, I planned to cry me a river, but not just now. Instead, I determined that come heck or high water, I would enjoy this day. I had a lot to be thankful for. My sister and I were on good terms. My daughter was happy and healthy. Sheila was coming home. My mother was out of my hair. I had a job. I was healthy. What more could I want in life?

Don't answer that!

I resolved to think of my problems as if they were two gigantic icebergs. I named them Murder and Mayhem, referencing Brenda's killing and Nathan's death. Armed with an ice pick of resolve, or stubbornness, depending on how you looked at it, I would chip, chip, chip away at the glacier. I would go about my life, ignoring the blocks of ice, except for those occasional opportunities to pick up my chisel and whack away.

"I can live with that," I told the woman in the mirror. "I can stay focused. I can do a little each day toward it. But those problems belong to other people. They can't consume me."

There wasn't a single thing I could do about Brenda Detweiler's pregnancy. I had to say a prayer for her and her baby and let it go.

As sick as I felt thinking of them together, the logical side of my brain found it difficult to fault Detweiler for having gone to bed with his wife. Sure the knowledge that Brenda was pregnant left my ego hurting as though I'd been the recipient of a smart slap. But like it or not, Detweiler and Brenda had still been married at the time that this must have happened. In fact, they were still legally husband and wife when she died. And as we all knew, marriage brought with it certain privileges, rights, and habits. Habits hard to break.

It was my dumb luck that he'd cashed in all his I.O.U.s only a month before he and I spent an evening alone together.

A new thought: *Maybe it wasn't Chad Detweiler's baby.*

A man so protective, so concerned about his child's welfare was unlikely to have unprotected sex with a woman on drugs. More than most, Detweiler knew the problems of infants born to addicts.

Grabbing my tube of concealer, I covered the dark circles under my eyes. No matter what Brenda had done, she'd paid the ultimate price. Worse yet, a baby had died with her. Had her pregnancy further fueled her rage at me?

Was it possible that she'd been killed precisely because she was pregnant? Maybe her death had nothing to do with her using drugs. Or her wild behavior. Maybe someone out there didn't want his name associated with Brenda Detweiler. Didn't want his relationship with her to be exposed to public scrutiny. Once she'd taken shots at Johnny and me, she'd become big news. Until then, she was just another junkie, another example of a wasted life.

As I brushed my teeth, I narrowed down the questions that needed answering:

Who was Brenda's baby's father?

Did the mystery man know she was pregnant?

Did he care?

There was only one person who might be able to provide answers: Detweiler's sister Patty.

FIFTY-FOUR

The Eugene Field House & St. Louis Toy Museum ranks high on my list as one of our city's least appreciated treasures.

"Boy, the name Eugene Field sounds familiar," said Amanda, as we parked in front of the museum. "But I'm drawing a blank."

"Wynken and Blynken are two little eyes," quoted Anya.

"And Nod is a little head," I added.

"And the wooden shoe that sailed the skies that night is a wee one's trundle-bed!" Amanda did a victory dance. "That's it, isn't it? He wrote the children's poems! And this is where he lived?"

"Where he grew up," I said. "In 1850, Field's parents leased one of twelve units in what was then known as Walsh's Row, a series of row houses. This one remains. By the way, his father Roswell Field was Dred Scott's attorney."

The Victorian setting of the museum charmed Amanda, as I knew it would. Whatever her faults, our mother raised us to revere history, and this place brought a bygone time to life. The dining room table was set as if expecting guests, the fireplaces reminded us how fortunate we were to have central heating, and when we climbed the stairs to the toy museum, I thought Amanda would expire on the spot from happiness. The collection brought back memories of our own playthings. Since the toys in the collection are rotated, each visit promises a new viewing experience. I couldn't have planned this one better because there in the center of one of the displays sat Amanda's all-time favorite doll, Chatty Cathy.

After the visit, we drove to Laclede's Landing, a district built on the footprint of the original city of St. Louis, a mere three blocks long. Rain started as we picked our way over the bumpy cobblestones, a reminder of how difficult travel must have been centuries ago. We ducked into Hannegan's, where Amanda treated my daughter and me to lunch.

When Anya excused herself to use the restroom, Amanda leaned close to whisper. "How are things between you and Detweiler?"

"Not so hot," I admitted. I summarized our visit to the farm.

To my surprise, my sister took his side. "Just because he wants to marry you sooner rather than later, doesn't mean he has an ulterior motive. Why not go ahead and get hitched? You want to and your baby will have his name."

"I'm not going to throw Anya under the bus to make life easier for him. She deserves better."

"Right, but have you discussed his position with her? She might change her mind if she knew that it could make such a difference."

I considered that. She had been happily chatting with Emily when Schnabel had explained his reasoning to me. I hadn't shared all of his thoughts with her.

Amanda paused, "But I have to be honest. I'm not sure that marrying Detweiler will make much of a difference to his case. All the prosecution has to prove beyond a reasonable doubt is that Detweiler shot her. Unfortunately the spent casings will go a long way toward that."

"But it doesn't make sense! He's been a member of the Major Case Squad here in St. Louis off and on for years. He's handled enough murder cases to know that leaving behind evidence like that would surely convict him."

"You're thinking he was set up?"

"I'm almost positive of it."

"And his alibi is ... ?"

"He was out for a run at his parents' house. To get to where Brenda's body was found and back, he would have had to have taken his car. The Detweilers vouch for him, but the prosecution will suggest they're covering for him or that they didn't hear him start the car."

"How did he know where to meet up with Brenda?"

"I assume Schnabel will pull cell phone records. Or text-message records. Whatever."

"Why would Brenda agree to meet him? That doesn't make any sense. Think about it. She's just taken a shot at his girlfriend. She's wanted by the law. Why go to Detweiler? He wouldn't have any sympathy for her."

Anya slipped into the booth next to me. I squeezed her hand.

"Where would Brenda run to? That's the big question. You find the answer and you'll know who killed her," said Amanda.

FIFTY-FIVE

When we got back to my house, my neighbor and landlord, Leighton Haversham stood on my front step with a large vase of red long-stem roses in his hand. At his side was my mother, wearing a peeved expression on her face as Leighton handed me the flowers. "These are for you."

I took the vase and watched as Anya and Amanda ambled over to visit Monroe. After inhaling the heavenly fragrance, I opened the envelope stuck in the flowers. The message read: *I love you. We'll marry when you decide the time is right. D*

Mom tried to grab the card out of my hand but I was too fast for her.

"Thank you for the lovely afternoon, Lucia." Leighton offered my mother his hand.

Mom launched herself at him, throwing her arms around his neck. He tried to kiss her cheek, but she artfully angled her lips to meet his. Her gnarly fingers dug deep into the fine fabric of his shirt. He tried to pull away, but she had a death grip on his shirt.

Finally, he wrestled free. Mom batted her eyes at him. "I enjoyed it, Leighton. But from now on, please call me in advance. My social calendar fills up so fast."

"Yes, of course. In the future I will. I guess I was just lucky you weren't busy today."

"You certainly were," Mom simpered.

What an odd pair they made. Leighton could have stepped right out of the senior edition of GQ. His neatly pressed pale yellow shirt was open at the neck, tucked into a handsome crocodile belt at the waist, and paired with grey slacks. My landlord hated socks, so he wore his topsiders on bare feet, his ankles flashing as he walked. By contrast Mom had on a tired white blouse, buttoned wrong, and marred by yellow circles under the armpits. Her skirt was a navy blue polyester dirndl. The contrasting colors chopped her stocky figure in half, making her look stumpier than she is.

"Bye Leighton. Thanks for bringing me these. Excuse me, Mom." I moved past her and into my house where I pulled my phone from my pocket and texted Detweiler a quick "thanks" for the flowers. Mom followed on my heels.

"Those are from him? That murderer? I heard the news in Leighton's car," Mom said. "That man you've been seeing is a cold-blooded killer. You sure know how to pick them."

After carefully setting the flowers on my kitchen table, I turned and grabbed my mother by the shoulders so she couldn't squirm away. "If you EVER say another negative word about Chad Detweiler, I will bodily throw you out of my house. If you think I'm kidding, you try me. You've crossed a line. I have totally had enough of you. For thirty-two years you have bullied me. You've teased me. Made fun of me. You've insulted me. And I'm tired of it.

I am not going to put up with your abuse anymore. Each time you are rude to me, I will call you on it. Furthermore, if you can't change your bad habits, you are no longer welcome in my home or my store or my life. Have I made myself perfectly clear? Because if I haven't, I'd be happy to go over it again."

Her mouth puckered as if she'd bitten a sour pickle. "Well, never—"

"You are right about that. You never expected me to stand up for myself. But trust me, you aren't dreaming. I've had enough of you, Mom. You are my biological parent, but you've never been a real mother to me. You've never been kind or loving or supportive. I am sick and tired of putting up with your bull. When I was staring down the end of Brenda Detweiler's gun, I realized that life is short. Really, really short. We don't know how long we've got. And it might not be long. So I'm not about to waste my time with people who are cruel to me. You are at the top of that list."

My throat closed nearly choking me, but I continued, "I've waited my entire life for you to love me. My whole life. All I ever wanted was to please you. Guess what, Mom? That's not going to happen. You are sick and twisted. You are nothing like the mother I want. I'm not the child you wanted either. But we're stuck with each other. So make the best of it and quit picking on me or go away."

She hesitated as she decided how to play this. Her eyes darted this way and that. I watched the cards flip over like a Rolodex as she chose,\ "Injured party." Ding-ding-ding-ding-ding!

Puckering up and sniveling, she worked up a tear. "I didn't come here for my daughter to insult me! You are so mean!"

I shrugged and said, "If you think that was my mean act, you ain't seen nothing yet."

FIFTY-SIX

After Mom and Amanda left, I went into my bedroom where I could read the text message Detweiler had sent earlier:

Autopsy shows B was pg. Have no idea who father is. Not me!

I believed him.

FIFTY-SEVEN

Monday, Day 7—after the shooting

Before going to sleep, I text-messaged Detweiler: *I love you. Everything will work out.*

The next morning I woke up bright and early when my phone vibrated to announce an incoming text message:

*Please join us at the memorial service for Brenda Detweiler ***
*1 p.m. Penney & Queen Funeral Home, Litchfield IL ***
Respectfully, JHS

With that depressing visit coloring my day, I dug around in my closet for a dress I had intended to be a staple of my maternity wardrobe. It was a somber gray, empire cut and gathered under the bust. The material was a soft jersey, making the outfit rather dull, which was probably why it had languished on the racks at Goodwill. It cost a whopping two bucks. By shortening the hem to a decent but more attractive length, I had managed to convert the dress from dowdy to plain. By adding a pin and a simple chiffon scarf to the neck this morning, my frock tiptoed over into the "nice but forgettable" category. Gray was as close as I could get to black under these conditions.

Anya seemed preoccupied as she ate her breakfast. I finished my morning chores, changed the water in the roses' vase, clipped the leash on Gracie, and we hopped into my car. As I dropped Anya off at school, I grabbed her hand and said, "There seems to be something bothering you. Something about Nicci Moore. When you are ready to talk, let me know."

"Yeah, yeah," she said, shaking me loose and reaching for her backpack. She started toward the brick building, and then paused and glanced over her shoulder at me. A sixth sense told me to wait. Anya did an about-face and walked toward our car. I rolled down the passenger side window. Gracie stuck her head forward, but since she was in the back seat, I could still talk around her to my kid.

"We probably do need to talk. But I want to give Nicci a chance to work things out. Okay?"

"Certainly."

"I'll ask Stevie to give me a ride to their house after school. Maybe I can convince Nicci it's time to talk to her mom."

I shifted the BMW into park, ignoring the dirty looks from irritated parents forced to drive around me. "Is she still being bullied? Jennifer told me Nicci was being picked on."

Anya's eyes turned furtive. She glanced around, watching other kids climb out of cars. "Um, that's part of it. But it's, well, it's complicated. Got to go!"

After checking the traffic carefully, I pulled out of the drop-off lane. We were definitely making progress. As long as Anya had a plan, we were golden. A weight lifted from my shoulders as I neared the store. Time in a Bottle had always been a sanctuary for me. I loved working there. Gracie's tail thumped the leather seat, reminding me how she enjoyed snoozing in the backroom. It was much better than leaving her at home all day.

Before opening the store, I reviewed my personal "to do" list. The card project had already been prepped for the evening crop, but I still needed to take our Monday quickie inventory. After finishing inventory I could work on a new tangle design to teach our croppers.

Since Mondays were slow, Margit came in at nine to check our shipments and to order supplies. My co-worker insisted on working until noon on Mondays and Wednesdays and not a minute after. She didn't work at all on Sundays. At first, I found her inflexibility a nuisance. Later I learned she was visiting her aging mother who had dementia. The set schedule helped both of them cope.

Five minutes after I flipped the sign to OPEN, a reporter walked in. Without preamble, she fired a question at me—"Did you know Brenda Detweiler was carrying her husband's baby?"

"This is private property. I am asking you to leave. If you don't go, I will call the police."

And I did.

But no one came.

Instead, the reporter followed me around the store, making a perfect nuisance of herself. I tripped over her twice. When I sat down to work on a new Zentangle® pattern, she bumped my shoulder trying to watch. The magic of Zentangle® is such that I was able to block her presence out of my mind until she joggled the worktable and sent my pen off on an unattractive tangent.

In Zentangle, you are taught there are no mistakes, only creative opportunities. The tangle might not have been a mistake, but this woman's visit was. The oddly incongruous tangent of my pen did indeed provide a creative opportunity, but not on paper.

I got up and walked quickly toward the backroom with the reporter hot on my heels. She started yammering at me. "Whose baby was Brenda Detweiler carrying? Did you know she was pregnant? Is it true that you and Detective Detweiler had an ongoing affair? Is that why she turned to drugs? Who's the father of your baby? How long have you been pregnant?"

I didn't say a word and I didn't slow my pace. My footsteps were heavy with anger.

Gracie is very sensitive to my moods. She would be curious as to who our guest was and why I was upset. I could hear her rustling in the playpen, but I couldn't see her because shelving blocked the way. I rounded the corner fast, coming right at my dog. The reporter tailgated me, her body nearly touching mine.

I skidded to a stop.

The reporter slammed into me. Pushing her to one side, I grabbed the door of the dog pen, swung it open and yelled, "Sic her, Gracie!"

Of course, my sweet pup didn't have the foggiest idea what "sic her!" meant. But the reporter did. She took one look at Gracie and went screaming out of the building.

"Nice job, girlfriend." I handed the big dog a yummy. For the rest of the hour, I let Gracie have the run of the store.

Margit arrived at nine, carrying the crockery half of a slow cooker and inserting it into the matching base she'd bought for the store. The smell wafting from her cookware set my mouth to watering.

"Sauerkraut and sausage. My husband's favorite. For the croppers tonight." She twisted the dial on the slow cooker. "Why are you dressed up?"

I explained about Brenda Detweiler's funeral at one o'clock over in Illinois. "Clancy will be in before you leave at noon. I'll take off when she arrives, but I'll be back to help with the crop."

"How is Dodie? Have you heard anything?" Behind her cat's eye glasses, Margit's eyes swam like twin green-gray goldfish.

"I don't know."

"I will stop by the Goldfaders' house after I visit my mother at Oak Haven." Margit and Dodie were long-time friends, whereas I'd only been to Dodie and Horace's home a couple of times.

Margit adjusted the temperature on the slow cooker. "I suppose I could call Horace, but perhaps it would be better to talk face to face. Ack, when you have an unpleasant task, best to do it in person and quickly, *ja*? This is why you will go to that woman's funeral. Despite the trouble she caused. But I think you should leave before Clancy comes. You do not want to walk in late."

I wasn't so sure I should walk in at all. My presence was bound to be an unpleasant reminder for the Kloss family that Chad Detweiler had moved on with his life. But I'd already turned down one of Schnabel's requests, so I couldn't very well ignore a second.

Besides, I was eager to see Detweiler, even if our meeting wouldn't allow us any alone time. Surely the attorney would accompany the cop to the service, both to shield him from unwarranted questions and to remind the District Attorney and the media that he, John Henry Schnabel, was on the case.

Once I'd climbed into my car, I used a stray rubber band in my map pocket to twist my hair into a makeshift ponytail. I also put on a pair of sunglasses. Not much of a disguise, but perhaps it would help.

Nosing the front end of the Beemer into the busy street, I glanced at my side mirrors. A local TV van pulled into the traffic behind me.

Drat, drat, and double drat!

MARGIT'S SAUTÉED SAUERKRAUT
WITH SAUSAGE AND APPLES

1 tablespoon butter

Smoked sausage cut into bite-size pieces

1 medium onion coarsely chopped

Large can of sauerkraut (drain and lightly squeeze to get most of the liquid out)

1 small/medium apple sliced into wedges (Margit likes to leave on the skin)

½ to 1 tablespoon sugar (to taste)

¼ cup white wine

½ cup water

Melt butter.

Add sausage and sauté on medium heat till it starts to brown and the center is no longer pink.

Remove excess fat from pan (so you're back to the amount you started with when you melted the butter).

Add onions and sauté a few minutes until onion is soft.

Add sauerkraut and sauté a few minutes longer.

Add apple, sugar, wine, and water. Simmer for 15 minutes till apple is tender. If needed, add more water.

Stir occasionally, don't let it burn.

Serve with mashed potatoes.

Note: Instead of serving with mashed potatoes, you can add small red potatoes cut in wedges to the recipe at the same time you add the sauerkraut and apple. You can also omit the sausage and serve the sauerkraut and apples as a side dish with pork roast.

FIFTY-EIGHT

THE PENNEY AND QUEEN Funeral Home didn't look like any funeral parlor I'd ever seen. In my admittedly limited experience, funeral directors repurpose beautiful, large homes—houses too large and unwieldy for your typical family—and convert them into funeral parlors. But out here, in the middle of a vast cornfield, Penney and Queen had remodeled a Quonset hut. I don't care how much tacky Victorian trim you glue to a Quonset hut, it's still a Quonset hut. That's all there is to it. Since I love crafts, you'd think I'd cut them more slack, but I couldn't.

Despite the low-rent locale, mourners arrived en masse. The entrance to the parking lot was a huge traffic jam. Sort of like one of those celebrity funerals in LA with one big difference... instead of fancy sports cars, I drove in behind a fleet of pickup trucks. The TV van had disappeared after we crossed the state line.

A man in a poorly fitting black suit waved me into a pretend parking space in the vacant lot across the street from Penney and Queen. Sparse clumps of grass dotted the damp earth. Every step of my way through the clumps, my heels sank into the dirt. Two rows from my car, the dirt had been churned into mud that sucked the shoes right off of me. Twice I moved forward to discover I was not only clueless but shoeless. Once I slipped and saved myself by grabbing at a bumper with an NRA sticker attached. By the time I got to the curb, mud covered me up to the knees. It looked like I was wearing thick brown anklets. Before crossing the street, I leaned against a tree, pulled a tissue out of my purse and did my best to clean myself up.

The big chunks came off easily. The small stuff I scrapped free with my fingernails. Mostly. Staring down at my legs, I saw what looked like a self-tanning experiment gone horribly wrong. My skin was tinted a greenish brown, and I stunk. But there was nothing I could do about it.

I joined the crowd standing in front of the unopened front door. The other people gave me a wide berth. Maybe they noticed my legs and the smell and figured I had contracted some sort of contagious disease.

While we waited for the place to open, I amused myself by picking a few remaining blades of grass off my calves. As I did, my sunglasses slipped down repeatedly. I doubted that anyone would recognize me, but figured a new look couldn't hurt. I hadn't counted on the mud.

Five minutes passed as we waited for the doors to open. Another TV van pulled up and joined the line of cars pulling into the parking lot. This vehicle bore signage announcing "News at Nine." But the man in black waved it on past the parked cars. A uniformed cop stepped out of the crowd to argue with the occupants, who eventually turned around and drove off.

I was beginning to wish I hadn't arrived so early as another five minutes went by.

At long last, Thelma Detweiler's old station wagon appeared in the line of cars. The man in black waved them into a reserved space. John Henry bounced out of the passenger's side and offered a hand to Thelma, who was sitting in back. Louis stepped out of the driver's seat, shook the hand of the parking attendant in black and helped his son climb out. As he did, the pants leg of Detweiler's black suit hiked up, making his ankle bracelet clearly visible. I heard a camera click to catch the image.

A beat-up gray Camry drove into the spot next to the station wagon. Patty and Paul, Ginny and Jeff all struggled out. Last of all, Emily pushed her way out of the back seat, looking around like she was lost.

As the Detweiler clan crossed the parking lot, cameras began clicking and flashes went off. Two men with long lenses stepped out of the crowd of mourners, but as soon as they did, the uniformed cop and another man who flashed a badge escorted them across to the other side of the street. At the far end of the parking lot, the TV van took advantage of the confusion to grab an empty space.

The Detweiler parents flanked their son. They turned neither right nor left as they walked toward the funeral home. All around me, whispers started first as a quiet murmur, and then as a distracting level. People craned their necks for a better look at Chad Detweiler. A woman behind me said, "I can't believe he has the nerve to show up."

A man added, "If I had my b-b gun, I'd set him to hightailing it out of here like the sicko he is!"

"You got that right! I'd make him sorry he was ever born!" snickered another male voice.

So that's how it was. "Us" against "them."

Well, today they picked the wrong woman to mess with.

"How dare you!" I turned and shook my fists at the gathering. "What happened to innocent until proven guilty?"

I ripped the rubber band out of my hair, shook my curls free, pulled off the sunglasses, and with head held high, went over to take Detweiler by the hand. He stared down at me, his eyes narrow with frustration. "I am so, so sorry to put you through this," he whispered with his lips nearly touching my ear.

"It's going to be okay," I said and gave his hand a squeeze. "The roses are wonderful."

Louis stepped up and took my free hand. The rest of the family nodded to me, something less than a smile and more than a casual acknowledgement. We moved forward as one, and the sea of darkly clothed mourners parted to let us past. The front door opened and a pair of ushers stepped forward to greet us. One of them spoke to Detweiler, in a way that suggested they were old friends. The other moved more stiffly, escorting us to a row of folding chairs near the front where the casket sat on a folding contraption that didn't look too sturdy to me.

Louis let go of my hand and dropped back to take Thelma's arm. John Henry moved forward, so that he and Detweiler bookended me. As we took our seats, the lawyer lowered his voice to whisper, "Great to see you. I know this is hard, but it's the right thing to do. For you, for Chad, and for our case as well."

A chill ran up my spine, but I put on a poker face. Mourners filled the seats around us. The ushers escorted Milton and Carla

Kloss to their seats near the casket. I noticed they weren't holding hands, and their faces looked more angry than grief-stricken. Once they were seated, all I could see was the back of their heads.

John Henry took out his cell phone and mouthed, "Vibrate." In response, we reached for our phones. As I did, I noticed a text message from Ned.

Hey! I need to check on my favorite patient. You up for coffee tomorrow? I'll come by your store around 3. LMK

I typed in a quick: *See you then!*

It appeared that the accounting firm had also left me a text message. That could wait. I silenced my phone and slipped it into my purse.

Floral tributes lent the air a cloying fragrance. The casket was surrounded by lilies, mums, and carnations. A color photo of Brenda rested against the simple walnut coffin. She usually looked unkempt, like a teenager experimenting with makeup, but not quite getting it right. In this picture, the photographer had captured a wholesome appeal, something I'd never seen in the woman.

A skeleton-thin woman with an over-active vibrato sang "Amazing Grace" to start the service. It's hard to ruin that song—I even love the bagpipe version—but bless her heart, this woman managed to mangle a beloved hymn.

A minister stepped to the center of the raised platform. He mumbled his way through a variety of prayers. After what seemed like an eternity, he called on members of the audience to share their memories. A former teacher went to the lectern and talked about Brenda's love of poetry. Her old softball coach spoke about what a talented player she had been. Then Patty Detweiler Kressig stood up and made her way to the front of the funeral home. In her trembling hands she clutched a slim stack of index cards. She shook so hard, it took her a few minutes to arrange the cards and find her voice.

"Brenda Kloss was my best friend. We met in high school while riding the bus. It took us a while to become friends because she ran with the sporty group and I was a real nerd. She wasn't a great student, but she had one goal—to keep her grades high enough so she could stay on the school team. So one day on the bus, she asked me if I would help her with her classes. I said sure, thinking how hard could it be? Of course, I didn't know that she hadn't cracked a book all semester!"

That brought a chuckle from the crowd.

"Brenda didn't care much about our classes, because she had another love: softball. The sport was her passion. In fact, she hoped to get a scholarship to play on a college team." Patty wiped at her eyes and spoke more softly now. "But as most of you know, she and her mother were in a bad car accident. Brenda's pitching arm was broken in two places. The whiplash caused her to have terrible headaches."

Mourners wiggled around in their seats. People who'd been watching Patty with interest, now stared down at their feet.

"That's how Brenda became addicted to OxyContin. It's also why she wanted to become a nurse. She wanted to help people, really she did, but the drugs slowly took over her life. At first, she knew she had a problem, and she wanted help. My brother Chad made a deal with her that if she got clean, they'd get married. I was her matron of honor. We all hoped she had broken free of the grip of addiction, but it wasn't long after that Chad caught her sniffing crushed pills. By then, Brenda refused to believe she had a problem. Or if she did admit it, she said the problem was ours, not hers."

Patty paused to get her emotions under control. Chad Detweiler's youngest sister resembled their mother. She had Thelma's strong features, and blond coloring, but her father's long chin.

"The woman we are saying goodbye to this day is not the girl I knew in high school. Nor is she the woman I welcomed as a sister-in-law. Drugs changed everything for Brenda. Her life spun out of control. No matter how often we would stage an intervention, and she would promise to quit drugs, she would go right back to them as soon as she could. Eventually, I wasn't her best friend anymore. Drugs were."

Turning toward a couple huddled together in the front row, Patty said, "Mr. and Mrs. Kloss, you have suffered more than anyone else here. I am very sorry about that. As I thought about what to say today, I tried to remember the sweet girl I knew who loved tossing around a softball. I know that's how you'll think of her, too. But the truth is ... we lost Brenda a long, long time ago. We're only gathering here today to say our last goodbye."

I always carry tissues in my purse. Now I distributed them up and down the pew to the Detweilers. I cried, too. The thought of losing a child to drugs scared me, and Patty's words were a chilling reminder how horrible addiction could be.

The minister seemed to realize he had been outdone by Patty's remarks, because as she started for her seat, he practically raced to the front and center to deliver a rambling sermon cobbled together with random and vague comments about the difficulty of knowing

God's will. He mentioned three times that Brenda had been cut down in the prime of her life. His storehouse of quotations about death seemed endless, but none of them were comforting. Building up to his big finish, he nearly shouted, "Ashes to ashes, dust to dust!"—and Mrs. Kloss burst into noisy sobs.

Ugh. Like she needed a reminder that her child was decaying as we sat there, staring at that walnut box.

I couldn't wait for that wretched man to shut up. When he finally ran out of steam, there was a small gasp from the audience. We'd all been holding our breath waiting for him to finish. The funeral director took charge, outlining the route that the hearse would take to the cemetery.

Since we were near the front, we were last out of the building. Like all the other mourners, we blinked in the sun and sent up prayers of thanks that the ordeal was over. Glances in Chad Detweiler's direction were kinder now. Patty's eulogy had been both heartfelt and effective.

"Come on back to the house with us," suggested Thelma, slipping an arm around my waist and pulling me close. "I promise no one is going to ask you to make any commitments other than asking what you'd like to eat."

"There's plenty of room in the station wagon," Louis said. "One of us can bring you back for your car."

He glanced down at my legs and did a double-take. "Gracious. That's some tan you've got."

I let that slide.

"Do you think we should go to the cemetery for the interment?" Patty asked.

"I suggest you take a pass. Chad has paid his respects. We made our presence known. It's your call," Schnabel said, turning to the tall, lean cop, "but without sheltering walls, you'll be easy picking for the press."

Detweiler nodded wearily. "It's hard to know what to do. I want to show Brenda and her parents respect, but I also don't want to agitate them. Maybe we should go before things get ugly."

Carla and Milton Kloss stood a few yards away, hugging mourners and accepting their condolences. Both wore pained expressions on their faces. Carla stood a few feet from her husband, far enough that he realized she wasn't by his side. Her dress sagged, its limp ruffles around the neckline and cuffs looking oddly clownish. Milton turned to locate his wife and draw her near. The expression on his face was unreadable, but it didn't seem warm or loving.

Detweiler paused, looked their way and said to no one in particular, "It's over. At least, my marriage to Brenda is. I never expected it to end this way."

FIFTY-NINE

THELMA TOOK MY HAND and pulled me toward the back passenger door that Louis held open. "Come on, Kiki. You and Chad can sit back there with John Henry."

Upon arrival at the Detweiler farm, I needed to use the restroom. I've always been a member of the frequent tinkler club, but pregnancy kicked my pee prompter into high gear. Once I finished my visit to the john, I sought out Patty. She was in the kitchen, helping her mother start coffee. "You did a wonderful job with your eulogy. I found myself wishing that I'd known Brenda before she … changed."

"Thanks," Patty said gruffly.

Ginny was taking down cups from the cabinets. "She's right, Patty. You did yourself proud. It was nice. Of course, Carla got off lucky."

Schnabel had wandered in and poured himself a cup of coffee. Leaning against the back of one of the kitchen chairs, he asked, "What do you mean, Ginny?"

Detweiler came and sat in a chair next to the one Schnabel was using as a prop. "Patty could have pulled the rug out from under our neighbor. Didn't you notice Milton turning white as she walked up to the lectern? If the minister hadn't left it open for people to comment, Patty wouldn't have been invited to speak. You can take that to the bank."

"I called the funeral director and asked him if mourners were going to be given the chance to say a few words," Patty said, taking the seat across from the attorney. "I explained that I'd been her matron of honor at her wedding, and I wanted people to remember her kindly. He said he didn't see why not. I asked him not to tell the Klosses because they had enough on their minds. I told him I wanted it to be a nice surprise." Patty spoke to her fingers as they traced a pattern in the weave of her skirt. She had worn a simple white blouse, a navy sweater with leaves embroidered on it, and a navy skirt. She looked more like a boarding school student than an adult, but in a pleasant sort of way.

"I still am missing something here. Why did Ginny say that Mrs. Kloss got off easy?" Schnabel persisted.

"Because this is partially Carla's fault and she knows it," said Detweiler with a loud sigh.

"Now Chad don't be so judgmental!" his mother quit spooning sugar into the sugar bowl and shook her head. "I know you're upset, but still…"

"Mom, it's true and you know it!" He looked from her to me and continued. "Carla was—is—an alcoholic. Back then, she was drunk more than she was sober. Yes, it's true that she and Brenda were t-boned, but they were hit because Carla was too loaded to drive. She ran a stoplight and the other driver plowed into the side of their car. What Patty didn't say is that the other driver was a young mom. She and her baby were both killed instantly. Afterwards, a local judge slapped Carla's hands and fined her. But I'll give her this, Carla started attending AA meetings shortly thereafter, and as far as I know, hasn't had a drink since."

"Which is laudable," Thelma said. "But it came too late to help Brenda. That broken arm finished her softball career. The whiplash caused severe neck problems. Poor girl couldn't sit longer than two hours without getting a headache. The doctors kept feeding her pain pills. No one worried about her getting hooked."

"Mom, it wasn't all the docs' fault," Detweiler said. "Brenda went from doctor to doctor getting scripts. They didn't keep track as well as they should have. Certainly not as well as they do today. She knew how to play the system. Got scripts from physicians on both sides of the river. While she was in nursing school, she would befriend young docs and tell them she had a sports injury."

"And Carla Kloss was responsible?" Schnabel mused, adjusting his somber navy and yellow striped bowtie.

Louis joined us and pulled up a chair. "Course not. No one forced Brenda to take pills. No family is perfect. Milt never was what you'd call a loving dad. Always acted like a son of a gun to Carla. He wanted a daughter so badly. Had two sons before Brenda came along. One boy died as a youngster, some genetic problem, the other in Iraq. Brenda, well, she was always a real tomboy and that bothered her daddy. She was happy playing baseball or golf or something her brothers liked to do. But Milton had his heart set on a girly-girl daughter. Said she should stay home and have babies. That man wanted grandkids almost as badly as he had wanted a daughter!"

"Louis!" Thelma shook a finger at him. "Don't say that. You don't know that!"

"The heck I don't. At the barber shop, he lectured me about how Chad should keep Brenda in line by keeping her pregnant."

"That's hogwash," Thelma said, crossing her arms over her chest.

"Keep her in line?" Detweiler's voice rose a notch. "Every time I tried to get her help, she'd run home to her parents!"

"Stop it!" Ginny formed a time-out sign with her hands. "That's enough! Since when did we start talking this way to each other? Huh? They did their best! They've lost all their kids. Isn't that punishment enough?"

Patty nodded. "Chad, they did try to get her to quit doing drugs. I heard Mr. Kloss screaming at her once over the phone. He asked her why she wasn't strong enough to quit drugs since her mother had been strong enough to stop drinking. In the background, I heard Carla crying. That's all Carla did. Cry and cry and cry."

By the time Thelma served dessert, that's all I wanted to do, too.

SIXTY

Iced tea only seems like it would be easy to make. Most people either brew it too long or dilute it so it's too weak. Some put it in a coffee maker and wind up with a nasty mixture of coffee and tea flavoring. But Thelma Detweiler's iced tea is outstanding. She even pours your tea over ice cubes with slices of lemon and a sprig of mint in them.

Emily joined us. Bits of hay stuck to her plain black skirt. She had wandered out to the barn to feed the many cats that Thelma kept rescuing and neutering.

"How are you?" I asked.

She shrugged. "Sad."

"You have every right to be," I said. "It's a sad day."

"How's Anya? Can she come visit soon?"

"I hope so," I said. "I know she enjoys spending time with you."

Sensing that the girl needed a task, Thelma asked Emily to cut and serve slices of homemade apple pie, while she doled out the cinnamon ice cream. The conversation about Milton Kloss and his daughter had dampened everyone's spirits. Of course, my last visit to the Detweiler home left me somewhat subdued, but despite my hasty exit before, I felt welcome here.

"What's the game plan, counselor?" Louis turned to Schnabel as he loosened his tie with all the gusto of a man ripping a noose off his neck.

That lawyer sure could pack away the food. I hadn't finished my iced tea but he was on his second piece of Thelma's excellent pie topped with two scoops of cinnamon ice cream. "First we'll try to get a dismissal on the basis that there's not enough evidence. If that doesn't work, we'll try to discredit the evidence. I hope by the time this goes to court, if it does, we'll have an alternate story to tell. My investigators are busy collecting information. I have experts looking everything over for us."

"What about phone calls?" I asked. "Brenda had to go somewhere after the shooting. She must have called someone. Was it her mother? Carla Kloss was at home alone when the State troopers came to tell her about finding Brenda. Right?"

"Carla says she didn't see her daughter after the altercation at the slough. I plan to question that. I have subpoenaed phone records for the Kloss parents, and Brenda's records as well. Of course, the phone company is dragging their feet. As per usual." Schnabel mixed his ice cream with his pie.

"Were Brenda's injuries consistent with those caused by a 9 mm Beretta?" I wondered.

"What do you mean?" Louis turned to me, questioningly.

"As I understand it, different bullets cause specific sorts of damage. I'm wondering if Brenda's injuries match those that would have been caused by a 9 mm Beretta. The newspapers reported that several of the crime labs in Illinois have been taken to task for all sorts of goof-ups. I realize this might be obvious, but I thought it worth asking," I said.

A slow grin spread across Schnabel's face. "I wondered the same. I'm not sure how carefully the autopsy results were compared to the bullet typing. Here in Illinois, our coroners are elected officials."

"Right," I said. "That means they don't have to have any formal training, do they?"

"Correct," Schnabel said. "However, they are expected to apply for the training course within 30 days of assuming office. After they apply, they have six months to complete said training. As per your question, I have called in an expert to review the coroner's findings. I suspect the bullet type and the wound will not be a match."

"In other words, if you hadn't done something, we might be relying on an elected official with no formal training at all!" Ginny said with a huff. "And even if he or she had gone through that course, goodness knows how extensive that training really is!"

"That's just jim-dandy, isn't it?" agreed Louis. "Gives me a whole lot of confidence in the system."

"Then you'll feel even worse when I tell you that in this case, they rushed to match the ballistics to Chad's gun because of an anonymous call to the state police." Schnabel's tone was as serious as his expression.

"You have to be kidding," Ginny said. "So who made that call?"

"We don't know," said Schnabel. "It was traced to a phone booth at a convenience store along Highway 55."

I toyed with the last chunk of apple on my plate. "Why would someone make that call? Think about it. The person making the call had to be the killer."

I took Detweiler's hand. "He or she must have wanted to incriminate you. And the killer wanted you fingered right away. Otherwise, how long would it have taken for the authorities to check those particular casings against your service revolver? The one you'd quit using on a daily basis?"

"They always look at the husband or wife or any family member, but considering this gun had been retired, it might have taken a while for them to point the finger at Chad," said Schnabel.

"Why would anyone have wanted to incriminate Chad so quickly?" Thelma finally sat down to a cold cup of coffee.

"I have done work for nonprofits, helping with their fundraising and public relations," Ginny said. "One of them brought in an expert who lectured us on positioning our services. She said that the group or individual who puts the story out there first usually wins the day. Her point was that the first rendition has the most sticking power. We don't always hear the correction or the rebuttal. And if we do, it might not matter because we've already framed the debate."

"That's true in the courtroom as well." Schnabel pushed his plate away. "That's the purpose of opening arguments, to posit your story, to frame all the evidence in light of your supposition."

"So, you're saying that someone, possibly the killer, wanted to create a narrative that cast Chad as the killer. And that this person was sharp enough to work the system. That means that the killer was a person who knew how the coroner's office worked, how to encourage the state police, and also knew that Chad had recently changed out his gun. Plus, this particular person had to have access to Chad's spent casings. So, Brenda's murderer has to be someone fairly close to you," I said as I took Detweiler's hand and looked into those gorgeous green eyes. "Because the person who set you up must have known that you kept your retired gun. Otherwise this whole scheme wouldn't have worked."

SIXTY-ONE

PATTY DETWEILER VOLUNTEERED TO drive me back to my car. I reckoned her offer was an olive branch, so I eagerly snatched it up.

"Let me tell Mom goodbye," she said. We both knew this was a complete ruse designed to give her brother and me privacy. Tucking my arm under his, Detweiler walked me to his sister's car. "You liked my roses?"

I kissed him. "Yes. They are lovely. I'm enjoying them."

"I want to tell you again how sorry I am. You were right; I should have cut Brenda loose a long time ago." He threaded his fingers through mine, but kept his gaze on the ground. "I don't know why I feel so sad. I wasn't in love with her anymore. I'd almost come to hate her for all the trouble she was causing."

"You feel sad because you remember the person you once loved. You know who she could have been. And because you're a good person." I hugged him, catching a whiff of the Safeguard soap he always used and a hint of cologne. I liked the fact he didn't douse himself like some men did.

Stepping away to study me, he asked, "You're not mad at me any more for being a bonehead?"

I laughed. "That's Detective Bonehead, right?"

To my great joy, he smiled. "D.B."

I laughed again. "I'm not mad. You did your best. We'll talk about our wedding later, okay?"

"And Anya? Does she hate me? Has she said anything? Is she okay?"

"You mean besides spending all day sticking pins into a cloth doll dressed in a police uniform?"

"Crud," he groaned, and a flutter in my belly reminded me how much I needed this man. "That bad?"

"She has other things on her mind," I answered honestly.

"What? Is she worried about the baby?"

"No, she's happy about that. It's a problem between her and Nicci Moore. Girl stuff." I waved the concern away.

"Tell her I love her and that as soon as I'm out of this pickle, we're going fishing. I had promised her a day of it, and I intend to keep that promise real soon."

This pickle. Well, that was one way to describe being a suspect in your wife's murder.

He hesitated. "Just so you know, I was being truthful. I wanted to ask her to be my daughter, but I wanted to talk with you first, and I needed to finish up the divorce proceedings. But I hope she'll take me up on the offer. I know she sets great store about being a Lowenstein, but maybe we can come to some sort of a compromise."

"What kind of compromise?"

"Patty suggested a hyphenated last name. Pretty smart, huh?"

"That's certainly an option. We'll have to run it by Anya. Speaking of Patty, your sister confuses me. Is it safe for me to get in the car with her? Or is she going to take the loss of her friend out on me?" Glancing at Patty telling her mother goodbye, I knew that Detweiler and I only had a few more seconds to talk freely.

"Here's the good news: Patty hates firearms. If she's angry with you, she's more likely to attack you with a glue gun than a pistol. The two of you are more alike than you know. Both of you love crafts. Both are loyal to a fault. Trusting. Sensitive." Then he grinned. "And boy, do you two have a temper on you!"

SIXTY-TWO

DETWEILER HADN'T WARNED ME that Patty was a speed demon behind the wheel. My seat belt snapped tight twice before we rumbled out of the Detweiler driveway, leaving me gasping for air. Patty was careful enough, looking both ways before pulling out on an empty stretch of county road, but her lead foot sent me bouncing this way and that over the poorly maintained pavement.

"I don't hate you."

"That's good to know."

"Given time, I might even come to like you."

"Or not."

"Or not." She laughed. "At least you don't take yourself too seriously."

"How could I? I'm the mother of a pre-teen. I get potshots taken at me on a regular basis. That reminds me, I heard that your brother and your father used to go to a shooting range and practice every Sunday. Where is it?"

"Down the road from my parents' house. Maybe five miles to the north."

We raced into an intersection obscured by rows of corn. She brought the car skidding to a stop and pointed a finger to the left. "Here's the crossroad. Harbinger Lane. The GM range is at the intersection of that and County Road 1200. Colby Nesbit added it to his farm to bring in extra cash. My house is ten miles northeast of here."

She sped away from the four-way stop, leaving a cloud of dust behind us.

"You and Brenda must have been good friends."

"You try spending two hours a day on a bus with someone. Gives you a lot of time to talk. Of course, things changed after we graduated, but we were still neighbors, sort of, so we stayed close. I think she had a crush on Chad for years."

We came to another crossroads. Patty pointed over her left shoulder. "The Kloss farm is six miles that way. It's a deep piece of land. The back of it runs up against County Road 1400, but the house is actually on County Road 1300. The place has been in their family two generations. Not as long as we've had our farm, but still…"

By my calculations, Brenda had been killed thirty miles from here, twenty miles past Patty and Paul's house, on the way to the city of Springfield, Illinois. I asked Patty if she knew anyone who lived along that stretch of highway.

"No. I know why you're asking. I've even gone through our yearbook and looked up our classmates. Most of them stayed close to home. Even though the employment situation here is pretty dismal."

"We gravitate to what is familiar, even when economic times are tough," I said.

"A few of our classmates have dabbled in growing pot. As you might imagine, if you know much about agriculture, growing hemp is easy enough to do. Especially if you have a greenhouse. A lot of farmers put in greenhouses to grow specialty crops like Beefsteak tomatoes, Big Girl and Better Girl varieties to sell at roadside markets. Of course, back in 1943, the government actually distributed hemp seed to Illinois farmers to meet wartime demands for rope, twine, and so on. You still see it growing beside the road. Today's plants are different, with a higher concentration of TCH in the buds, so it doesn't take a lot of marijuana to turn a good profit."

I channeled Sheila for a second and had to stop myself before her voice came out of my mouth, or I would have said, "Really?"

Instead, I tried to sound noncommittal. "Uh, that's interesting. You think it has anything to do with Brenda's death?"

She hesitated. "I don't know. It's possible. I mean, maybe someone local was supplying her."

"But marijuana is different from prescription drugs."

Patty sighed. "I know. I'm just trying to make sense of it, you know? Find a connection somewhere, somehow to help Chad! Besides she could have been trading prescription drugs for dope. It happens. Dope is easier to sell."

She sounded desperate. I put a hand on her shoulder. "It's going to be all right. We have to trust that it will. Schnabel is the best there is. Chad didn't do this, and we'll all stand by him."

"Yeah, you're right. I'm just telling you something I was thinking about. I mean, maybe Brenda knew about a marijuana operation, and that caught up with her. She could have threatened to rat someone out."

"Anyone you know?"

"No!" she said too quickly. A slow blush stained her face. Was it possible that Patty and Paul grew dope for Brenda to sell and harvested a peck full of trouble? Was this the "investment" that went bad? Paul had been out of work for a year or so by my calculations. Jobs were hard to replace in rural communities. Houses tough to sell.

Could it be that Patty Kressig knew a whole lot more about the circumstances surrounding Brenda Detweiler's death than she let on?

SIXTY-THREE

On my drive back to St. Louis, I talked with Robbie Holmes. Fortunately, there's a lot of flat highway between Illinois and Missouri, so being on the cell phone wasn't endangering other drivers. A couple of times, I resorted to what we call "knee driving," where you steer the car with your kneecaps so both hands are free. Not recommended, but hey, long flat stretches of road can be tiresome! Robbie asked a few questions about the funeral and what I'd observed. He listened carefully to all I'd seen and heard. "Sounds like a hot mess. I think you're right that Patty might know something. The question is what? I sure hope the case doesn't go to court."

My heart started racing with fear as Robbie continued, "You never know with a jury. Ever. If one person in the jury box has a problem with cops, Chad could be sentenced even if the evidence is weak. It's always a crap shoot."

After that depressing thought, I wanted to change the subject. "When's Sheila coming home?"

"I'm picking her up tonight after work. Want to come over?"

"I have a crop."

"What's a crop? I've heard you talk about them."

"Basically a scrapbook party. Think of a quilting bee with paper. And I'm in charge. I couldn't get to her house until eleven."

"She should be fast asleep by then. How about if you stop by in the morning?"

SIXTY-FOUR

MARGIT'S FOOD PUT OUR croppers in a super mood, and my projects were well-received, especially the one teaching croppers new ways to use gesso on Zentangle® tiles.

Yifat Glassman Cestare came up to me after the demonstrations and gave me a hug. "Those of us who know you and Detweiler know he's innocent. He couldn't have had anything to do with his wife's death. We think the world of you, Kiki. Always have. Always will. Don't let the turkeys get you down." Her kind words meant a lot to me, and her hazel eyes glowed with sincerity as she spoke.

A half an hour before we ended the event, my cell phone rang. I ignored it, but the store phone rang immediately afterward, a sure sign of a problem. A peek at the clock told me that Sheila might be home by now. Could it be her? But then, Robbie would be by her side.

Reluctantly, I picked up.

"Mom? I need you. Come quickly. It's Nicci. Something's wrong."

"Where's Jennifer?" I tugged at the strings of the apron I wore during crops. The ties came loose and I wiggled it off.

"She's at a meeting. Something to do with business."

"And Stevie?" I asked as I fumbled with my purse. Since he was older, he could help as I raced to the scene.

"He's with Nicci. Mom? Are you coming or what?"

"I'm on my way. Do you need an ambulance?"

"I don't think so. I'm not sure."

"Call nine-one-one. If you aren't sure, it's better to be safe."

She hung up.

SIXTY-FIVE

CLANCY LOOKED UP FROM helping a cropper with a project, took one glance at my face, and made a beeline to my side. "Anya?"

"An emergency." I had my car keys in hand.

"I'll take Gracie to your house and wait there."

"This might take a while."

"That's fine. I can sleep on the sofa. You might want the company when you get back. You've had a rough couple of days."

Without a backward glance or a goodbye to the troops, I raced out the door. My hands shook so much I had trouble getting the key into the ignition, but I managed. Then I outdid Evel Knievel in my daredevil attempt to cross 40 into the fancy Ladue neighborhood where the Moores lived. Fortunately, their house wasn't more than a couple of miles from the store.

I jumped the curb in front of the perfectly manicured Moore house. Didn't care. As long as I didn't blow out the tire, I was fine. Turned the car off and sprinted to the front door. Once there, I pounded on it. Anya appeared, paler than a bedsheet soaked in Clorox. "Upstairs. In the bathroom."

Anya and I bounded up the stairs, faster than I would have ever dreamed possible. She pointed to an open door and I stepped in to see Nicci on the white tile floor, her inner thighs covered in blood. Stevie sat under her, propping her up, squished between the toilet and the bathtub. My first thought was that the girl had miscarried or hemorrhaged. But the blood started three inches or so down from the top of her thighs. She was wearing a loose tee-shirt and knit gym shorts with a drawstring waist. The humidity in the room told me that the shower must have been running recently. Nicci's hair was wet. Had she slipped, fallen and hurt herself?

Where was all this blood coming from?

"You called nine-one-one?"

"Y-y-yes," Anya stuttered.

"I think she's passed out," said Stevie as he cradled his sister's torso.

"Get me a wet washcloth, Anya. Please." I touched Nicci's pulse, which seemed strong to me. I could see her chest rise and fall, so I knew she was breathing. Her lips were pink, so I could tell she was getting oxygen. "Stevie, any idea what happened?"

"I was playing video games when I heard a thud." He wiped away a tear. "She going to live?"

"I hope so. I think so. Looks to me like this blood is coming from cuts on her leg."

He nodded. "That's what I think, too."

"Nicci? Nicci, honey?" I tapped her cheeks lightly and she moaned. A good sign.

It seemed to take forever before Anya passed me a warm, damp washcloth. An area of Nicci's thigh about six inches long by three inches wide was bloody, but it wasn't spurting blood. Some of it had actually dried on her skin, forming a rusty border. Very, very gently, I dabbed. As I did, I noticed that the center seemed to be coagulating. Bit by bit, I worked my way from the outside toward that center, discovering as I wiped, a crisscross of cut marks. Working carefully so as not to encourage more bleeding, I noted with relief that the area affected was not nearly as large as it had initially looked.

"Could you rinse that out?" I handed the cloth to Anya and heard water running in the sink behind me. "Nicci? Nicci, honey?"

She roused a little. Her eyelashes fluttered and she tried to sit up. I lightly pinched her nostrils shut. Nicci's eyes snapped open. "Wh-wh-what?"

"Nicci, are you all right? Where are you hurt? Just your legs?"

She nodded.

"What happened?"

She tried to push herself to a standing position. Stevie and I each grabbed an elbow to help. Metal clattered to the tile floor. I looked down to see a bloody razor blade.

HOW TO USE GESSO ON A ZENTANGLE® TILE

Gesso is a primer made of gypsum or Plaster of Paris and glue. It's used to put a coating on rough surfaces, but we've found a couple other reasons to add it to your Zentangle® supply kit.

Black Gesso

Although tanglers are taught, "There are no mistakes. Only creative opportunities," occasionally we all feel disappointed in how our tiles turn out. Not to worry. You can re-purpose a Zentangle® tile by painting it with black gesso! Black gesso does a wizard job of covering up your mistakes—giving you a new surface to tangle.

One of the outstanding properties of gesso is how quickly it dries. Once it feels dry to the touch, usually fifteen minutes, you're good to go. You can tangle on your black tile with white ink, white pencil, gray pencil, black pen (for cleaning up or definition) or those specialty pens like the Souffle pens by Sakura.

White Gesso

Gesso also comes in white. You're probably wondering why would you paint white gesso onto a white tile? Traditional Zentangle® tiles are a very absorbent paper. If you paint the tile with a coating of gesso, you can use markers that would otherwise bleed. In other words, now your markers will deliver a crisp line, giving you more control over your design.

* A tile is a pre-cut square of high quality paper.

SIXTY-SIX

After Nicci regained consciousness, I phoned Jennifer. I didn't want to scare my friend, but I told her that I thought Nicci needed to be seen by experts. "We called 911. She doesn't appear to be seriously hurt, but she did faint, and she might have hit her head."

Jennifer thanked me profusely and instantly agreed with my assessment. Of course, there was more to the problem than I'd said. But as the shriek of the siren grew closer, I didn't have time to talk. This was a job for professionals.

The cuts on Nicci's thighs weren't deep, but there were a lot of them and they had bled a lot. I suspected she passed out from blood loss or from shock or both, but I wasn't qualified to make that call. After they loaded Nicci in the ambulance, Stevie, Anya and I followed in my car.

Emergency rooms are such strange places. Everything moves at breakneck speed if you're bleeding or obviously hurt, but at super slo-mo if you're not.

We hadn't been at the hospital long when Jennifer and Steven burst through the automatic doors. Jennifer was out of breath, flushed and frightened out of her wits. Steven simply seemed irritated. The staff told them that Nicci was okay, being seen to, and the doctor would be out to talk with us in a while.

After she sagged down onto the seat next to me, Jennifer started crying. Her teeth chattered audibly. I sent the kids to get her a Coke and flagged down a nurse to bring her a blanket lest she go into shock. Steven didn't seem to notice his wife's distress. Instead, he tried to look manly, strutting around and playing with his Blackberry. What a jerk. I don't have much use for him. He does make cute kids, but otherwise he's a waste of space and air. There are cardboard boxes I'd rather spend time with.

A staff person came out and handed us each copies of a pamphlet on self-harming.

That got Steven's attention. He nearly dropped and stepped on his Blackberry. Jennifer grabbed a handful of tissues and mopped her eyes. "Why? What?" she said.

"The admitting doc thinks this will help. There's good information in there," said the staff person.

At long last, the doctor came and talked to the Moores. He suggested they keep Nicci overnight until a psychiatrist could evaluate her. "Strictly as a precaution."

Reluctantly, they agreed.

By the time Anya and I found my car in the parking lot, I could barely keep my eyes open. The drive home seemed endless. The warm yellow porch light outside my little cottage never seemed so cheery. Clancy met us at the backdoor. She had changed into one of my long T-shirts. Over the top she'd pulled a sweatshirt that bore the legend "Lowood Institution Lacrosse." Of course, that's a joke, because Lowood was the charity school that Jane Eyre attended. There surely wouldn't have been a lacrosse team or any other sort of recreation at that gruesome place.

After Anya stumbled off to bed, Clancy poured herself a glass of my wine. Since I couldn't drink, we decided she could be the designated drinker. Actually, that's what I want to be when I grow up: A designated drinker. People can take me places and I'll drink for them. I wonder if there's a career opportunity there.

Clancy made me a cup of that nasty chamomile tea.

"Cutting. It's an epidemic among young girls." Clancy shook her head. "How long had it been going on?"

I rubbed my eyes. The kitchen clock told me it was nearly one in the morning.

"Jennifer thinks Nicci's problems started last year when Stevie came out of the closet. I guess the attention he got only exacerbated all the negative feelings she had about herself. Anya told me Nicci had been teased at school about Stevie being gay. A couple of weeks ago, a boy she liked dumped her. Said cruel things about her on Facebook. I guess Nicci's emotional cup runneth over."

"Did Jennifer know what was happening?"

"She knew there was a problem. Wasn't sure exactly what. She'd never heard of cutting. Nicci refused to bare her legs when the family took a vacation in Aruba. Jennifer chalked it up to body image issues. That's what she was worried about. She didn't think to worry about this."

"What brought everything to a head?"

"Tonight Nicci cut herself more deeply than usual and passed out."

"Anya found her?"

"Stevie did. He yelled for Anya."

"Did Anya know this was going on?"

"Yes. Poor kid couldn't decide what to do. She was afraid to tell on Nicci, for fear that her friend would get more upset and eventually commit suicide. She was equally scared not to tell anyone about it, for fear of the same. She worried that if she ticked Nicci off, things might get worse and no one would know until it was too late. The two girls quarreled over it. Nicci insisted that she wasn't planning to kill herself, only that the cutting felt good. Called it a release. Of course, that explanation left Anya totally baffled. Tonight Anya planned to tell Nicci that if she didn't tell her mother, she would."

"But Nicci *is* suicidal, isn't she?"

"No. Health care professionals have recently re-evaluated cutting. They call it NSSI, for non-suicidal self-injury. They theorize that the act of self-harm releases endorphins. That release feels good, so the cutters become addicted."

"You have to be kidding me!"

"Nope. One cutter compared it to getting high. Which is especially appealing if you feel like you need to escape. To walk away from your life." As I spoke, Gracie growled in her sleep, her large body twitching in response to a bad dream. With my big toe, I rocked her shoulder to rouse her. She raised her heavy head, glared at me, snorted, and immediately fell back to sleep. "Hand me my purse," I said to Clancy, who willingly got up from the couch. After she passed my bag over, I dug around for the pamphlet. "Wait until you hear the stats on this. Experts say nearly one in five girls today is or has cut herself."

On her way back to her sofa, Clancy scooped up Seymour and put him in her lap so she could stroke his fur absent-mindedly. Martin jumped up onto the back of the sofa and watched. He's a bit more shy than Seymour, so he watched Seymour soaking up the love.

"Growing up I never heard of anyone cutting herself. But lately I've read about it with Angelina Jolie, Princess Di, Amy Winehouse, and Lindsay Lohan. I guess I didn't think about it with high school girls. Those celebrities are a pretty high-flying group of women. I mean, they all are—or were—terribly successful role models. What gives?" asked Clancy.

"I wish I knew. The brochure says that cutting seems to be catching. It's much, much more common in girls than in boys. When one girl does it, her peers try it, too. I bet it's an epidemic at CALA. They work so hard to keep up a good front. I wish the people in charge cared half as much about taking care of our kids."

"That's not fair and you know it." Clancy sat up straighter. "When I taught high school, parents threatened to sue us all the time if we shared confidential information about their kids. No one wanted Little Jenny or Little Johnny labeled as a kid with a problem. And who can blame them? It's usually just a stage. Kids grow up and move on."

She was right. I agreed with her. "But I have reason to think there's a bigger problem at CALA than anyone is admitting. On the way home tonight, Anya told me about cutting parties in the school restrooms. Can you believe it? What do I do now? Tell the administration? What does my daughter do? Become the cutting spy and tell on everyone?"

"I'll tell you what I would do if I were you. I'd watch my kid like a hawk. Shake her down regularly for sharp objects."

"Huh. That wouldn't do much good. According to that pamphlet kids can be very cagy about where they hide their tools. One mother searched her daughter's room but didn't find anything. The girl had hidden a blade in a picture frame between the photograph and the cardstock backing. She taped another blade to the inside of a CD case."

"Regardless, I'd still watch Anya carefully."

I didn't tell Clancy the details of my talk with Anya on our drive home. My daughter admitted being grossed out by Nicci's problem. "I want to be Nicci's friend, Mom, but I sure hope she stops doing this because the sight of blood makes me want to barf. I know that's like totally selfish, but it's true. It took me forever to get you the washcloth because I got sick in the other bathroom. Anyway I'm kinda glad this happened. I've been really, really worried about Nicci. Now I don't have to rat her out."

Clancy's yawn brought me back to the here and now. I joined in.

Snug at home at last, Clancy had done an admirable job of turning my sofa into a makeshift bed. I told her goodnight, woke Gracie, put my hand on the dog's collar, and walked the big girl into my bedroom. Once I was under the covers and Gracie sprawled on the other half of the bed, I started to fall asleep. I had a lot I could worry about. But I remembered what a German theologian named Meister Eckhart taught his followers, "If the only prayer you said in your whole life was, 'Thank you,' that would suffice." And it seemed to me, as I snuggled next to Gracie's slumbering bulk, that as worried as I was about Detweiler, I had a lot to be grateful for. So instead of reviewing my worries, I told myself: My daughter is safe. Her friend is getting the care she needs. Clancy is my rock. My sister lives nearby. Sheila is home. My friends have my back. Mert will forgive me someday. Dodie is in God's hands. My boyfriend has a top-notch attorney, plus he's innocent. And I have a baby to welcome into this world.

Life was good.

Mainly.

SIXTY-SEVEN

Tuesday, Day 8—after the shooting

THE PHONE RANG EARLIER the next morning than I would have liked.

"Come on over for breakfast," boomed the voice of Robbie Holmes.

"Be right there. Can I bring Clancy?"

"As long as she doesn't eat anything. Hey, I'm pulling your leg. You can bring anyone you want," and he hung up.

Boy, someone was in a good mood now that his honey was home!

No one makes better breakfasts than Robbie. He's great with eggs, hash browns, pancakes, biscuits and gravy.

I called CALA and told them Anya was taking a mental health vacation for a day or two. Fortunately, the receptionist didn't press me for details. Margit was scheduled to open the store at eight, and Dodie would come in soon after. Robbie's timing was perfect, even if Clancy and Anya weren't happy about getting up so early. I reminded both of them that Robbie was an excellent cook, and they grumped a little less.

I sniffed the armpits of my gray dress and pronounced it clean enough for another day's wearing.

A short time later, I tapped on Sheila's front door. It flew open and there stood my mom. As we tried to come in, she blocked our entrance. "Well! It's about time, Kiki. You haven't called. You haven't been by to ask how I am. Here I am, all alone in this strange city and you haven't made an effort."

She swept her eyes up and down, studying me. "In that gray dress, you look like a whale."

"Son of Blubber, huh? Or Daughter of Blubber as the case may be? Nice to see you too, Mom," I pushed past her. "Robbie? Sheila? Hello!"

Clancy and Anya also edged their way past my mother, who continued to complain while following them into the kitchen.

The Sheila sitting in a kitchen chair was much, much smaller than the woman I knew. Pain diminished her, although her bright blue eyes snapped with intelligence. Leaning over, I gave her a kiss on the cheek. On the trip here I'd warned Anya that her grandmother might be fragile.

"I know, Mom," said Anya. "I saw both of you in the emergency room, remember?"

My child's face was suffused with love as she approached her Gran and slipped her arms around Sheila's neck so lightly, she could have been a butterfly landing on a petal. "Gran! It's so good to have you back. I missed you."

"Harrumph," my mother fussed in the background.

Amanda came in and I gave my sister a hug. She'd met Clancy at my house during the welcome home party, but I reintroduced my friend to my sister and started to introduce her to my mother when she interrupted.

"My daughter has forgotten her manners. Of course, I am Lucia Montgomery, Amanda's mother. Kiki's as well," said my mother stiffly, extending her hand the way Henry VIII must have done for Thomas More to kiss before he had him beheaded.

"Mom, Clancy is the nice person who's renting us the house in U City," said Amanda. "Remember? You liked that place a lot. Very large. Great location. Nice yard."

"Then I need to talk to you. Those windows haven't been cleaned in a long time. That simply must be done. And you need to get a water softening system, as I have very delicate skin," Mom patted her own face as if Clancy might need visual reinforcement to get the drift.

"Tell you what," said Clancy. "Why don't you make me a list?"

As Mom toddled off to find notepaper, Clancy leaned close to me and whispered, "So I can tear it to shreds and forget it. How's that working for you, girlfriend?" And she gave me a high-five.

I snickered. "Really well. You might be able to keep her busy for weeks writing it over and over."

Without my crabby mother, the kitchen was a warm and happy place to gather. Robbie's hash brown potatoes with onions and green peppers gave off a tantalizing aroma. An accomplished sous chef, Robbie had all his ingredients for omelets at hand so he could take our orders and whip them up in no time.

"I filled the French press with coffee from Kaldi's," Robbie said to me as he slid the first omelet onto Sheila's plate.

"Oh, you doll you." I hugged him. I filled the eight-cup coffee maker with hot water from the special spigot at Sheila's sink.

Mom walked back in. I watched her look around and I read the expression on her face. She was a deeply, deeply unhappy woman—and her sour disposition caused everyone to want to avoid her. Robbie and Sheila were joking and stealing kisses. Amanda and Anya talked about U City. Clancy caught me up on what had happened when she closed the store the night before. An empty chair sat open, waiting for my mom, but she simply stood there, staring at all of us. When no one immediately dropped what they were doing to cater to her, Mom pouted. "Well, I can see I'm not wanted," she sniffed before leaving again.

The conversation turned to light-hearted matters. Sheila's sling. Local news. The annual appearance of moles in Sheila's lawn. Visitors who wanted to come by and wish my mother-in-law well. A few had dropped off packages at the house, leaving books and chocolates and magazines.

After an hour or so of chit-chat, Anya wandered into the great room to read her grandmother's fashion magazines. We could hear the television in that room booming, which I rightly assumed was a passive-aggressive statement from my mother.

"I'll take Mom a plate," said Amanda. "You know she's pouting because she isn't the center of attention."

"I know," I said with a sigh. "How do you put up with her?"

"By ignoring her. Look at it this way, Kiki. She doesn't have much of a life, does she? She's run off most of her friends. She creates imaginary dramas with people to have a reason to be put out. She's too insecure to simply ask for what she needs. Instead, she twists things and manipulates people. Although she wouldn't call it that. It isn't a conscious act. It's just the way she's learned to view the world and her place in it. This is all she knows. And she's too old to change. Pretty pathetic isn't it? By acting helpless, she exerts her power. My therapist calls it the tyranny of the weak."

I thought about that a minute. "I call it sick."

SIXTY-EIGHT

CLANCY STARTED RINSING OFF dishes. She's one of those people who wash their dishes before stacking them in the dishwasher so that it can—wait for it—wash the dishes. This seems doubly redundant to me, but each to his own. Or her own, as it is in this case.

"You wouldn't believe how kind people have been. My bedroom looks like a florist's shop," said Sheila. "So many people have been so nice. That reminds me. How was Brenda Detweiler's funeral service? I heard that you decided to attend."

I told her about Patty's remarks at the service, and about what John Henry Schnabel was doing in terms of having an expert check Brenda's wounds against the sort of damage a 9 mm Beretta would do. Robbie made a huffing sound and said, "The use of untrained people as coroners continues to be problematic. I'm sure the coroner who pronounced Brenda dead called in a medical examiner, but even if he did, it's better to have an expert at the scene from the git-go."

"Why do states use elected officials as coroners? I mean, wouldn't it be smarter to have a forensic pathologist or at least a physician doing the job?" Clancy asked.

"Most counties don't have the resources to hire a professional. Fortunately, they rarely need one. In rural areas, the coroner's job largely consists of showing up at a farm house, staring down at a cold corpse, and saying, 'Yep, he's dead. Now it's official.'"

"Like in the Wizard of Oz!" I said.

"Exactly. But once in a great while, there's a problematic situation. Like this one. Then things get dicey."

"Any luck tracking down who supplied Brenda with drugs?" I asked Robbie.

"It looks like she might have gotten her most recent supplies from Bill."

"How? Was he buying them on the street?"

"He had a supplier. Until recently, a lot of prescription drugs have come from drug mills in Florida. They bill themselves as pain clinics—and some actually are legit—but many of them are simply storefronts, and they make their money by supplying pills to junkies. Here's how it works: A drug dealer solicits mules, sort of quasi-employees. The mules make appointments with the clinics. The dealers coach the mules, teaching them exactly what to say about their symptoms. After the mule gets the script, he turns it over to the dealer. The dealer either pays the mule in money or drugs."

"Why Florida? What's so appealing about the Sunshine State?" asked Clancy.

"Until recently regulations were loose there," said Robbie.

Sheila stirred her coffee. "They gave me OxyContin in the hospital, but I told them I didn't want a prescription for it. I don't want a bottle of pills like that in my house. I want Anya to be able to invite friends over without having to worry that someone, sometime, might raid my medicine cabinet."

That reminded me about Nicci, so I shared what had happened.

Sheila shook her head. "I hope things turn around for her. She's a sweet child."

"I hope so, too."

"And for you and Detweiler," she added.

"There's nothing I can do for him, it seems. John Henry Schnabel warned me to keep my nose out of the case lest I make things worse instead of better. I can't do anything for Anya, except take her over to visit Detweiler's niece Emily, which I plan to do tomorrow since she needs a break. But I do need your help with another problem."

I told Sheila about Cherise Landon's visit to the store, her claim that she'd killed Nathan, and Dodie's response. "Horace told me that Dodie's cancer has spread to her brain. I'd like to give her closure."

Sheila sighed. "I've known Dodie and Horace for years. We didn't socialize, but I've always thought well of her. She's certainly been good to you. What a shame."

"What do you know about the Landons?"

"Shep is a jerk. One of those men who always thinks he's the smartest guy in the room. Cherise is his darling. Margie Landon is nice enough, but rather plain. Cherise got the best of her parents' features and then some. I think Margie is rather in awe of her daughter, and she's lived through her child. Shep is a legacy, so I often saw the Landons at CALA events. He was quick to whip out the latest photo of Cherise. Margie would brag about how popular the girl was. I believe she was the May Day Queen as a senior."

CALA was famous for its May Day ceremonies. To be named Queen was an honor bestowed on one girl by her classmates. I thought about what I'd learned about Cherise and decided I really didn't know much more than when I started.

Instead of coming to the store with me, Anya decided to spend the rest of the day with her grandmother. "Why don't you text-message Emily and ask her if you can visit tomorrow?" That would give me a chance to see Detweiler again, and perhaps offer Anya something to look forward to.

Gracie looked so comfortable on the dog bed that Sheila had bought for her that I didn't have the heart to make the big dog move. So I told everyone goodbye and headed for the store by myself, leaving Clancy to talk with Sheila and Amanda.

On the way, my thoughts circled back to Cherise Landon. I couldn't figure out a way to learn more about Nathan's death. I'd tried the school. I'd tried my limited contacts. I'd tried the police records. What was needed here was a burst of creativity. An out-of-the-box solution.

Margit had, of course, opened the store precisely on time and gone through our daily procedures according to the laminated sheet. Dodie sat in a folding chair behind the register. "Her balance isn't good. I thought she might fall off a stool," explained Margit in a whisper.

I greeted my boss with a hug. She held me extra tight, as if I were her anchor to this world. "Let me get you a Coke, okay?" I offered because I didn't want to break down and cry. The sight of her, so thin and fragile, sickened me. Where was she going? What would her journey be like? I hoped it would be an easy trip.

After I handed Dodie her Coke, I checked with Margit about what our priorities were. I noticed the self-contained German lady sniffled a bit. Her eyes were red. I guessed she'd been crying, but I didn't remark on it.

"I have been reviewing our numbers. More and more we are doing well with Zentangle®. Why don't you teach a beginning class?"

I explained that a Zentangle® teacher should be certified. Margit pulled up their website and pointed. "So if we could get you into that session in Rhode Island, would you like to go? I recall Dodie offering to pay your way."

"Wow, would I ever!"

With a skip in my step, I went back to my worktable. I decided to work on a few new tangles, the patterns that make up the method's vocabulary. Getting the certification was definitely a move in the right direction. With pen in hand, I started copying tangles by other people, working to expand my own knowledge. As the founders of the art form, Rick Roberts and Maria Thomas, said on their website, this repetitive, deliberate stroking produces a type of meditative calm. What they didn't say was that it expanded a person's creativity—but it did!

I was tangling when it came to me in a flash: I couldn't ask Rebekkah to befriend Cherise Landon on Facebook. But that didn't mean I couldn't contact her myself!

I hopped up and ran to the computer. With a few keystrokes, I landed on Cherise Landon's Facebook page and poked around. Like most young people, Cherise hadn't enabled any of the privacy settings that would keep her personal life personal.

Cherise Landon's life was an open book.

Using the timeline feature, I scrolled through her postings for the past year. Most were banal, and self-absorbed. She had indeed graduated from Princeton. Her parents had obviously, and rightly, been pleased. Her posts grew increasingly bleak as she hunted for a job. Eventually, she announced to her friends that she was taking a temporary post as an intern in her father's law firm. One album on her Facebook page showed her and a work colleague at a sidewalk eatery in Clayton. Her friend was in a sundress and Cherise wore a long-sleeved blouse as she raised a glass of wine to toast the photographer. Scrolling quickly through the pictures, I tried to find the name of the establishment. I passed pictures of huge urns of flowers, a photo of a salad, a crooked shot of a smiling waiter, and finally, a small picture that included the front door. Aha! I recognized the restaurant as Chou-Chou, a place I once went with George.

I stared at the spot. Glanced at the clock at the bottom of the computer screen. Eleven o'clock. Almost lunchtime. Maybe I'd been going about this all wrong. Cherise had walked into the store because she wanted to confess. She wasn't trying to hide what happened to Nathan. She wanted to get it off her chest.

I could help with that.

SIXTY-NINE

PARKING IS ALWAYS A challenge in Clayton. I circled several blocks, got turned around, tried for a parking garage, discovered it was full, and finally zipped into a space as a man was pulling out. By eleven-thirty I was seated at an outdoor table on the Chou-Chou patio. My budget couldn't absorb the cost of a lunch at such a pricey eatery, so I nursed a glass of iced tea, figuring I'd make it up to the waiter by leaving him a big tip.

The day was warm for May, but not so hot as to be uncomfortable. By June only the heartiest of the outdoor patrons would want to sit outside. Although pregnancy had turned my thermostat to pre-heat, as long as I could sip the tea, I could stand the sun beating down on me.

By the time one o'clock rolled around, I'd gotten up to tinkle four times. The waiter kept asking me, "Are you ready to order?"

I kept saying, "I'm waiting for a friend." Of course, we weren't friends—and the waiter was quickly turning into a sworn enemy—but that was beside the point.

I'd requested my bill when Cherise and two other girls walked in. All of the young men at the bar turned to admire the trio. One was a pretty blonde who wore a sleeveless wrap dress in shades of orange that showed off a wonderful tan. The other a dishwater blonde whose cap-sleeved, A-line dress in a pink pastel cotton was totally businesslike but also appropriate for summery weather. Several sets of silver bracelets jangled as Cherise tugged at the long sleeves of her light-blue cardigan paired with a gray skirt. She'd pulled her long auburn hair into a loose bun that was very flattering.

After they sat down and ordered glasses of wine, I tucked a ten dollar bill under my glass and approached their table. The blonde in orange was telling a funny story, but she stopped and frowned at my intrusion.

"Cherise? My name's Kiki. You came into the store where I work to talk with Dodie Goldfader. I was wondering if I could have a moment in private."

The girls took in my gray dress and my growing bump of a belly and said nothing.

Cherise nervously fingered her wine glass and took a long drink, nearly draining it. "Okay, sure, but I can't talk for long. We're having lunch. Lisa? Order the Cobb salad for me. No dressing, okay?"

We walked inside the restaurant, trying to get our bearings the way you do when you leave the light and move into darkness. A booth in the back was open, but dirty. It would work for our purposes. I led the way. We sat down, and I made sure her back was to the door. I figured if her friends came looking for her, she'd have a reason to bolt.

Cherise twirled and twirled her glass of wine. A slight stain of dark burgundy was all that remained in the bowl-shaped bottom.

I figured it best to jump right in. "Dodie Goldfader has cancer. It's gone to her brain. She's dying. We think she only has a few months."

"Oh!" Cherise jerked her head up to look at me. When she satisfied herself that I was telling the truth, she mumbled, "That's too bad," and held up one finger to order another glass of wine.

"She wants closure. About Nathan. I told her I'd try to get answers for her." I took a deep breath. "I'm not here to judge you or anything like that. It's just that … well … why did you say what you did? About his death being your fault?"

Her body language changed. Cherise began to scoot out of the booth. I grabbed at her forearm. "Wait! She's dying! Can't you help her! You must want to!"

Cherise's eyes traveled to where I gripped her wrist. "Let go of me."

I pulled my hand away but as I did, I saw the marks. Her bracelets barely covered them. They were fine, white, and crisscrossing her wrist.

"You're cutting yourself, aren't you?"

"What business is it of yours?" she sank back into the booth and glared at me.

"My daughter's friend does that. We took her to the hospital last night."

"So?"

"So, I know you hurt inside. I know that hurting on the outside is easier. That when you cut, there's a release."

She looked away. The waiter hurried over with her second glass of wine. "You want anything, ma'am?" he asked me. I shook my head no.

Cherise took a big swallow of her wine. "Yeah, that's how it works. Sort of."

"How long have you been doing this?"

"Off and on since eleventh grade."

"It must be hard … to have all those feelings inside."

She shrugged. "It got worse after Nathan … died."

"Why don't you tell me about it? No one can overhear us. I'm a good listener." I shut up.

"There's nothing to tell."

"Has to be. Otherwise it wouldn't bug you so much." I channeled Piers Morgan. "So he had a big crush on you. He was probably the smallest guy in your class. A nerd but nice. Probably got teased a lot. You were used to guys having crushes on you. You had a boyfriend. For some reason, you invited Nathan to come along that night."

Her mouth quivered. "My boyfriend Spenser thought it would be funny. A joke. Like Nathan was a mascot or something."

"You picked up a case of beer. Jeff Horton had a hot car, and he loved showing it off. He drove all of you to the gravel pit that was supposed to be haunted. The moon was full. One of the boys suggested jumping off the cliff. He'd done it before, but during daylight. You were all a little drunk. It sounded like fun."

Her glass was empty. She wore the dazed look of a dreamer. "See, Spense and Jeff were on the swim team. Spense is the state record holder in the IM, individual medley. Jeff was a diver and did the last leg of the relay. Nathan didn't want to jump. The boys laughed and told him not to be such a wimp. Jeff got a flashlight out of his car and told me to hold it so they could climb up. They jumped twice. Tiffany and I thought it was cool, seeing them against that big orange moon. Nathan was getting tired. Spense and Jeff were in great shape, but then, they were on the swim team, so sure. Spense was getting jealous because each time that Nathan went off the cliff, I told him Nathan jumped the farthest out. That wasn't true. I mean, I knew that would honk Spense off. He always thought he was such a big man."

The waiter brought her one more glass. I worried about how much she'd had to drink, but I reasoned her friends would look after her. Just like I was trying to look after Dodie.

"Spense said let's go again. Nathan said he didn't want to. Jeff said come on. And I said, please, Nathan, please do it for me."

In the dim light of the restaurant, I watched twin half-moons of silver tears form in Cherise's eyes. "If I hadn't encouraged him, he would never had jumped. He was too tired. He knew it. I knew it, but I liked having that power over him, you know? So it really was my fault. I killed Nathan Goldfader."

SEVENTY

BACK AT TIME IN a Bottle, I called Horace from the office. I told him he needed to come in and see me when he picked up Dodie. "I have an answer for you two. I know what happened that night."

"All right, but how is my darling girl?"

"She's fine. I haven't shared what I've learned with her. Margit tells me she's greeted a few customers and taken several naps."

"More and more, she will withdraw from us. They have told us this would be her path. Well, this is good that you have an answer for her. Maybe she can go in peace."

The sadness in his voice hurt to hear.

Margit overheard my call. She set down her pen and shook her head. "*Alles hat ein ende nur die wurst hat zwei.*"

"Translation, please."

"Everything has an end. Only the sausage has two," she said with a sigh. "So this sad story, it is over, *ja*? She will know why her son did what he wouldn't do. For the love of a girl."

"A girl who can't forgive herself. I hope she gets help. I'm not sure she can go on unless she does."

I went about my work with a heavy heart. Customers had called in orders, and it was my job to pull merchandise because I knew it best. The tangle I'd been working on stared up at me. Picking it up carefully, I decided to tuck the tile away, into my notebook of tangles, and create another design for our scrappers to use. This one would forever remind me of that crying girl, and I wouldn't be able to teach it.

I was sitting on a low stool counting stickers when a pair of men's shoes took up an unusually large section of the floor. Ned bent down and waved a paper punch to get my attention.

"Hey, lady, what about a punch? A Hawaiian punch?" With his loud Hawaiian shirt and his blue jeans, Ned could have been a tourist coming back from the big island.

I laughed. "Only if you're buying. I spent my last dollar extracting a confession."

"That sounds interesting."

"It is. Help me up and I'll tell you all the ugly details. Before we leave, I need to give Margit a shout so she knows to watch the sales floor." After I was on my feet, I stuck my head in Margit's door and explained I was taking a break. She wanted to finish sending in an order, but she'd join us momentarily.

I gave Ned a quick tour of the store. He and I walked over to the front counter where Dodie was still sitting in her chair. She regarded Ned curiously. I introduced Ned to her and tried to start a conversation about scrapbooking, buying time until Margit would join us from the backroom. Dodie is usually keen to chat up her favorite hobby and livelihood. This afternoon, she rambled in nonsensical sentences, all the while plucking at her clothes. Finally I asked, "Is something bothering you? Do you have hives? Should I bring you something? Ned and I can stop by a pharmacy."

"No. I'm fine." She kept pulling at her top, nonetheless, and after pinching it repeatedly, her hand moved to her thigh where she repeated the gesture, tugging at her loose-fitting pants.

I was ready to ask Ned to examine her, being that sure she was in distress, when Margit appeared. In fact, I turned to him and said, "Dodie says she's fine—"

But he cut me off. "And she is. Let's go."

SEVENTY-ONE

"SHE'S PRE-ACTIVELY DYING," NED explained as we took our coffee over to a park bench outside Kaldi's. "Dodie is plucking at herself, acting restless, and not eating, right? I bet the store doesn't matter to her anymore, does it? She wants to tie up the loose ends in her life. She's said she's dying because she is."

His matter of fact delivery calmed me. "This is normal? How long does it last?"

"Usually two weeks. Occasionally, a person will rebound, especially if there's a special reason to delay, such as an upcoming holiday or a visitor. But in general, she has two weeks and then she'll move into the actively dying stage." He smiled kindly at me. "Think of it as detaching. Her soul knows it no longer belongs here. She doesn't need that body anymore. She longs to shuffle off her mortal coil. The activities of this world don't interest her."

Now that he explained the situation, I remembered that Dodie hadn't asked me where Gracie was. Usually, Dodie visits with Gracie frequently during any workday. If I leave Gracie at home, Dodie always asks about the big dog. But not today.

I told Ned about my visit with Cherise Landon. "I'll share it with Dodie and Horace tonight when he picks her up to take her home."

"Don't expect her to come back."

"Why?"

"Because she doesn't need you or the store anymore. This is the end. She'll want to spend it with her husband and daughter."

I took my fingers and pressed them against my eyes so I didn't cry.

"You need to let her go. Don't try to keep her here. Don't beg her to eat, or demand that she stay awake. Respect this as a natural process and let her ease her way from this world to the next."

I sniffled and nodded. "Okay."

Ned changed the subject. "How's that jailbird boyfriend of yours?"

I filled him in on all that had happened. Ned was a good listener who interrupted only for clarification. "Tell me more about Brenda's body. You said it was wrapped in a blanket? What kind of blanket?"

When I finished he smirked. "Shades of David Hendricks."

"Pardon?"

"Before your time. It was a notorious murder that happened in Decatur, Illinois. Hendricks was accused of killing his entire family, but he got off. It was difficult for the authorities to pinpoint the time of death. See, the killer wrapped the kids and Hendricks' wife in electric blankets, plugging them in before he left. Time of death is calculated by the drop in body temperature. The heat of the blanket heats the corpse and throws the timing off.

Look the murder up. Two books have been written about it. The scenario is also similar in that no one could figure out how Hendricks might have gotten from Chicago to Decatur and back in time for his scheduled business meetings."

"How did he?"

"He had his own plane. He probably flew back and forth. But we'll never know. He was retried and acquitted. The man is a genius, and if he did murder his family, he was smart enough to keep his mouth shut. That's how most killers get caught. Blabbing."

SEVENTY-TWO

NED LEFT BEFORE HORACE arrived. Dodie had fallen fast asleep, her head lolling to one side as she sprawled in the chair. I helped Horace walk his half-asleep wife to their car. Although I wanted desperately to tell her what I'd learned, I remembered Ned's advice. Perhaps it didn't matter to Dodie anymore. Perhaps it would. But her life, such as it was, now moved to a rhythm that had nothing to do with this earthly world. I helped him get her comfortable in the passenger seat. He handed me the seat belt, and I laughed inwardly at the irony of that. As if we could pin her down! Keep her here!

Not likely.

I told him what I had learned about Nathan. "Too late smart and too soon old," he said. "I cannot hate the girl for that. When we are young, it is all about us, isn't it? We want what we want and we do not think any further than our desires."

"If it's any consolation, I think she deeply regrets what happened." I told him about the cutting.

"A shame. Nathan would not want that. I am sorry for her. When my darling girl wakes up, I'll tell her. If she still wants to know. She cares about less and less. Used to be, she hopped out of bed, rushing through her breakfast to get to the store. Now, she only rolls over." He withdrew a white handkerchief from the inside breast pocket of his jacket. Meticulously, he rubbed the lenses of his glasses and gave a nod to the building. "I am thinking about this place, Kiki. This store."

Here it comes. He's going to tell me he's pulling the plug. I'll be out of a job again!

"It makes me happy to think it will go on," he said. "It has meant so much to my darling."

Whoa. I didn't see that coming. "That's true. As long as it's here, it's a remembrance of Dodie's passion for saving memories."

"I am hoping you will buy it."

"That would be nice, but I don't have any money."

"I know. I am thinking you can make payments. Ones that we know you can afford, because we will base the amount on what the store produces. Does that interest you?"

"Of course it does. But is that fair to you? Wouldn't you rather get a lump sum?"

He shrugged. "Does Dodie have need of money? Does Nathan? Neither do I."

Bending down to her quiet form, I gave Dodie a kiss on the cheek. She only grunted. Studying her, I said, "You have been such a gift to me. When I needed good counsel and a shoulder to lean on, you were there. Thanks to you, I grew up. And now it seems as if it's time to say goodbye. But I don't want to, so instead I'll tell you goodnight, dear friend. Sleep well. I hope your journey is an easy one."

SEVENTY-THREE

ANYA AND I SPENT a quiet evening together. I talked to Detweiler on the phone. I told him about my visit with Cherise Landon and my conversation with Ned about David Hendricks. "I'll pass that on to Schnabel."

"Are you coming to see me anytime soon? I really, really miss you and the squirt."

He was confident that Emily could be enticed to visit her grandparents' farm. "Then expect us around one," I said. "Anya could use another mental health day."

"Better yet, come for lunch. You know how Mom loves to feed people."

The next morning spawned a cornflower sky wearing a crown of white clouds. I let Anya sleep as long as she wanted. While she did, I cleaned house. When I finished, she was still snoozing so I opened the browser on the computer and went to a wonderful site called tanglepatterns.com to look up a few new tangles to try. Just for kicks and grins, I also Googled "9 mm" to see what popped up.

To my surprise, one click took me to Etsy, the online marketplace for handcrafted and unique items. There I found jewelry fashioned from spent casings. Bracelets. Necklaces. Pins.

Cool stuff.

The best vendors tell stories about their offerings. How they gather the materials. What inspired them. Their creative process. The vendor for "HotShots" where they turned bullet casings into jewelry and art explained that he lived near a shooting range. "The noise used to bother me. One day I went over to complain. I noticed all the casings on the floor of one of the gun lanes. 'What do you do with those?' I asked. The manager said that they swept them up and packed them, sending them off to be recycled. I offered to take them off his hands. I'd been into crafts my whole life, so I figured I could turn his scrap into something cool—and I think I did!"

What was it Patty said? There was a shooting range near the Detweiler farm.

Maybe the killer wasn't a cop who practiced with Chad Detweiler at the range used by the St. Louis County police. Maybe the killer wasn't a cop at all. What if it was someone who knew that Chad and Louis liked to visit the range together for a little father-son bonding time?

Anya padded into the living room. "I thought we were going to see Emily today."

"Are you planning to go in your PJs?"

She stuck her tongue out at me, and we both laughed. "Hustle up. We were invited for lunch."

I was backing my old BMW out of the driveway when my phone rang. I pulled off to the side of the road to answer it. Anya and Gracie stared at me impatiently.

"Thank you," said Horace. "You kept your word, and I told her what you discovered. It seems to have put her at peace."

Although I was sad, I also felt relieved. I was glad to perform this final service for my old friend. "You're very, very welcome," I said as I ended the call. We headed down the side street leading to the main thoroughfare of Webster Groves.

My cell phone rang again. I checked the number. It was Tuttle, Watson and Pettigrew, that stupid accounting firm. I pulled over. Anya rolled her eyes and mouthed, "Moo-oom."

I thought about letting it go but I figured I'd better respond. If I took Horace up on his offer to buy Time in a Bottle, I would need a good accountant. This group knew the store and its track record. Besides, Horace and Dodie seemed to think highly of these people.

"Hello, this is Kiki Lowenstein. May I help you?"

"I'm Arlen Tuttle, CPA. Are you the wife of George Lowenstein?"

"Yes, I am. Or was. He's deceased." What a weird way to start a conversation. But then, some men—especially older ones—always prefer doing business with a man. I vowed to set Arlen Tuttle straight.

"Is this about buying the business from the Goldfaders? Because if it is, I'm the person you need to talk to. We'll need to negotiate fair terms. I will need to prove the value of all the assets, review any outstanding liabilities, check any UCC filings, and determine a fair value for goodwill. "

I'd learned all these terms from Jennifer Moore, who was not only a terrific friend but a wonderful businesswoman. I didn't entirely know what they meant, but she and I had often discussed what it took to buy a business. She'd had a lot of practice at that. When we spoke, I was only daydreaming about owning my own store, but now it might become a reality. I only hoped that I could afford to buy Time in a Bottle!

There was a pause.

"Well," said the accountant, "that's not why I'm calling you. Didn't you get my messages?"

"No," I said rather crossly. "I've been busy."

Anya snorted, a sort of controlled chuckle. Under her breath, she mumbled, "I'll say."

My caller cleared his throat. "I need to talk to you about Dimont Development."

Rats! Here I'd been avoiding these calls, thinking that they came from the accounting firm that Horace had hired, and I'd been wrong. The messages I'd avoided were from another accountant, one I'd also probably wanted to avoid. The last thing I wanted to hear was that my late husband, George Lowenstein, owed more money. Money I didn't have. More debts might sink my chances at buying Time in a Bottle. I felt my shoulders droop with disappointment.

"To whom am I speaking? I didn't catch the name." I tried to sound tough, business-like. Anya screwed up her face to frown at me and Gracie whimpered from the back seat.

"Arlen Tuttle," he repeated.

"You don't know me," said Mr. Tuttle quietly. "But George was my friend—he once did something for me. Something that meant a lot. I'm trying to return the favor." After a slight pause, he continued. "If I were you, I'd hire an attorney to check into Dimont Development's finances."

"Unfortunately Mr. Tuttle, I've already looked into Dimont's finances, and I know they owe money, but I don't have any money to pay."

"No, no, that's not it," his voice dropped to a whisper. "You didn't hear this from me, but they found a bank account."

I sighed. "I know already. The one in the Cayman Islands. Bill and his friend Roxanne Baker opened it. The police looked into that, and into the buy-sell agreement Bill had with George. Believe me, I've tried to get money back out of Dimont. There isn't any. According to Bill, George squandered it all."

"Not exactly," said Mr. Tuttle. "That's what Bill wanted it to look like. He set George up. Falsified the paperwork. The buy-sell agreement between Bill and George was incorrectly executed. Most importantly, there was another bank account."

"And you know this how?" I wouldn't let myself feel hopeful. I'd been let down too many times.

"I overheard two other accountants discussing it. That's why you can't tell anyone that this information came from me. Apparently, Bill Ballard was siphoning off funds from Dimont without George's knowledge. He had been for a long time. Now that Bill's dead…" he paused. "Things have come to light from the audit of the books."

"It is very kind of you to let me know about this, Mr. Tuttle. But I am so busy right now, I just don't have time to spare to chase down bank accounts."

"Mrs. Lowenstein, I don't think you quite understand." In a quiet, even voice, Mr. Tuttle continued. "There's money owed to you. A lot of money."

Anya saw the grin on my face. "Good news?"

"I think so. You've been talking about remodeling your bedroom. It's possible I might have a little extra money. What would you like to do?"

"I was thinking about painting my room in a peacock blue with green, the color of a new leaf. Can I?"

We were discussing the pros and cons of painting her old dresser when I realized I'd missed the turn to the Detweiler farm. I've driven there a half dozen times, but the markings on the country lanes can be tricky. Fortunately, this detour would take us past the shooting range. A glance at my phone told me we were actually a half an hour early for lunch.

"Do you mind if we stop for a minute? I want to ask a question about collecting bullet shells. I saw some cool jewelry on Etsy."

Anya texted Emily and discovered that she hadn't left for her grandparents' house yet.

"Sure."

At the GM Range, Anya, Gracie, and I tumbled out of the car, which I'd parked between two monster trucks. All in all, probably six vehicles sat on the worn-down grass, and my car looked the best of the bunch. The range wasn't much to brag about. A converted shed with rusty siding that might once have been green served as the "office," where you could pay to shoot and buy ammunition. To keep costs down, Colby Nesbit had tacked a porch onto the front of the shed. The struts were painted a cherry red, and a tar-paper roof covered a rickety card table where a young man checked in would-be shooters. To his right, a metal coin box served as cash register.

Behind the shed, you could see the lanes. Six were open-air, and a simple frame building bore a sign announcing six indoor lanes. Two shooters were loading as we walked up. Twenty-five yards away black silhouettes with red targets flapped in the light breeze.

"Hi," I said cheerfully to the young man taking money. He looked to be all of Anya's age, awfully young to be working, unless he was family. Taking one gander at my adorable daughter, the boy pinked up.

"Hey." He smiled shyly at Anya and completely ignored me.

I tapped on the table. "Could you answer a question for me? I'm into crafts. I was wondering, what happens with the leftover casings?"

"We sweep 'em up," said the boy. "Colby sells 'em to reloaders."

SEVENTY-FOUR

NOW THAT MY QUESTION was answered, Anya and I took time to pick a bouquet of wildflowers for Thelma's table, as we worked our way back to the car with Gracie in tow. I looked up to see an old man come out from the office and shuffle toward us. His scuffed shoes were covered with dust. The Dickies worksuit he was wearing had seen better days, and the stains and small tears on it proved the coverall had earned a rest. A faded John Deere cap, once a bright green, was jammed down on his head. He moved with purpose as if he wanted to talk to us.

Once the man drew near, he raised his head. Our eyes locked. A dull weakness started in my legs as Milton Kloss angled toward us. I spotted the revolver in the holster under his arm. He was still twenty feet away.

Surely he didn't plan to shoot me where I stood. There would be too many witnesses!

If that was his plan, there was nothing I could do. Nothing. I was unarmed. But I could protect my daughter. It was highly unlikely that Milton would hurt her. Especially if she was out of his reach.

"Anya, honey? No questions, okay? Listen carefully. Take Gracie with you. Go stand over by the clerk. Over there at the front desk. Get moving, now, and don't come back until I say so."

The urgency in my words caused her to start walking, Gracie at her side. But halfway there, Anya stopped to glance back at me. Using my hands, I shooed her away. She moved forward reluctantly. Turning my back to her, I faced Milton.

"Rupe told me you were asking questions."

"Rupe? The guy behind the counter?"

"Nah. Rupert McLean. The young one who takes care of the lines. Those corrals where the shooting occurs."

"Oh."

"Rupe cleans the butts. The packing behind the targets is where the bullets are lodged."

"I know what the butts are. I've been to a shooting range before."

Milton raised a hand to the back of his neck and rubbed it, as if the tension were unbearable. His gaze traveled a semi-circle, stopped when he noticed Anya, and then returned to me. "Your girl?"

"Yes."

"How old?"

"Thirteen."

His face puckered up and his mouth trembled. "Pretty thing. Reminds me of Brenda at that age. All legs and arms and hair. Bet you love her to pieces."

"Yes, I do." It was as if someone had instantly frozen me, the way a villain might level a weapon at a superhero. I can't recall ever feeling so cold, so helpless.

"I loved my daughter, Mrs. Lowenstein. Loved her desperately." His eyes, an indeterminate color, were wet. Using the back of his hand, he wiped at them. "Once, when I was a young 'un, my dog got bit by a raccoon. Don't you know that blasted coon had rabies. My dog got it. My pa made me shoot my dog. My own pet that I loved more'n anyone in my whole family. Said I owed it to my family and to the dog to end it before anyone else got hurt."

The edges of my vision turned black. A buzzing started in my ears. He meant to kill me! Shoot me where I stood! I set one hand on the quarter panel of my car to steady myself, but I must have turned green, because Milton Kloss asked, "You okay."

"A little woozy."

"You've got a bun in the oven, don't you?"

"Excuse me?"

"You're expecting."

"Yes." Was this an admission to seal my fate, but it surely wasn't a secret.

"Chad got you pregnant."

"Right."

"You cannot imagine how much I wanted to be a grandpa. It was all I dreamed about. I kept thinking, she'll get pregnant and she'll straighten up. She sure will. When there's a baby involved, it's bound to change her ways. But it didn't, did it?"

My fingers ran along the hot metal of the car hood. I couldn't believe I was going to die in the middle of a parking lot. What a way to go. I thought about trying to grab a handful of dirt to toss in his eyes, but then what? I was unarmed. If he was any good with that gun, he could easily turn and shoot Anya. From the sounds of it, he came here often.

I couldn't see a way out of this.

"Of course, being pregnant didn't change nothing. Not a thing. She didn't even tell us she was expecting! She called me right after the shooting and said she'd been in a bad accident. I was in Chicago, so I told her to go home and stay put. My plane was in for scheduled maintenance, so I rented one from a fellow I know. I flew to Springfield. Picked up my car at the airport and drove down to our house to meet up with Brenda. Wanted to talk things through."

He stopped to sigh. "Brenda was higher than a kite. Couldn't talk straight. Wouldn't tell her mother what happened, just went straight up to her old room. Carla took her a cup of hot chocolate, hoping to talk. Brenda was sitting there on the bed. With a mirror. Had a rolled up dollar bill in one hand. Running it over the surface like it was a vacuum cleaner hose. So Carla calls me on my cell phone and asks, 'What on earth could she be doing?' I hated to tell my wife. It was awful."

I shook my head. Despite my being afraid of him, I could empathize with his misery. "I can't imagine it."

"You wouldn't want to. Nothing mattered to Brenda but her next fix. Nothing at all. You know she stole all the money out of our household account? Ran up our credit cards to the max so she could sell stuff and get money for drugs? Even took poor Carla's rings, the ones she inherited from her mama, and hocked them. Swiped our DVDs, took my watch. Anything she could get her hands on. She was like that mad dog. She was crazy and sick and it wasn't going to end ever!" With that, he choked on a sob. "I pity you, Mrs. Lowenstein, if that ever happens. If you ever see your whole world fall apart. If you ever know your little girl has turned into a monster and the only way you can stop her from hurting someone else is to … stop her yourself? What would you do? What?"

"I honestly don't know," I said.

From her spot at the counter, Anya turned slightly toward us. Watching. Staying vigilant.

With a long, low sigh, Milton slowly withdrew his gun from the holster and rested it against his knee.

Anya must have seen the gun because her expression changed. Turning to the kid behind the counter, she pointed at Milton. I didn't need to hear her to know what she was telling the clerk. The boy rotated to face us, and his face went white.

Milton resumed talking, this time waving his gun in the air. "This was all her fault, Carla's! If she hadn't been in that accident, none of this would've happened. But how could I be mad at Carla when she's been sober all these years? So then I was angry with Chad. How come he couldn't control her? I was mad at everyone but the person who deserved it."

"I kept praying," and the man's voice broke, so he started again. "Going to church and praying Brenda would change. I asked God to let her see how she was hurting other people. I kept thinking she would change. But then I realized. She was just like that dog of mine, don't you see?"

The boy was leaning inside the doorway of the shed. Anya had her hand over her mouth. Gracie, bless her, faced the opposite way. I was glad about that. I didn't want her to get the raw end of this deal by trying to rescue me.

"I was running for public office. Telling folks I'd do the hard jobs. The ones that had to be done. Making cuts. Balancing our local budget. But a hard job was right there before me. Staring me in the face. I was the only person who could do it. If I let her keep going, I'd be passing the buck. I brought her into this world. It was my job to do what was right. Hard as it was."

"How did Brenda wind up in that house? So far from your place?"

"Carla helped me get her into my car. That girl was stumbling like a drunk. I told Carla I knew a place where Brenda could sleep it off. See, I knew that place was in foreclosure and empty, because I'm on the bank board. So I took her there, thinking we'd talk the next day. But then as I was driving, I heard the news report. Heard how she'd shot you and that man. Left you both to die."

He sniffed and used his sleeve to wipe his eyes.

"I had to do the hard job. I had to stop her. No one else could do it, so I had to. So I did it. Fast and clean. Then she looked so little, so young that I wrapped her up. I had a few casings in my pocket. I'd picked them up after watching Chad and Louis here at the range. So I sprinkled them around and pocketed my own spent casings. Then I realized if I plugged that blanket in, no one had to know I was down here. But I couldn't just leave her! I couldn't, so I stopped halfway to the airport and made a call. I wanted them to find her and to blame Chad. They did."

A man stepped out of the office. His cell phone was in one hand and he was talking and waving his other hand. Probably calling nine-one-one, not that it would do any good. We were so far from help. I knew from experience how long it could take for an ambulance to come. By then, I'd be dead.

I wanted to move away, to run to the shed, but I stood rooted to the spot. The longer Milton talked, the more time I had to live.

He wiped his eyes again. "Here's the worst of it. You get this smidgeon of hope, and then it's dashed. Again and again and again."

"I think I understand," I spoke slowly and looked Milton in the eye. "My dad had a problem, drinking. I kept thinking if I said or did the right thing, he'd change."

He nodded. "I think you do understand. That's exactly right. That's the way it is. Did he?"

"No. In fact, after he died we learned he'd been in multiple car accidents. I don't know if he hurt anyone, but I wouldn't have been surprised to learn that he did."

"See? That's what I'm talking about. Exactly what I'm saying!" The hand by his side still held the gun. I tried not to focus on it. Not to draw attention to the weapon. Maybe he'd forget he held it. Slowly, he rocked back onto his heels and rested his weight on them. He turned his head in Anya's direction.

"That little girl of yours. She's a sweetheart. You don't let anything happen to her, you hear? Or that baby? Promise me."

My mouth was so dry I could barely croak out the words: "I promise."

With that, he raised his gun to his head and blew his brains out.

SEVENTY-FIVE

LATER THAT EVENING, DETWEILER and I sat side-by-side on a bench in his parents' backyard and watched Emily and Anya chase fireflies. Soon the girls would be too old for this sort of nonsense, but a new baby in the family might tempt them to return to these carefree ways.

"I would have never guessed that Carla Kloss could have been so strong," said Detweiler. "But she told Milton that enough was enough. She wouldn't put up with the lies any longer. He got up and walked out of the house. Hopped in his truck. Didn't go far. When he spotted you at the shooting range, he had to stop and spill his guts."

I shuddered. "I'm sorry Anya had to see that."

He sighed. "I am, too. But at least it's over. Thank goodness. Schnabel says Carla told the police the same story you heard from Milton. He's confident all the charges will be dropped. That reminds me, what's the latest on Johnny?"

"I phoned Ned and he told me that Johnny's been waking up. Just for short periods, but still…"

"But still…" Detweiler kissed me tenderly. "That's encouraging. And Dodie?"

"It's not good."

"Ah."

My turn to sigh.

His cell phone rang.

I walked over to the girls. They had twenty or so captives in a Ball jar with an apple core in the bottom for the lightning bugs to feast on. Anya threw her arms around me and hugged me tight. "It's over! Isn't it great? Now we can get married."

"Excuse me?" I couldn't believe my ears.

"Well, maybe. But if Detweiler isn't going to jail, we can talk about it, right? I know what kind of dress I want to wear."

I shook my head and marveled. Honestly her moods shifted so quickly, that once again, I was caught unaware. "Right. We have a lot of talking to do."

"Kiki!" Detweiler yelled to me. I trotted over to his side. He was staring at his phone, and he finished his conversation with, "I'll call you back. Yes, yes. I understand. Right away."

"What is it?" I slipped my arms around his waist.

He hesitated. "That was a worker at a child welfare agency in California. We'd better sit down."

Leading me to the wooden bench, he struggled for words. "It's about Gina. My first wife. Um, there's been an accident. A car crash. She's dead."

"Whoa. Two dead wives in one week." I rubbed my arms against the coming chill of the evening. "That has to be some kind of a record."

"Uh, that's not all. It seems she left behind a son."

"Poor little guy."

"He's my son."

THE END

AUTHOR'S NOTE

As Kiki discovered, "cutting" is an epidemic among young women. Signs to watch for include wearing clothes that cover the wrists and thighs even in warm weather, scarring, and keeping sharp objects on hand. Most of those addicted to self-harm do so in secret, so another clue might be bloodstained towels, tissues, and clothes. Self-harm usually escalates, with the addict spending more time alone and more time hurting herself/himself (boys are not immune to this practice). For more information please go to http://www.helpguide.org/mental/self injury.htm and http://www.twloha.com/vision./

Zentangle® is an easy to learn method of creating beautiful images from repetitive patterns. You can see samples of Zentangle® art at http://pinterest.com/joannaslan/. Rick Roberts and Maria Thomas are the creators of Zentangle. Zentangle® is a registered trademark of Zentangle, Inc. For more information, go to Zentangle.com. You can also visit Linda Farmer's wonderful TanglePatterns.com for inspiration and ideas.

ACKNOWLEDGMENTS

As usual, I have many people to thank: my niece Katigan Campbell Hutts; Joe Burgoon, law enforcement officer extraordinaire; my sister Jane Campbell; my assistant Sally Lippert; and my ace computer team at NCI Systems. Any mistakes are my own.

Thanks to Julie Failla-Earhart and Margit Hanna for the great recipes. Margit also supplied the nifty German saying about the sausage!

My Beta Readers did a fabulous job of helping with this book. I want to thank: Candi Bise, Yifat Cestare, Brooke Gale, Mary Havlovic, Mary Kennedy, Carrie Simpson, and Aldean Tendick. If you would like to be a Beta Reader for an upcoming Kiki book, be sure to follow me on my Facebook page (http://tinyurl.com/JCSlan) to learn of opportunities.

Yifat was randomly selected to become a character in this book after she told me how much she loves Kiki. To read what other readers have said, go to www.JoannaSlan.com.

My fabulous husband, David Slan, helped me with all aspects of Kiki's business dealings. He's my patron of the arts, and I love him.

My team at Midnight Ink continues to keep Kiki alive and looking good! Thanks to Terri Bischoff, Connie Hill, and Kevin Brown.

Kelley at Iconix Biz has produced my bookmarks for ages. If you write to me at JCSlan@JoannaSlan.com I'll send you some.

I am incredibly thankful for my talented and wise agent, Paige Wheeler, of Folio Literary Management.

And last but not least, I want to thank my readers. You communicate with me. You show up for my signings. You follow me on Facebook. You write reviews. You tell your friends. You suggest these books to your book clubs and libraries. In short, your response to my work keeps me tapping away at the keyboard.

ABOUT THE AUTHOR

Joanna Campbell Slan is the award-winning author of the Kiki Lowenstein Mysteries (an Agatha Award Finalist) and two other mystery series. She is an internationally recognized expert on scrapbooking and is a certified teacher of Zentangle. In her past life, Joanna was a television talk show host, an adjunct professor of public relations, a sought-after motivational speaker, and a corporate speechwriter. She is married to David Slan, CEO of Steinway Piano Gallery-DC. The Slans and their two dogs make their home on Jupiter Island, Florida. Visit Joanna's website at www.JoannaSlan.com.